Anglish
Spoken
Here

. . .

Anglish Spoken Here

—

DON ZAHNER

. . .

THE STEPHEN GREENE PRESS
Lexington, Massachusetts

Copyright © The Stephen Greene Press, Inc., 1986
Introduction copyright © Charles Kuralt, 1986
All rights reserved

First published in 1986 by The Stephen Greene Press, Inc.
Published simultaneously in Canada by Penguin Books Canada Limited
Distributed by Viking Penguin Inc., 40 West 23rd Street,
New York, NY 10010.

LIBRARY OF CONGRESS CATALOGING IN PUBLICATION DATA
Zahner, Don.
Anglish spoken here.
1. Fly fishing—Anecdotes, facetiae, satire, etc.
I. Title.
SH456.Z34   1986   799.1'2   85-30502
ISBN 0-8289-0568-1

Printed in the United States of America by
The Book Press, Brattleboro, Vermont
Set in Baskerville
Design by Mary Wirth

Page 227 constitutes an extension of this copyright page.

To Nick Lyons—*EMERITUS* Professor of Anglish

Contents

Foreword

I WAS INTRODUCED to Don Zahner, cheerful evangelist of fly-fishing, by the wise old angling dean, Robert Traver. I wanted to learn the art and Traver was wise enough not to try to teach me. So it was Don Zahner who took me to a store in St. Louis to buy my first chest waders, drove me to a river in the Ozarks, pointed to a trout, and stood aside to watch my first effort with a fly rod. I hooked his hat on my backcast.

I don't think I caught any trout that day, but I didn't catch Zahner's hat again, either, and we parted as friends. He had made a convert. As a passionate fly fisherman, I went on to hook many bankside willows and weeds over the years. As an evangelist, he went on to found *Fly Fisherman* magazine at his kitchen table and watch it grow into a canonical journal as eagerly awaited by anglers all over the world as letters from St. Paul were awaited by the Corinthians. (Probably Paul also started out at his kitchen table.)

No pursuit on earth is so burdened by arcane lore as fly-fishing, beside which brain surgery and particle physics are simple backyard pastimes. The aim of most writers about fly-fishing always was to further mystify the sport, thus making it seem unapproachable to outsiders, thus keeping these outsiders away from the writers' favorite trout streams. This was perfectly plausible strategy; fishing alone is the more satisfying, and in solitude the hat one hooks will be one's own. Don Zahner's unique contribution to the literature has been to show that fly-fishing is a pleasure. He honors all the snobbery and tradition of it and *still* writes about it as a pleasure, because he loves it and can't help himself. He has given away the secret: there's no kick like flinging a bit of fur and feather into a rapid current and watching it float toward a fish, or possible fish, or imagined fish.

The punning title, *Anglish Spoken Here,* should give you fair warning that you'll find a lot more pun and fun and extravagant overstatement in Zahner's writing than you will find perfect casts to rising rainbows. But there is much practical wisdom here, too: short casts catch more fish than long ones; long leaders catch more fish than short ones; a roll cast can sometimes dislodge a sharp hook from a rotten log. And there is sentiment and good fellowship, for this Zahner is a sentimental good fellow who knows that a lot of wonderful fishing goes on at bars and cribbage tables.

His columns, made into a book, make lovely reading—or, for devoted fans who never missed his columns, of whom I am one, delicious re-reading. Our work has taken us in different directions (I have a good job, wandering and reporting on it for a living, but he has a better job—wandering and *fishing* and reporting on it for a living) and I haven't seen much of the man since the day I raised his size-7⅝ gray fedora with my size-14 gold-ribbed hare's ear, but I have followed his rambles down rivers, his fumblings through fly boxes and his plays on words with rapt admiration. I am still a confused Corinthian, and he is a good-humored saint from afar, writing letters to keep me interested and to set me straight.

Charles Kuralt
CBS News

Preface

As I TOLD MY PUBLISHER, I was paid to write this stuff, not to read it. For the past few months I have been forced—and I speak with precision, forced—to revisit the scenes of some hundred of my earlier crimes against angling humanity and to view, for the purpose of imminent exhumation, the gory remains of one angler's view of the fly-fishing life.

Quite frankly, the experience has been like falling from a high building and reliving my life—but never hitting the sidewalk. This brief Preface, it turns out, is the sidewalk.

Someone, whose previous literary high had probably been *Black Beauty*, remarked that the department called "Anglish Spoken Here" was the keystone of *Fly Fisherman* magazine. Actually, he was correct, for it was originally designed as a buffer to absorb the last-minute ads that usually trickled in at presstime. Three pages were usually reserved for this accommodation, but happily for everyone concerned, the ads flowed in at an ever-increasing rate over the years and the space, if not the prose, became more precious. "Anglish" was "writ to fit."

Oddly enough, it did fit. Fly-fishing has, for centuries, through blood, sweat, and tears, contributed far beyond its numbers to the lore and literature of the sporting life. This dedicated cadre of fly-fishers, warmed to the chase by Izaak Walton in the seventeenth century, then fired by his fly-fishing disciple-mentor, John Cotton, pursued their finny Grail with growing fervor until their writings became a literal laying on of hands—one that eventually deposited at the contemporary angler's felt-booted feet a body of scripture transcending the secular.

It afforded the unchurched and the freethinker an alternate spiritual style, and enticed the religious. I can recall, after a wedding ceremony during a particularly warm Christmas week, persuading the presiding Anglican bishop to take the next day off for a foray into the Ozarks for trout. The fact that this would be a Sunday obviously created no conflict in the mind of his angling Anglican. Happily for the establishment, it snowed, but I decided that any bishop who loved the fishes more than the loaves could not be All Good. There was hope, I realized, and a few months later I published the first issue of *Fly Fisherman* magazine.

While I exulted in the apostolic frenzy of the converted nonbeliever early on in my angling career, I was quite aware that I had taken no vows or heard no sudden call. But all around me were the devout, donning their vestments at stream-side and walking, at least in spirit, across the waters to pursue their daily devotions. As the evening hatch tolled its angelus, I saw them move out into the mists, their chilled fingers fumbling over their flies and their faint voices mumbling the gospels according to Halford, Gordon, Wulff, or Schwiebert.

Later in the evenings, during post-vesper libations, I often listened to their apocryphal tales of revelation and redemption astream, but this soon became a bore—like hearing the confessions of saints.

Thus was born the concept of Anglish-speak. I would post my own banns of reformation on a convenient door, telling them, if not like it really is, like it should be. The very act of fly-fishing, if examined step by step by the analytical eye, shares much with the act of procreation—a most pleasant fulfillment but one not to be too closely viewed by the casual observer.

And that's how I came to be a piscatorial Peeping Tom, viewing the act of angling with love and affection but with a weather eye cocked toward cant and a lance at ready to prick pomposity wherever it might arise—even within myself.

If the voice of the angler is still heard in this land, this is how I have heard it.

· I ·

Tools of the Trade

States of Our Art

THE BASIC PHILOSOPHY BEHIND THE CHARM AND CHAL-
lenge of angling with the fly rod is one of ultimate simplicity: to place as little mechanical contrivance as possible
between the angler and the angled.

It then becomes the role of the fly fisherman to elaborate
on this pure, yet rather spartan, theme. There is no restric-
tion, either implied or to be inferred, on what minor im-
pedimenta the fly angler may harbor within the inviolate
sanctity of his fishing vest.

On the basis of this interpretation of the angling canon,
an international industry has been created. The industry
recently raised a monument to itself and the poor souls it
serves by creating a wading vest with fifty-seven—count
'em—separate pockets. Well, I bought one and I did, but
only found fifty-five, but I would have to give up fly fishing
if I returned it.

They've got you coming and going.

The Last Fly Rod at Abercrombie & Fitch
(*1978*)

ABERCROMBIE & FITCH was the store for the man who had everything—and he went there with some regularity just to make certain.

But now, those who care will never know for sure, because just before Christmas A&F folded up its down-filled, Everest-tested tent and "stole away."* Which, some wags would say, they had been doing successfully for over a century.

For several years, the rumored reports of Abercrombie's imminent death had not been over-exaggerated, but the finality of the somber bankruptcy-announcement ad in *The New York Times* caught the carriage trade with its traces down. Like "dollar day at Tiffany's" or a "fire sale at Cartier's," it's just not done.

But the times hadn't kept up with A&F. The leveling effect of taxes and inflation had taken its toll, and to be quite truthful, there was nothing sold at Abercrombie's which was required to sustain life. I remember just last Christmas season my visit to Abercrombie's with Dermot Wilson, England's premier dry-fly angler, who was looking for a gift for his wife. In an attempt to keep him away from the A&F tackle department, by then in a state of almost total decay, I steered him toward the games department on the first floor. There, displayed under a soft spotlight within a roped-off viewing area and looking altogether like an alabaster sarcophagus from King Tut's tomb, was a huge gold-marble-and-ivory chess set, priced to sell quickly at just $12,000.

"I wonder if they take Barclaycards?" Dermot asked, quietly calculating to himself just how many miles of his beloved Itchen he would have to sell to snap up this bargain. Happily I diverted him to luggage, where he acquired a relatively modest

* A&F reopened in October of 1985.

3

· 4 ·

picnicking set, fit for any *al fresco* fare Piccadilly's Fortnum &
Mason's might conjure.

NOW, ONE YEAR LATER, I was entering A&F's canopied door
for the last time. The store was jammed, but the only remnant
of the carriage trade I could identify was a lone cab driver por-
ing over a loose pile of A&F bush jackets, the kind Hemingway
used to buy there while picking up his latest custom magnum at
Griffin & Howe's establishment in the gun department. I don't
know if the cabby found his size, but I'll keep my eyes open for
him on my trips to Manhattan. I do know that he paid in cash,
though, because Abercrombie announced to everyone entering
that no credit cards could be honored, not even A&F credit
cards. The very thought of an Abercrombie & Fitch credit card
in my hands caused me to break out in a rash. This was one test
of my moral mettle I had never allowed myself.

Before elevating to the tackle floor to pay my respects and
view the remains, I reflexively detoured to my favorite corner
on the main floor, the counter that had for several decades displayed an enchanting German-made microbarograph, its pol-
ished-brass rotating drum encased in glass, the secrets of
nature's elemental plans locked within. For all those years I had
managed to pass it up, a steal most recently at just $895. It
wasn't there. I envisioned it reposing on some marble man-
telpiece in the halls of affluence on Long Island—instead of in
the cluttered den of an unreconstructed former Air Force
weatherman still waiting hopefully for his veteran's bonus. I
made a mental note to write a letter of succinct social commentary to the *Daily Worker,* if it were still published.

But now it was near that final closing time, and the elevator
carried a mournful and obviously illegal load. It was like the last
barge down the River Styx to Lethe.

But as the doors opened, the scene was nearer to the bargain basement at Gimbel's. Bronx matrons, bewhiskered and
aging flower children, and Madison Avenue slicks already late
for their commuter trains seemed all to be engaged in a single
and consummate act of looting. I did recognize a rather dis-
tingished older gentleman with whom I had met briefly nearly
a decade ago while he was pricing a Payne rod there. We

nodded our mutual recognition almost funereally, then passed on to find our bearings.

Bare bulbs glared obscenely overhead. The glass counters were stripped, and merchandise, such as it was, was spread out over folding tables, convenient for pawing and clawing. I finally located the remnants of what was once one of the country's finest tackle emporiums. On the display wall there was a Martin automatic reel with a broken spring and a classic Medalist reel with a bent spool. The same wall from which I had selected my first Hardy fly reel some fifteen years before. The few remaining spinning and saltwater reels were moving fast.

I asked where the fly rods were, and the clerk pointed across the floor to a sprawling construction of pine 2 × 4's that resembled an elephantine complex of umbrella racks. Sticking out of each segment were fishing rods of various persuasions.

"You'll find the fly rods," the clerk added knowledgeably, "in bin number one hundred eighteen."

Was this the Abercrombie & Fitch that I had known for thirty-five years? Was this the same shop that became the weekly home-away-from-stream for hundreds of Manhattan-based fly anglers? Where you could finger Paynes and Leonards and Pezon et Michels and Orvises "off the rack" on your lunch hour, a headier draught than any martini? The *sanctum sanctorum* where I window-shopped one time with Charles Ritz while he told me of his days, early in this century, as night manager of his father's New York hostel, when he spent the wee hours rebuilding fly rods he had released from pawn, then turning them over to Abercrombie & Fitch for re-sale? Where he eyed, as we talked, the tiny little A&F Passport fly rod, a four-footer that broke down into a vest-pocket companion—the same rod I later gave him to use in his informal casting in the Rue Cambon Bar at the Paris Ritz?

Not the place, certainly, where hundreds of anglers would gather at noon-time to adjourn to the long casting pool on the A&F roof to test rods and watch casting demonstrations by such people as Leon Chandler?

THEN I FINALLY LOCATED IT—the last fly rod at Abercrombie & Fitch. An 8½-foot graphite, even grayer in its loneliness among the spinning and plug-casting rods. We contemplated a documented purchase of the rod, appropriately witnessed this day by the referees in bankruptcy waiting in the wings. But then, I thought, perhaps the cab driver. . . .

As I finally stepped out into the fresh brisk air of Madison Avenue—not by the 45th Street doors as A&F was impotently attempting to direct traffic—I realized that this was the end of an era, the last fly rod from the last Manhattan fly-fishing emporium. (Except, I suppose, for Jimmy Deren's Angler's Roost, with Jimmy posed precariously on his stool, daring anyone to find him in and then actually persuade him to sell them something.)

In a last grasp for roots, I crossed Madison Avenue for a quickie at the old Biltmore Men's Bar, the last stronghold of Manhattan *machismo*—the place where, many Christmases ago, a chubby, pink-cheeked nun started to enter for her charitable solicitations, only to be greeted with a rising sound of polite applause designed to send her scurrying to her cloisters.

I was at the door of the Men's Bar before I saw the flashy new sign: "Fanny's." I looked in and saw all the pretty ladies sitting on theirs.

Too much culture shock for one day. I would never again drop in to the Biltmore Men's Bar for a short one, occasionally to hear the reverberations of the classic argument *cum* fisticuffs between Hemingway and Scott Fitzgerald still bouncing off the framed, well-lighted nudes on the walls.

Nor would we all, ever again, go down, as they used to say, "to Abercrombie and Fish."

The Replete Angler
(1975)

ELSEWHERE I have, for the edification of newer fly fishermen, discoursed upon my earlier days astream and in doing so told of my reactions when suddenly, through the pages of Arnold Gingrich's book, *The Well-Tempered Angler,* I discovered the world of fly fishing as it existed at that time. Up to then, my only source of information on fly fishing had been several rather outdated volumes, and I described my feelings as similar to those of my boyhood hero, Buck Rogers, who awoke from 500 years of "suspended animation" to step into a world of unthinkable fantasies and delights.

However, angling in the twenty-fifth century was not all I had hoped. Like the housewife of my generation I had bought freedom from toil by selling my soul. Problems of maintenance and logistics became greater than those which the devices were designed to overcome. My collapsible, and aptly named, wading staff *did*—majestically and with unerring timing—and I had acquired a net to match it. I owned nine fly reels, each with three spools for extra lines; this created somewhat of a problem of identification, so I soon acquired a micrometer to gauge the weight of each line (which required a conversion chart for the line-widths and profiles for the half-dozen different manufacturers' specifications, a chart considerably smaller than the National Geographic Society's Map of the World), and eventually a second micrometer for checking the accuracy of the first.

I carried a wicker creel of sufficient authority to have attracted the interest of Captain Ahab. I wore what amounted to a bullet-proof vest, made so by the living presence of at least thirteen metal fly boxes with cunningly hinged doors which opened at critical moments to release unexpected hatches onto the water. Optically, I was impeccably equipped. I had sunglasses with prescription lenses to match the light-level of any hour of any day, as well as an attachable light to allow me to use my magnifying granny-glasses to tie on midges at dusk. For

7

several years I carried an eye-cup filled with Murine to alleviate the stress caused by the inherent optical accommodation required by this battery of lenses, but I kept confusing it with my bottle of silicone fly floatant. Occasional application of the floatant did keep rain out of my eyes, but Murine seemed to do nothing for the flies, which had a hard time locating any rising fish.

An incipient hernia and distress in the sixth lumbar soon required ballast to counteract Moby Dick's creel, and I eventually added a lovely English fish bag to hold two cameras; a large stock box for the flies that the thirteen other boxes could not absorb; a first-aid kit forced on me by fishing companion and later publishing associate Bob Bassett, an ex-med student constantly praying for disaster, and containing an assortment of that paraphernalia which would enable me to perform emergency appendectomies on a moment's notice; and a streamside lunch, washed down with a light claret. I had formerly carried my lunch in that convenient pocket at the rear of the vest, but had never been able to reach it without causing further lumbar distress.

The cameras were useful, but primarily to record the exploits of others. Immobilized as I was, landing a fish became a major undertaking. More than one companion suggested that I acquire a gillie to accompany me, but in truth I needed more the services of a loyal and able squire to attire me properly in my armor and mail to join the lists, and to mount me finally securely in position on the water. I soon became known on several streams as "high-density Don," for I was able to get to the bottom—"where the fish are"—faster than any of my sinking lines. I performed some valuable underwater research in those days, and some delightful acrobatics.

From tip to toe, I was The Replete Angler. I even added, from time to time, an occasional fish to back up this claim. No one personified the oft-quoted statement of angler-conservationist Le Wulff—that "a trout is too valuable to be used only once." Oh how true. I once calculated (not while on the stream, unfortunately, because the pocket calculator had not been invented at that time) that the trout I caught in my first years of fly fishing, measured against the logistical support required to land them, carried a value of $122.57 each. This is roughly in proportion to the fuel and ground support needed to maintain a squadron of SAC long-range nuclear bombers on air alert.

However, after ten years, and a long and agonizing strip-tease, I have managed to maintain more than a hedge against inflation, and I calculate the value of Lee Wulff's trout—or at least mine—to have dropped considerably. I could probably acquire a mistress for less—and my wife has always wondered why I didn't.

The Spartan Life
(1969)

IT IS ABOUT this time of year, after a stock-taking tour of our piscatorial warehouse in one corner of the basement, that we feel somehow we have managed to come through the year with more tackle than fish. Of course, turnback is fair play and we return much of what we catch—the loss of which would scarcely dent the ecology of a sunporch aquarium—but little or no fishing tackle ever gets returned, traded back or passed on to the worthy or needy. We often have the distinct impression that we are disrupting the marketing ecology of the tackle industry.

In fact, our creel runneth over—not with fish, but with the instruments of their intended demise. It all began, we recall, less than ten years ago, with one rod and the rather misbegotten image of the lone fly angler, gleaned primarily from an early Leslie Howard movie, moving cleanly along the wooded banks of a Canadian mountain stream with a light rod, a small fly box, and a large sense of being at one with nature.

We realize now that it was the introduction of a second rod into that pristine world of a decade ago that led to its inevitable violation. Male and female ferrules met and multiplied, feeding upon the frustrations of a city-bound and job-harried angler like a school of oversexed bluegills. Until we undergo the electric-shock therapy of our annual year-end inventory, we will not be able to confirm whether we have this year two reels for every rod or two rods for every reel. We did determine earlier this season that we had 3.5 lines for each reel, with matching spools, and we've spent the remainder of the year worrying about which rods have only one-half a line allotted to them.

After the introduction of the second rod into those virgin waters, we proceeded to add further exotic species. This year we have managed to introduce the following items to our increasingly befouled waters:

- Six gut leaders, stained by Hewitt, and a brushed aluminum (or would it be aluminium?) English leader box with drying pads—as yet undefiled.
- A silk fly line, #3 IFI floating, but no rod to float it (make a note of this!) and a line-storage reel to dry it, should it ever become wet.
- A strange apparatus, resembling to all purposes an orthopedic truss, designed to train the novice angler to stop his backcast at one o'clock high; one end is taped to the rod handle, the other held firmly against the biceps in the manner of a crutch to keep the arm and rod from descending below the one o'clock position on the backcast. We have decided that it has merit, but not necessarily in its use. Up to now, the mere thought of this device taped to the handle of our Leonard rod during an evening hatch on the Beaverkill has been sufficient to deter us from coming closer than 12:45 on the casting clock.
- A nicely tailored canvas rod bag to contain some six or eight of our most-often-used rods and rod cases, and a heavy-duty aluminum carrying case to carry the canvas-bagged rod cases in. Lately we have been eyeing a fitted cloth bag to cover the aluminum carrying case. But this would probably appear to be a trifle pushy.
- A five-foot-long cabinet of fly-tying materials, purchased from a reformed fly tier, and sufficient to match all the hatches known to Ernie Schwiebert and Art Flick. It reposes at the back of our fly-tying table, but the two most vital drawers cannot be opened without our first cleaning off the entire table—suggesting more than a few unmatched hatches next season.
- Seven new bamboo rods and four additional glass rods, bring our current total—quoted from time to time by our sons' friends as one might the closing stock market prices—to thirty-one. But not including a handmade glass rod that we loaned, in a rare moment of compassion, to a rodless novice; what would ensue should thirty-one of our most intimate angling companions from around the country descend upon us, ill-equipped but eager, is enough to make us quite apprehensive. We must get it back.

To go beyond this brief inventory would be stretching the boundaries of good taste. Suffice it to say it has been a good year. We even caught a few fish.

However, the threat of imminent overpopulation of our angling environment has not gone unnoticed, neither by us nor by our wife. An overnight fishing trip into the Ozarks has gradually taken on the aspects of a fully mounted invasion, and we find ourself wondering how Leslie Howard ever pulled it off.

Our wife, not one of our regular angling companions but nevertheless conservation-minded (keep our bank account green), has spent an undue amount of time casting about in our pool of tackle lately. Over the dark months ahead we shall manage to do a bit of additional stocking, but we predict that, by the time of the spring run-off, there will be a disastrous winter kill.

How to Get Rid of Your Hang-Ups
(1973)

IT'S ALWAYS A PLEASURE to demonstrate one's expertise—especially if one's ration of it is limited. *Fly Fisherman* magazine colleague Dick Friz and I had taken a few stolen moments from the office to run up the road to a newly found stretch of the Mettawee, the excellent local stream we frequent when we're too chicken to trek some fifteen minutes away to the Battenkill. Dick had gone downstream while I investigated a particularly enticing pool near our put-in point—one of those "places I would go if I were a fish," a technique which has only proved to me over the years that I think neither like a fish nor a fisherman.

I eventually moved downstream, and rounded a double bend in the stream, to find Dick puzzling over a rather difficult yet promising lie. The violent early summer flooding had built a veritable beaver dam in an elbow of the stream's course, but the tricky current and the keystone log had made the eddy pool something less than inviting.

"I've been holding off until you got here," Dick confessed in the still blooming innocence of his second season of fly fishing. "I didn't want to hang up in there and ruin the fishing. There was a rise a minute ago."

"Well, now then," I chuckled knowingly in my most paternal manner, "I think this can be handled. We'll just cast this Cahill above that log, then float it for just . . . a . . . few feet . . . then . . . retrieve it carefully j-u-s-t as it . . .

". . . but before I do, I'll show you how to remove a snagged hook from a goddam log without disturbing the fish!" My keen reflexes had prevented me from actually setting the hook in the log. But it was still an awkward situation, and I reached for any available cliché. "One thing you'll learn is that, if you aren't hanging up occasionally, you aren't fishing. You've got to cast where the fish are, and there's nothing they like better than a half-submerged log like this one."

And truthfully, I didn't mind it myself, because I was at last on firm ground. Over the past ten years, I had hooked and released more logs than Lee Wulff had trout, and I knew how to do it, and perhaps better than any angler in the free world today. "I thought you'd like to see how this is done," I added.

Dick's interest span was obviously limited, but after striking him across the wader seat with a convenient stick with 2 × 4 dimensions to regain his attention, I proceeded to demonstrate. Pulling a few yards of line off my reel and drawing my rod tip well back over my right shoulder until the running line curved up from the water at my side, I executed a well-turned and sharp roll cast. The loop rolled the length of the line, its momentum lifted the hook back and out from the log neatly, and then, without disturbing the surface beyond the log, my snap backcast carried the fly safely out of danger.

Dick couldn't have been more impressed. Well, not totally true. After looking back over his shoulder, perhaps he would have been even more impressed if my fly hadn't snagged on a limb some ten feet above and behind me. "Notice," I mumbled, "how I always keep my backcast high. That way, you never snag bushes on the backcast. Only trees."

My fall from grace had been rapid, but I had not reached bottom yet. Because if you think you are gathered here by the river just to learn how to get your rusty old hooks out of soggy old logs, you're completely separated from your gourd. This becomes a morality play, with touches of Greek tragedy, complete with chorus.

I had gotten out of the frying pan, but it would be hard to pull *this* one out of the fire. "There is a way out of this, of course," I explained as I tried to think of one. But desperation is often the unwed mother of inspiration. "And here's how," I suddenly blurted. "I merely turn the rod over and use the reel as a hook to pull the snagged limb within reach."

Dick watched in fascination as I stumbled deeper into the Dismal Swamp. I held the rod upside down, with the butt-section, topped by the Hardy reel, swaying precariously back and forth like a circus high-pole act as I attempted to hook the limb with the reel. I strained on tip-toes to bring the two together, finally consummated this unnatural act, and began to pull the limb within arm's reach when suddenly, I felt a sharp pain in my groin and heard a sickening snap.

Oh, if it had only been that incipient hernia! But life is not that easy. It had, instead, been the deep-digging tip of my treasured Winston, and the snap the final thrust as the rod tip reached the crotch of my waders. What an ironic twist, literally, to bring pleasure to Doctor Johnson, even in paraphrase—"a fly at one end and a fool at the other," and the wrong ends at that.

I HAD ASKED FOR IT. In fact, I had always wanted to acquire a 6½ foot Winston, like Phil Wright's, to go with my 7½ footer—and now I had one. But the irony of it all went even deeper. As Dick and I had gathered our gear from the trunk, I realized that it was too warm to wear my long-sleeved fishing jacket, so I transferred "the bare essentials" from that jacket to my short vest. To me, "bare essentials" usually means bringing only one small hand-ax and eliminating the mini-chain saw, but against my better judgment, and because we had less than an hour to fish, I had knowingly *not* transferred my handy Fly Retriever.

This had been an unfortunate oversight, as Dick Friz well knew, because on a stretch of the Battenkill earlier last season I had demonstrated quite graphically how well this new fly-retrieval device worked. I had gotten down to my last Hendrickson, and then proceeded to hang it up—"you aren't fishing if you aren't hanging up," someone said—on a scraggle of bushes over-reaching an undercut bank that had been the launching pad for several frantic rises by some hungry Battenkill brownies.

I merely placed the Fly Retriever—actually a sharp pruning hook—into the end of my rod's tip-top. After reaching out carefully and anchoring it on the offending branch, I then removed the rod tip from the hook itself and used the strong cord attached to the well-sharpened pruning hook to sever the light branch and retrieve the last Hendrickson without disturbing the pool. It worked, just as the man said in the ads, and for me, it wasn't the first time. P.S. I didn't take one of those Battenkill browns back with me—but I *did* return with the entire 8 feet of my Leonard!

How to Get Gut-Hooked
(1970)

THE JOY OF DISCOVERY in fly-fishing never totally diminishes, but I would suppose that the level of pure ecstasy is never higher than during one's first years astream with the willowy wand.

Truthfully, it was less than fifteen years ago when, approaching middle-age as tangentially as possible, I realized that there would be soon little else to do, so I went fishing. Like many others before and after me, I had fished sporadically in a most desultory and unlearned fashion in my early years. As any youngster, I found the *idea* of fishing quite exciting but the *process* itself rather overwhelming. My memories are of $5.98 plug-casting reels, quickly enriched with rust; of magnificent bird's nests of a line similar to that used by my younger daughter today in doing her macramé; and of grand and massive plugs so large and gaudily painted that I realize now they were not designed to be cast but to be launched. I do not even have any firm recollection of "fish that got away."

I do recall, however, the kind services of a neighbor—the father of a friend and a man who sensed my own father's parental delinquencies—who took me with him and Jack on my first angling excursion to what I like to refer as "my home stream"—the Mississippi River. We fished with unutterable devices for unspeakable varieties of underwater life, and I do have a faint memory of actually hooking up on something, although I cannot be certain whether it was organic or inorganic. The Mississippi still managed to harbor both in those days, although "Mississippi mud" had already become firmly implanted in the language by that time.

However, this very fact—peering into a brown and silty liquid for a fleeting object that my elders had hinted might be there—prepared me for my later incursions into fly-fishing. I *believed* that there was actually something down there! Just as I believed, in my first fly-fishing excursions—and in my last one last season—that a wisp of wool and a hank of hair would personify Escoffier to that most wily of fish, the trout. For fly fishing is an act of faith.

You've got to believe. You must believe everything I say here, and certainly the words of the major prophets, such as Schwiebert, Wulff, Fox, Kreh and the two-headed entomologist Swisher-Richards. Believe us—until we are proved guilty. And, of course, we never will be, for our guilt must be judged by a jury of our peers—and no self-respecting "expert" fly fisherman will ever admit to having any.

But we will not lie to you. We will tell you the truth as we have seen it revealed over the years, the decades and the centuries. It is just that the Wulffs and the Foxes and the other reigning kings of the angling bestiary have learned to make less mistakes than you—and even less than I.

And, as for myself, I have probably had more time and opportunities to make these mistakes—opportunities I took full advantage of, I must admit—but I find myself making less and less of the same mistakes, at least, each ensuing year . . . and I haven't been at this business so long that I have forgotten them.

Take Ernie Schwiebert, for example. Take him anywhere, but not fishing. He doesn't make mistakes—he makes angling history every time he casts. Schwiebert's father loved him best, and took him up to Michigan from the time Ernie could walk. He was potty-trained on the Au Sable, and weaned to the dry fly on the Pere Marquette. He teethed on a vintage Leonard. Every time I think of him I get sick to my stomach. But I believe him; I believe everything he says in *Matching the Hatch* and *Nymphs*. Again, it's an act of faith, like eating stew: you've got to believe that everything in there is good for you.

But people like Schwiebert don't remember things. They forget their mistakes, and they read their own books and *they* believe them. I, on the other hand, piscatorial basket-case that I still am, don't believe anything I've written—except when I'm writing it. Then I never read it again. But I remember my mistakes—often in the middle of the night, in the middle of a pool of sweat. And I remember how it was, back there in the early '60s, in the dim, gray dawn of my fly-fishing genesis as I flailed away unceasingly, even on the seventh day when the Lord Himself rested. "Pity him," I'm certain He said, gazing down at me, "for he knows not what he does."

Somehow a fly rod had appeared in our household—purchased, as I recall, *in absentia* by my wife for my elder son in behalf of his uncle. Regardless, none of us knew anything about using one, and especially the purchaser, who to this day thinks fly fishing is silly and that all fishermen smell. She doesn't even believe in Schwiebert; she's been close enough to him to sniff him, and she likes him, but she doesn't believe him.

A few weeks later I stood by a large pond. Alone. I held the long, slim rod in my hand, and I was suddenly Adam with the urge but without Eve. I was the man who just invented the wheel and didn't realize it and instead tried to use it as a table. Once or twice I was even able to cast the fly beyond the rod tip. I made a dozen forward casts before I got the fly wet—and the water was lapping at my toes. It was totally frustrating, and I say "totally" advisedly, because, despite my ineptitude, I subconsciously realized that there was more to all this than met the eye. I was the short-circuited end of a laying-on-of-hands begun, I suppose, with Walton and Cotton, passed on by Halford and Skues along the "holy waters" of the Test and the Itchen in England and then to Theodore Gordon and the other earthly hosts who kept the faith over the centuries. A few more casts, if I may describe my lurching heaves thus, and I was, literally and figuratively, hooked. Suddenly I was off—off to seek the Holy Grail, wherever the quest might take me.

I have not found it. In fact, the only thing I've found is that no one has, and that there are keenly honed anglers of 80 years, and who have fished like hell for 70 of them, who will go to their rest still hoping to make the perfect presentation to the perfect rise of the perfect fish. Perhaps it's a disservice to tell you this, because in other less gentle recreations there is a certain score to be reached, a specific goal to be attained, and total satisfaction is then realized. In fly fishing, this is not true; one can keep score, but the point total always adds up to one. With each cast you begin again; there is no point in the fly-fishing experience at which one yells "Bingo!" Occasional "hells" and "damns," perhaps, but never "Bingo!"

Take Me to Your Liter
(1975)

MY COMPANION AT THE BAR had me confounded, so I did what I always do when confronted with a difficult problem-solving situation. I apply the weight of sheer logic and order another drink.

"Are you people over there at *Fly Fisherman* magazine," he posed, "ready for conversion to the metric system? Almost on us, you know."

Well, the gentleman was celebrating his eightieth birthday, and I had to humor him. I rapidly calculated that he had been alive during about forty percent of our country's history, and then wondered why the hell he didn't just live in the past like old geezers are supposed to.

Our founding fathers had deemed it "meet and right so to do" to adopt the British Imperial system of weights and measures when they broke the tie that binds some 200 years ago. I've managed to live with most of this legacy, except for pints of warm beer, and we're going to hold out to the last here at *Fly Fisherman*. Measuring King William's pedal appendage from heel to toe, and then calling it a foot—which it was—seemed like a rather straightforward and honest thing to do.

But Senator Claiborne Pell tells us that the United States is losing some $25 billion each year because of the conversion problems (or would it be twenty-five gigabucks?), and Congress doesn't like to throw away that much money without putting its imprint on it. England has already moved to get rid of King William's foot, and apparently we'll be moving into our third century under the metric system, instead of the socialist system which my companion had been darkly predicting ever since "that man" moved into the White House.

"Kilogram for kilogram, centimeter for centimeter, the black bass is the gamest fish that swims!" Dear old Dr. Henshall would never have said that back in the nineteenth century when he was running around the country planting bass like an angling Johnny Appleseed—or at least no one would have re-membered it—had we been under the metric flag in those days of yore.

Now, meters I can go along with. Most of us can live with those. A meter is just about four inches longer than a yard—so we can make a cast of twenty meters instead of sixty feet and gain another six feet. Ten percent longer casts without the ex-pense of buying a graphite rod!

Of course, anglers like Charlie Ritz and Lee Wulff and Er-nie Schwiebert have been fishing for metric monsters for years in various exotic waters, and they'll manage to convert rather easily. I still remember commiserating with Ernie when he re-turned from a week on the Laerdal and told me that he only picked up "two salmon over twenty kilos." I thought this was a shame to go all that distance and pay all that money—until I realized that the guy had knocked off a couple of forty-five pounders-plus.

My kind of fish don't hold up under Schwiebert's "over-kilo" measurements, however, because around here a half kilo is a good fish. But, come to think of it, a "twenty decagram brookie" sounds pretty good—even if I know that it's just seven ounces. "I beached a twenty decagrammer this morning." That would be good for one free drink at the local pub, at least for a year or two.

But, of course, there will be the trouble-makers. Swisher-Richards, the two-headed monster of angling entomology, will undoubtedly market a handy streamside "No Hassle" Metric Converter and then we won't be able to get away with anything.

I thought again of our founding fathers and the Bicenten-nial year. The breakaway from England was now complete. I looked with admiration at the grizzled but dapper gentleman next to me (a founding father himself, of sorts—mine), amazed that he could accept the metric system so readily with four score years under his belt.

Speaking of belts, he ordered another deciliter of bourbon, but, holding out to the last, I demanded two fingers of scotch.

I sipped on, confident that anglers would quickly learn to lie under *any* system of measurement.

· II ·

Only When We Laugh

For Those Who Have Known Pain

THEY TALK OF THEIR "EVENING VESPERS" ASTREAM, THESE fly-persons, of their "holy waters" among the Hampshire chalkstreams, and of the "laying on of hands" as they steal old fly patterns from each other. But we don't start to worry too much about them until they try to head for the opposite bank without wearing their waders.

For some of them, the act of angling seems to be a constant act of contrition for not having gone directly to the seminary—an apology for having taken up the rod instead of the cloth. This bothers some of us, even though we clearly recognize that ours is a higher calling than most mortals are heir to.

But we also recognize the inherent foolishness in the sight of grown men and women deep in their piscatorial pursuits, fully believing that they can entice a wily trout into a consummate deathwish with a hunk of steel and a hank of hair. We see them beguiled by myth and wive's-tale as they mount their gentle crusade—and then we often see them later for a sacramental snifter or two, just to ward off those evil spirits who constantly plague the basically good. Especially if the good were not good enough that day.

I once met a drunken angler astream, and thought it a horrible sight, until I met a sober angler who had fished beyond the local pub closing time.

There's Nothing Like a Dame
(1979)

SPRING HAD COME UNSPRUNG. The rains came, the snow stayed. The rivers rose, and the fish didn't, so why should the contemplative angler? Instead, I remained in bed and sought refuge in literature, trying to catch up on the dozens of angling books that seem to spew forth each month—a growing stockpile to which *Fly Fisherman* has recently made a substantial contribution, at least in bulk.

Naturally, we've had to be selective here at *Fly Fisherman* in the books that we review. Had we covered them all each issue, few of us would be here now. However, all this is by way of an apology for a major oversight that we would like to correct in this issue. We're a tad late, but it is a book with some redeeming piscatorial value, so we present it now for your delectation.

A Treatife of Fifhing with an Angle, Berners, Dame Juliana. St. Albans Press, Sopwell, England, 1496 price: (hardback) 50 groat (70 groat in Gaul).

DESPITE THE POOR PROOFREADING, *Treatife* does bear looking into. It is a thoughtful work, and we must compliment Dame Berners for not rushing it into print—although such a decision was perhaps not totally in her hands, since the authoress is reported to have written the manuscript as early as 1406 and thus had to wait around until moveable type was invented in the mid-fifteenth century. (There are reports, however, that several Xerox copies were made earlier by a small, balding monk.)

The publishers lay claim on the dust-jacket—and our review copy was excessively dusty—to have produced, with the issuance of *Treatife,* the first book on angling. I suppose we can allow some literary license here, although most of us accept the canon that fly-fishing as we know it was invented in the late 1930's by Ernest Schwiebert.

Regardless, the work does deserve attention, if only for the culture shock we experience when we realize that the first fishing book was written, not only by a woman, but also a working nun, a prioress, in fact (see *Canterbury Tales*, G. Chaucer). The Priory at Sopwell was the mother house of a particularly uncloistered order, for the original manuscript contains sections, not only on angling, but on hawking, hunting and fowling. It is with more than inference that we can assume that Dame Juliana and her swinging nuns both ate and lived well, for she commends to us in her introductory passages the three principles by which she guides her own life style:

"Merry thought . . . work in moderation . . . and a good diet of pure food and suitable drinks."

We can fault her on none of these, adding only that a person of Holy Orders who follows them cannot be All Good. To us, however, this was the high point of a rather tedious introduction; we were elated to arrive at the meatier sections of the Dame's *Treatife*.

BASEMENT RODMAKERS may disagree with Dame Juliana's recipe for fabricating a rod, however, as it involves a rather exotic heat-treatment process requiring an oven, a bird spit, ferrules of hooped iron, and "fair shoots of blackthorn, crabtree, medlar and juniper" for the tip section. We also question the cooling and drying period of four weeks after heat treatment, but Ms. Berners does suggest that all this be done off-season, or more accurately "between Michaelmas and Candlemas."

In her discussion of line making, the good Prioress of Sopwell offers a rather stimulating alternative to the ready-made convenience-packaging of today's fly lines. She prescribes the single hairs from a tail of a white horse, each colored differently and woven together, then boiled, with an admixture of walnut leaves, in a kettle of ale! Enjoyed with one's angling companions, such a pursuit could possibly promote a high order of good fellowship during the lengthy process.

DAME BERNERS' WORK does come into its own when she deals directly with the pursuit of trout with the fly. Her chapter "In What Place is the Best Angling" is appropriately "catholic" in its recommendations. "You should angle in a pool or in standing water, in every place where it is at all deep and clear at the bottom . . . and especially if there is a whirly-pit of water, or a covert—such as a hollow bank or great roots of trees and long weeds. . . . Also in deep, swift streams and in waterfalls and weirs, floodgates and mill pits, and wherever the water rests by the bank and the current runs close by and it is deep and clear at the bottom."

Now, should you think that Dame Juliana has already covered the waterfront, you would be mistaken, for she leaves us with an inspired coda to this "survey of hot spots" by adding: "And in any other places where you can see fish rising and feeding at the top." Nowhere have we seen the art of reading the water so completely revealed.

We must nevertheless question her loose usage when she recommends times of the year to fish. She speaks interchangeably of "fishing with the anglerod" for trout during "leaping time" or during "biting time." We feel that she shows a certain shallowness of experience by not explaining to the apprentice angler that these two key events do not always coincide.

Even in a dissertation on matters temporal, it is appropriate that a medieval religious should be influenced by Biblical numerology—as in the case of her three recommendations for a sound life—and we are not disappointed in Dame Juliana's listings of "Twelve Impediments to Catching Fish" and "Twelve Flies with which You Must Angle for the Trout."

Berners leads off with typical directness:

1. If your tackle is not good and well made (although there is no supplier directory in the appendix).
2. If you do not angle in biting (or even "leaping") time.
3. If the fish are frightened by the sight of man.
4. If the water is thick . . . from any flood recently fallen.

5. If the fish will not stir either for cold or fair weather.
6. If the water is very hot.
7. If it rains.
8. If it hails or snows.
9. If there is any tempest.
10. If there is a great wind from any direction.
11. Poor choice of bait.
12. (An interminable discussion of wind directions in which she boxes the compass, possibly in anticipation of the Solunar Tables.)

Although most readers will have experienced most of these derelictions, all will find solace in such a conveniently condensed tabulation.

ONE WOULD EXPECT a woman of Dame Juliana's high calling to dwell also upon the ethical and esthetic aspects of our recreation, and page after page after page, one will not be disappointed. In summarizing her philosophy, Dame Juliana consoles us should we break off a fish—she urges us to look on such experiences as "wholesome and as merrie walks" in which we "hear the melodies of the sounds of birds"—and then admonishes us against trespassing, raiding other men's fish traps, poaching and in general against "using our artful sport for covetousness."

She strikes a telling blow for stream management and ecological good works when she charges the reader to "busy yourself to nourish the game in everything you can, and to destroy all such things as are devourers of it."

And in closing, the Prioress of Sopwell gives us a distilled bit of angling morality that, we must admit, puts to shame the pithy but rather trendy slogan of the Theodore Gordon Flyfishers ("Limit Your Kill . . . Don't Kill Your Limit!").

Chides Dame Juliana pungently: "When you have a sufficient mess, you should covet no more at that time."

WE COULD NOT HAVE SAID IT BETTER, and we commend our fellow publishers over at St. Albans Press for their foresight, if not their alacrity, in bringing this praiseworthy tome to the angling public.

We understand that it will be a "Book of the Millennium" selection of the Field & Stream Book Club in September, and that selections from *Treatife* will be published in a forthcoming issue of *Sports Afield* under the title "Unlocking the Angling Secrets of the Ancients!"

A Treatise on Writing with an Angle
(1981)

1500
Approx. ~~3500~~ words
(12) transparencies (35mm)
ONLY 10!! 2 LOST

Submitted by Sam Jones

THIS NEEDED SOME TOUCH-UP
WORK, BUT IT SHOULD BE A
CLASSY PIECE FOR OUR NEXT ISSUE.
                                    EDITOR

A Catskill Nocturne

~~Hauling 'Em In On The "Ash Can"~~

Joseph
/~~Joe~~ Berger, my ~~fishing buddy~~ (angling companion), and ~~me~~ I try to get to the Catskills together at least once each season to fish the ~~Ashokan Reservoir~~ storied waters of the fabled ~~"the Ash Can,"~~ ~~dumps into it~~. Joe, who's known to his ~~Joe calls it where the lower~~ Esopus River friends as ~~'Stinky', works for a White Plains exterminating company, but~~ J.B. is a Westchester County chemical firm executive,

in the summer he lives ~~on an old party boat at a slip near 85th St. on the~~ near his yacht on Upper Manhatten's exclusive East Side. ~~East River in Manhattan.~~

cruises
Between ~~trips~~ he can usually be found advising ~~derelicts~~ members at ~~the Harbor~~ his club Wall Street ~~Light refuge in the Bowery area~~ dist., giving the benefit of his experience to his friends from the street, ~~just as he promised the judge.~~

But now it was September, and Joe had tired of ~~dragging~~ cruising the ~~river~~ Sound for shark ~~sea robins~~ with ~~a boat load of beer and baloney Jerseyites~~ the jet-sets beautiful people, and we were headed once more for the ~~Ashokan~~ beckoning challenge of the Esopus. This year we would be following the adv late Arnold Gingrich ~~the old nighterawler fisherman~~ gave us years ago—"fish ~~will bite fine an~~ ~~if you go far enough off~~ the point there you'll take them ~~in like you we~~ ~~shootin' em~~ with 22's." oligochaeta

I had worked up a good ~~earthworm~~ oligochaeta pattern on a ~~#12~~ #22 hook, and old Jo

28

IF ONLY FOR PENANCE, anyone who fly-fishes should essay to write an angling article of some redeeming piscatorial value. Getting it published is another piece of business, of course, but today, with fly-fishing becoming increasingly popular, there are many opportunities available in some of the fine organizational and regional angling magazines, as well as the general outdoor publications, for the novice writer. The information that follows should help lead you down that primrose path to publishing success, in your own basement, and for fun and profit.

FIRST, A FEW GENERAL TIPS. While it is not true that those who can't fish, write, and those who can't write, edit, it is generally the case that angling editors are an inherently touchy lot, basically frustrated and insecure—publishing's walking wounded. Treat them gently.

Drops of water on the covering letter will not lead the editors to believe that the manuscript was composed on the stream; rather, their twisted psyches will interpret these as tear stains, however falsely contrived they might be, and editors do not like to become emotionally involved with contributors unless they are of the opposite gender (which they have a difficult enough time handling when they edit).

Keep the covering letter short, giving only salient facts, such as your name and address. For example, if you have included color slides, give the number of slides sent—adding one or two to the number actually sent so that the editor will eventually become personally involved in your submission. Again, keep the cover letter crisp and brief—if it is too long, the editor might not know which submission to reject. (I once rejected an article but published the covering letter.)

Number the pages of your manuscript. Editors like to know right off how many pages they have to cut out.

Send return envelope and postage with the manuscript. Be certain to allow some twenty percent additional in stamps in anticipation of future postage increases to go in effect before the editor makes a decision on your submission.

Don't daub a spot of rubber cement on the second or third page of your manuscript to see if someone actually read your rejected article. One doesn't have to eat an entire goldfish to realize that it's a carp. (I once returned such a gummed up submission with a nice note telling the author that "we all found your opening paragraphs intriguing but we couldn't read the rest of the piece because it seemed to be glued together." I never heard from him.)

BUT ENOUGH OF THE MECHANICS of manuscript submission. There's an awaiting audience of fly fishermen out there who will believe almost anything you tell them. It must, however, be phrased, couched and cleanly set in the form to which they have become accustomed. As you know, all fly fishermen are affluent, educated, literate and highly cultivated, and they will not accept hackneyed, cliché-ridden prose. Perhaps a little guidance would be appropriate at this point.

No "Me and Joe" stories. In these "classics," Joe is usually holder of the local Roto-Rooter franchise or the village Amway distributor, who receives a late-night call from the author to see how "they're biting" down at Hawkins' Hole. Joe speaks of an unspeakable device, generously baited with Roman Meal bread, that will take every sucker in the hole by beertime, and before he finishes the conversation Joe's already caught one. Such writing has no place in the fly-fishing literature—unless, of course, Joe turns out to be chairman-of-the-board of a *Fortune* "500" corporation, in which case the opening would be edited, so as not to offend the reader's sensibility, to "Joe and I."

Wine selection is important. Fly anglers do not live by fish alone. Streamside luncheons are very important, as well as victory dinners later that evening. If there is any question in your mind as to the appropriate chateau or vintage, place a call to Ernie Schwiebert, Philip Wright or Sylvia Bashline, outdoor-writer Jim Bashline's wife and recognized fish-and-wine authority— but in the latter case, if a man answers, hang up.

Lace your article with well-known names. "I used the special knot that Lefty showed me on our way out to the Dry Tortugas," or "It reminded me of that day at Lee's salmon camp up in the Labrador when we took six fine grilse between us by sunrise." Of course, this can get sticky if it turns out that these notables claim fuzziness in their recollection of specific events.

In that case, use *deceased* anglers. A few choice phrases can heighten the pungency of your prose—such as "I've always considered it presumptuous of Halford to have suggested. . . ." or "there are those of us who still question Gordon's dubbing technique," can put you in the best of company and the safest of hands.

But if you can't drop names, drop streams. "I'm lucky if I hold a rod on the Grimsa for a week or two each year, but the West Branch of the Old Silty, just an hour away from my home, continues to hold a dark challenge within its murky depths." The average reader immediately identifies with you, a world-class angler, as you step down to his level from that chilled Icelandic river to fish the Old Silty with him in southern Illinois.

Don't carry around tape measures and scales. These just bog down a writer, both physically and creatively. Recollect in tranquillity; possibly in front of a log fire on a crisp autumn evening, applying mild libations of scotch to start those creative juices flowing. Tell it like it is—but six months later.

Don't fall victim to the grammar/spelling/neatness fetish. Such submissions bring out the most base of latent neuroses and frustrations to which angling editors fall heir. A crisp, clear manuscript, seemingly untouched by human hands and resembling the Dead Sea Scrolls as written by Henry James, practically screams out "Charge!" to angling editors. The last refuge of their funky spirits lies in the enticing presence of that dangling participle, the errant misspelling and the undecipherable typo; don't take this away from them.

Use action words, especially if the trip was unproductive. Don't let a "fish take your fly." Allow it, and the reader, the luxury of seeing the "great leviathan spin on its fins and lust hungrily after my spectral mini-midge." But, in livening up your lines, do not jar the reader to the point that his train of thought is totally derailed, as did the imaginative author of an otherwise excellent article submitted to us recently: After carefully trimming with scissors the hackled body, he then asked us to "take the carefully circumcised fly and. . . ." But, like you and the future reader, we got no farther. *What* kind of fly? What kind of *hackle*? From the neck of the Barred Mitzvah? He temporarily lost us.

One must use a certain restraint in describing Homeric achievements astream. The thoughtful editor will prefer that a sorely tested reel not "scream in a sirenlike wail," but rather that it "whine in controlled anticipation." And certainly, ". . . with bared fangs the great lunker brown exploded the pool into a mushroom cloud of water droplets" has little charm to recommend it to the more contemplative angler. References to nuclear fission have no place on our fly water. Might it not have been phrased more subtly: "Perhaps it was the sting of spray in my eyes that led me to misjudge the size of my companion at the other end of my line, but . . ."—and then proceed to make quiet suggestions as to the handspread between the eyes of the fish in question.

ALTHOUGH I'VE ONLY TOUCHED on a few fine points in this discussion of writing fly-fishing articles, it's quite possible that, with some minor extrapolation and major imagination, the quoted phrases in this article could be cunningly strung together into your first fly-fishing article and submitted to angling magazines (nicely Xerox-ed, of course, so that copies can be mailed simultaneously to a dozen prospective publications).

But don't call us, we'll call you. We're going to be very busy updating our old rejection notices.

· · ·

An Anthology of Short Casts

Comparison Is Odoriferous

WHILE ON A BASS-FISHING TRIP to the Ozarks a few months ago we arrived at our fishing-camp cabin and noticed a rather pronounced animal odor. We searched the cabin for any dead animals or rotting fish, found nothing, and went about our fishing. It wasn't until we were packing up to leave and were searching through a dark closet that we arrived at ground zero—two pairs of waders and a lump of rancid fishing clothes left, likely by choice, by some earlier anglers returning to the bosom of their families.

This adds new depth, if only by paraphrase, to the oft-repeated pronouncement of the venerable Dr. C. M. Henshall about the sporting qualities of his favorite gamefish. Thus we can state that, without qualification, inch for inch and pound for pound, smallmouth bass anglers are the gamiest fishermen in the world.

Weighty Matters

Perhaps it is only the rather delicate physique of most of the trout we take, but we have never made a habit of weighing our catch. The closest we have ever come to acknowledging the avoirdupois of our creeled catch has been an unconsciously affected list to port upon return to camp or car at the end of a day. Weigh-ins are for prizefighting, not for fly fishing. If God had intended trout to be weighed, He would have given them bigger scales.

· · ·

· 34 ·

Raise Cane, Not Hell

We ran across an interesting piece of information recently which we covered in more detail in this issue's "Complete Fly Fisherman" department—to the effect that about 20 percent of the 694 models of fly rods available today are still made of split Tonkin cane. We also pointed out that the first modern split-bamboo rod made of Tonkin cane—as opposed to the unsatisfactory Calcutta cane used prior to that—was made by William Mitchell in 1869. Thus *Fly Fisherman* magazine cannot possibly let this anniversary pass unnoticed—the centennial of the modern Tonkin bamboo rod.

Of course, as all bamboozlers know only too well, Tonkin cane has been in short supply for more than two decades. The cane fields of Tonkin Province—formerly in China, but now in North Vietnam—have been noticeably unproductive since about 1948 when they were overrun with nonangling types. Stocks of Tonkin cane have dwindled, both here in America and in England, because the better artisans select only the finest cane from their stocks with which to make their rods. Part of the premium one must pay for good bamboo rods is the cost of select cane—measured against the limited supply.

We have a friend who has been worrying about this for twenty years—until it has become an obsession with him. He has nine lovely bamboo rods in his stable, but he is afraid to use any of them because of the uncertainty of the future. Life as he knows it has been directly threatened by the dropping of the Bamboo Curtain.

Normally peaceful, if not outright dovish, he has convinced himself that the Vietnam conflict is actually a war to liberate Tonkin Province and its fallow cane fields. In reporting this, we do not intend for a moment to make light of a war that has taken the lives of some 30,000 American men and shows no immediate signs of abating—but up to this moment, our friend's proposed reason for being there is about the most logical that we've heard.

The last report from our friend informed us that he was training a small force of dedicated anglers for a possible invasion of the mainland. But happily, his normally peaceful instincts are prevailing, and rather than any immediate effort to hit the beach at Tonkin, he is planning instead to teach President Nixon to fly fish. With a rod made of Tonkin cane, of course.

On Presidents

It is interesting to note, for what it is worth, that our country has never fought a major war during the administrations of Presidents who were fly fishermen . . . Taft, Teddy Roosevelt, Coolidge, and Hoover.

In fact, we seem to recall that practically *nothing* happened during the administration of President Coolidge!

The Skues Appeal

Thirty years ago as we write this a gentleman named G.E.M. Skues passed away in his native England after a long and productive life. He is, of course, known to many fly fishers in this country through his books (including *Minor Tactics of the Chalk Stream* and *The Way of a Trout with a Fly*) and as the "father" of the nymph. He had been fishing his beloved Itchen one day—with a dry fly, upstream, after the manner of the chalkstream folk—when he was forced, as a last resort, to bend on a particularly scrimpy store-bought pattern that immediately sank—and almost as immediately was taken by a large brown.

This happy event led to a long investigation, many articles in the journals, a long battle with F.M. Halford, *paterfamilias* of the dry fly, and, on some Hampshire waters, his banishment to angling Coventry. But the nymph, and the nympher, survive, and British anglers are planning to honor his memory.

When Skues died in August of 1949 at the age of 91, his will stipulated that his ashes be scattered over the Itchen along the Abbots Barton stretch above the town water at Winchester—and specifically on "the tussocky paddock on the East Bank of the main river."

Unlike some of his somber and pedantic predecessors,

Skues was a talented writer who could occasionally relax and drop in a bit of verse or light anecdote. In fact, in the introduction to a recent collection of Skues articles, *The Chalk-Stream Angler,* British angler-writer Conrad Voss-Bark reminds readers with a sly wink of Skues' "schoolboy jokes" perpetrated within the pages of the often-austere *Flyfishers' Journal.*

I was personally fetched by the colorful instructions in Skues' will, and the result was a schoolboy reversion similar to his occasional lapses. I do not intend to submit the lines below for enshrinement on his headstone, but I feel that Skues would understand.

> There was a nymph angler named Skues,
> Whose doctrine brought nothing but "phooeys."
> Now he fishes for haddock
> From his tussocky paddock
> To let the "old boys" know just *who* he's.

At the least it will teach thousands of fly fishermen to *pronounce* his name as well as honor it.

While fishing, we were wishing . . .

. . . to fish that one distant stream—fished only by anglers who write books and magazine articles—the banks of which are composed of that rare clayey mud that, when rubbed on leaders, sinks them.

. . . to encounter that forgotten little fly in one corner of the fly box, just before the day's last cast, that suddenly causes the pool to explode in a mushroom-like cloud.

. . . to make a reservation to fish a far-off water, and then arrive one week earlier—that week when "the fishing was so great" and "we should have been there."

. . . to follow one of those outdoor magazine cover artists who draw the pictures of savage salmon and vicious brownies with panther-like incisors and see just where it is they do their fishing.

. . . to find one of those fabled fly-fishers who bends on a #28 midge to a 7× tippet between rises of gigantic rainbows at dusk—and spike his carrot juice.

Ancestor Worshiper

This is nothing to worry about, just the forces of evolution at work—natural selection and all that. A fellow we once met in the Men's Bar of the Biltmore in Manhattan while screwing up our courage to enter the tackle department at Abercrombie & Fitch reminded us of this, and of the fact that this evolution extended far into time beyond the anthropoid to that stage of our development at which we had gills instead of ribs, proving that we were all descendants of the fishes. He had actually gone so far as to trace his lineage with the help of a Yale ichthyologist and had found that his people had originally been brown trout. We started to pursue this a bit further, but he suddenly rose to a dry martini and was never seen again.

This is a bit extreme, of course, but there is certainly room within our more gentle definition of "angling purist" to allow for the cultivation of minor conceits and lesser fetishes—and without resorting to the militant reactionism of the small but vocal Establishment groups which are usually identified, and not without some basis in truth, with the Eastern portion of our country. True one may-fly doth not a hatch make, but it would be a delinquency on our part if we were not to report on a significant streamside encounter we witnessed on a fabled Eastern river a few years ago. . . .

Angling Amenities

We had been fishing an upper reach of the revered Overkill and were pausing on the bank for a moment to wash off our waders prior to entering a particularly hallowed pool. As we were completing our devotions we noticed a rather distin-

guished old gentleman moving slowly and methodically upstream as he plied his dry fly with delicacy and precision. As he
neared our vantage point we detected the dull glint of gut at
the point of his supple silk line. His rod was a vintage Leonard,
the reel a Hardy, his apparel pure Abercrombie & Fitch.

Suddenly he stiffened perceptibly, and we awaited with
some anticipation the quick flick of the wrist which would signal
the setting of the hook. But his eyes were not on the water
ahead of him, but rather on an approaching form stumbling
clumsily downstream—we repeat, *downstream*—above him.

He recovered his composure in a moment, for there was
no precedent in his five decades of angling to prepare him for
an encounter with a person who would fish Gordon's Pool
downstream. More likely he assumed that the approaching angler had merely forgotten something and was returning for it.

As the clod approached, our fly fisherman gave him a dis-
creet but friendly wave, then called out "Good day, sir! What
are you using?" in the time-honored stream greeting of those
who long ago had acquired the grace and skill which rendered
invalid the cliché salutation of "any luck?"

"I've got a wet fly, sir," came the equally friendly reply
from the man above.

"A wet fly?" replied the old angler with a puzzled expression. Then, suddenly, he burst out in a relieved and jovial
shout.

"Don't worry about it, old man! Happens to me all the
time. You're probably just wading too deep!"

False Cast

It is both a matter of recorded fact and happy coincidence that
a fly rod of the proper size, action, line and terminal tackle is, in
the majority of cases, the most efficient, fulfilling and sports-
manlike tool for the care and feeding—and even the catching—of fish. We add "catching" advisedly, because the fly
fisherman can become so involved in the esthetic delights of
casting that he forgets to aim his fly at a fish. This type should

be watched carefully, but if the condition reaches manic proportions there is a place for him—although not on the stream.

Q. and A.

Why do fishermen on the lower Madison River wear waders with red suspenders?
    To get to the other side.

Beating the High Cost of Angling
(1979)

In KEEPING WITH White House guidelines, I plan to limit the increase in the number of fish I catch this season to no greater than seven percent. I once calculated the cost of the various support services, equipment and apparel required to catch a fish, and the total came out somewhere between the costs of operating a Strategic Air Command bomber and a small nuclear energy plant (not including safety measures in the latter, which seem to be optional).

The figures were based on the number of fish caught at the height of my skills, a frenzied peak of activity that spanned some three hours during a prolonged may-fly hatch on Wisconsin's Wolf River in 1967. I allowed for inflation in my calculations—inflation of prices, not, of course, of the number of fish taken.

Without going into the sordid financial details, and without a quantitative breakdown of the number of fish taken, let it suffice that the final per-fish cost came out to roughly $847. Some readers might consider this excessive for a recreation that offers few tax write-offs for the typical angler, especially if he catches more than one fish during any given tax year.

It becomes even more overwhelming when one extrapolates these figures to account for the number of fly anglers loose on our waters today. We will be conservative and accept the modest figure of one million anglers who have given themselves to our gentle recreation instead of acquiring box seats to the Dallas Cowboys games, joining indoor tennis clubs or participating in any of the less esthetic excesses available to red-blooded Americans today. Assuming an average of thirty days astream during the angling season—in line with *Fly Fisherman* surveys—during which our anglers catch an average of five one-pound fish, one quickly sees that we are already guilty of a terminal case of inconspicuous consumption.

Although it may be difficult for many readers—to whom my angling skills are legend and who have elevated me to a position in angling folk myth somewhere between Paul Bunyan and Kilroy—to suspend willingly their natural disbelief and accept me as an "average" fly fisherman, we have only to take my carefully calculated cost-per-pound of $847, multiply it by the anglers, their fishing days and their catch of fish to determine that fly fishermen invest more than 125 billion dollars per year in their contemplative recreation!

Even a seven-percent increase in this expenditure during 1979 would amount to $8.9 billion, exactly what was spent in fiscal 1976 by the Department of Defense on all research and development. Any greater increase and it would no longer be Big Business or Big Labor that would disturb lovable old White House inflation fighter Alfred Kahn, but Big Angling. We certainly don't want that trembling, bony little finger pointing at us on the evening news, threatening us with total guilt and a deep and wracking "banana."

Rather, we should look within ourselves—and then around us. For, while we have been literally casting our hard-earned bread upon the water, there is another large segment of fishing America that has been getting paid for it.

MY DAD RECENTLY SENT ME a clipping from the St. Louis *Globe-Democrat,* and I read it with some interest. In recent years I've come to suspect that he wasn't as dumb as I thought he was back in the days when I was still smart. He's spent some sixty years in the advertising game and can usually sniff out a good thing when he sees it—if the St. Louis weather isn't getting to his sinuses.

The piece was Bill Seibel's outdoors column, "Rod & Gun." (Bill took over the column many years ago from his father-in-law, George Carson, beloved among Ozark anglers and who started writing the column some months before there were fish in Missouri.) This particular column was about the bass-fishing tournament circuit and a real eye-opener. These guys have got something going for them. They get paid to catch fish!

Specifically, the event in question was the 1978 Bass Caster's Association-Schlitz Grand National bass tournament, or, as Seibel describes it, "a big bucks fish-off" involving the top 22 fishermen on the BCA's tournament circuit. The fish-off was held at the original Playboy Resort and Country Club, on Wisconsin's lovely Lake Geneva early last fall. Conditions, at least for fishing, were not good. The water was cold—especially for Southern bass fishermen, who could have fallen out of the boat at any time during the tournament—somewhere in the low 50s. Both the skies and the water were agonizingly clear, Seibel reports.

Of course, the uninformed reader could conjure bizarre fictions of weed-popping by day and Bunny-Hopping by night, but they would be wrong. These were professionals with their eyes on the Grand National purse of $3,500, not to speak of the additional Schlitz $1,000 bonus award.

After a day of practice, the money casting began. BCA vice-president Larry D. Heath, apparently functioning as a rather shifty tipster on the side, touted Dave Carroll of Oak Ridge, Tenn. "Carroll is used to fishing for smallmouth in the same kind of water at Norris Dam in eastern Tennessee. He'll win it."

Questioning the accuracy of Heath's track odds, outdoor editor Seibel countered with his own summation. "If Carroll doesn't, Jim Nolan should." Seibel was demonstrating a certain regional bias, of course, for a top-seeded Ozark basser within the coverage area of his newspaper. He wrote, "Nolan, of Bull Shoals, Arkansas, has been pounding the Big Bull for brownies for many years. Both men know the tricks."

They knew all the tricks of professional bass-catching, and Seibel persuaded them to reveal many of them for his readers. Both Nolan and Carroll, for example, confronted with clear skies and cold, clear water, abandoned their usual rigs for light four-pound-test monofilament and spinning rigs early in the tournament. Sly old Carroll's technique was to fish the weeds and keep his eyes on his line as he made his slow retrieve. "You have to reel slow and watch your line," he explained. "You can't feel most of the hits." Then he disclosed: "That's another trait of cold fronts—smallmouth just barely suck the bait in."

Giving us an even deeper insight, Seibel described Carroll

in action. "At the slightest twitch, Carroll would crank the reel handle fast to pick up slack and almost in the same motion set the hook with an upward sweeping motion." Wisely not fishing as a competitor in the tournament but merely as a "press observer," Seibel kept his eyes glued to Carroll. "Once he hooked a fish," Seibel continued, "Carroll played the fish very carefully on the light equipment. 'You can't horse a fish to the boat on light gear like this,' he grimaced as the fish made a surge for deep water and freedom. 'A smallmouth has the power to pop this light line if you try to rush things.'"

On the day of Seibel's press observation of Carroll, Dave boated a 2½-pound small-mouth. "It took him 7½ minutes to land it," Seibel documented. He also reported that Carroll used a three-inch curly-tailed Squealer plastic grub on a ¹⁄₁₆-ounce jig head that day. Carroll called the color "br-ed" because the brown and the red grubs got wet and then mixed up in his tackle box and bled color onto one another. "I think these things imitate *leeches*," Dave confided in an entomological aside to Seibel.

By this time Seibel had understandably abandoned Nolan and put his money on Dave Carroll, hometown loyalty be damned. Nolan used two lures, Seibel reported, a Rapala and a Roadrunner. We assume they were not used concurrently. Nolan preferred "yellow and white colors."

Joe Verbeck, a St. Louis-area favorite from across the river in Belleville, Illinois, "used a leadhead dressed with multiple rubber legs and a small split-tailed eel." Verbeck didn't divulge what this imitated, but told Seibel that "brown was his favorite color."

Larry Landers, another suburban St. Louis qualifier in the Grand National, felt the pressure early on. "I was hurting," he reported, "so I went to Rebel's Humpy and Deep WeedR." Landers liked chartreuse, but went fishless the first day. Two fish the final day weren't enough, though, for the Carroll-Nolan parlay was unbeatable.

Dave Carroll took top honors with four fish. Jim Nolan netted three. Carroll won the Grand National first-prize purse of $3,500, plus the Schlitz bonus of $1,000. Nolan placed and carried off $2,500, but nothing from Schlitz.

· · ·

EVEN THOUGH THIS FISHING is on a different scale and level from that which most *Fly Fisherman* magazine readers are familiar with, we thought this report would offer some revealing insights into the secrets of the angling pros. But, of course, there is more to this revelation than a cursory reading might suggest.

At $3,500 for four fish, Dave Carroll *made* $875 per catch, even disregarding the Schlitz bonus. If we accept my calculations, we fly fishermen *spend* $847 for each fish we catch. Jim Nolan did about as well as Carroll on a per-fish basis, taking in $833 for his three testy retrieves.

Is this a signal of the demise of fly-fishing? At first blush, we thought so, but as they say in the commercials, you only go around once. Although I will watch the seven percent increase guideline this season, I won't let it obsess me. I will cast on, warmed by the thought that, for every $847 I spend, a circuiting bass pro will be raking in from $833 to $874. It's really a matter of ecological balance-of-payments.

Yes, Mr. Kahn, we have no "bananas" today!

---- · · · ----

That'll Be Fifty Dollars, Please
(1980)

HAVEN'T WE ALL experienced it? An acquaintance discovers, perhaps because of the slight facial tic, or possibly by smell, that we are of the angling persuasion, and this revelation is soon followed by the reflexive confession: "I've always wanted to try fishing, but I just don't have the patience to sit there all day waiting for the fish to bite."

Some of us can dismiss this with a knowing smile, while others become militant and deliver long and angry discourses to the poor, stunned infidels. Personally, I try not to hang around people like that at all, but when the confrontation occurs, I usually drift back in memory to one of Nick Lyons' short stories in an early issue of *Fly Fisherman,* in which the angler, after a testy candlelight dinner at the inn with his wife, dons his waders and steps into the dusk for a go at the late-summer evening hatch.

A fine trout is working; the angler moves out into a heavy current to position himself properly, just between that big submerged rock and a nearby hard place, and suddenly finds himself trapped between his lust for trout and his love for life. It was that point-of-no-return that many of us have experienced, and I can't even remember just how long it was, or whether he caught the trout; I only remember that he eventually returned to the inn later that night, and that his wife looked up from the novel she was reading with a casual, even conditioned, "Catch anything?"

Of course there is more to the story than that, but my clumsy exegesis points up the problem. How do we explain all this to the unenfranchised layperson? Why is it that we return from our day or evening astream and fall exhausted into the embrace of a $15-a-night motel mattress? Why the fact that our waders are always drier on the outside? Why do we end our

45

daily safaris with medicinal doses of corn, barley or juniper dis-
tillates? Why all this if, as two psychologists tell us, we can "sit,
waiting for the fish to bite" and "let our minds drift off into
fantasy land."

Such is the news from New Haven, Connecticut, where two
psychologists tell us that "when tensions and stress threaten to
bring on nervous collapse, it's time to go fishing." Dr. Jerome L.
Singer, a Yalie, and Dr. Armin Thies, a Townie, have been running about giving such therapeutic advice to today's harried
and huddled masses yearning to breathe free, and there are
few among us who would not applaud the spirit in which they
have refurbished and re-issued this arcane cliché.

Equally, there are few among us who could willingly identify with the further statements of Drs. Singer and Thies, utter-
ances that seem to become strangled in Yale's surplus of ivy.

States Dr. Thies—after the writer of this revealing newspaper story warns us that "no fisherman is going to argue" with
the gentleman—"the effect of this recreational activity is one of
reducing stress and increasing relaxation . . . perhaps the result
of the *sedentary* nature of the sport." (The italics are mine; the
error is the doctor's.)

Now, I don't care if Dr. Thies *is* the son of veteran St. Louis
Globe-Democrat sportswriter Bud Thies, who authored this tale.
Given twenty-four hours and full recovery from early-season
fractures, contusions and wounded psyches, I could round up a
pride of fly-anglers who would quickly straighten the boy out.
My sons say things too, but I don't write them down and publish them.

The sedentary nature of the sport! The last time I sat while
fishing it was rather wet, and it hurt a lot. I haven't tried it
again. The article itself includes, as illustration of the "peaceful
on-the-water surroundings, as well as the sedentary nature of
the sport," a rugged-looking young man with a pre-
kindergarten-type kid and a wife who looks like one of "Charlie's Angels," all sitting in a motorboat with the beer cooler and
portable radio at ready. They all have spin-rods in their hands,
so they must be fishing.

Such a situation inspires Dr. Singer to evoke images of
Huck Finn and Tom Sawyer "drifting down the Mississippi and
letting their boyish minds soar in pleasant reveries."

I suppose that most of us, in a burst of daring, have at one time or another willingly tested our marriages and the loose bonds that tie us to our children by taking them on a fly-fishing trip. And, just as we learned to be wary of submerged "dead-heads" while wading and not to step out into fatal currents, we also learned that a similarly foolhardy venture such as taking a serious fly-fishing trip with the family can only lead to disaster—and certainly not "turn our thoughts far from the anxieties and harassment of modern living," as the article suggests.

We will, it reads, "enjoy the quiet companionship of loved ones." Especially, it continues, when "all join in cleaning the fish, in cooking and enjoying them together."

I can only speak for myself, of course, but such nonsense evokes some of the darkest moments of my life. On our first "family fishing trip" one son fell and broke my fly rod; on the second trip the other one left the tip section on top of the station wagon as we took off for home. Now, except for an incident during his maturer years when one son redesigned my seven-foot Payne with a trunk lid, the success of our fishing trips together is measured by the distance we maintain between each other while on the water.

And the idea that fishing trips are built around pastoral, streamside family "luncheon parties" eludes me. Cleaning and cooking trout *al fresco* and *en famille* brings out the worst in everyone, even inducing loathsome disfunctions still unknown to Mexican doctors. Only our *last* angling safari as a total social unit ended on an upbeat note—when my wife suddenly stood up, quivering and pale, to announce that "we're never going to do this again." And at that time she didn't even *know* about the water moccasin!

At the end of the article, Dr. Singer—just after Thies the Younger chimes in with an ex-cathedra pronouncement that "the man who can drift and dream is blessed"—successfully convinces us that psychiatry, or in his case, psychology, is "the disease of which it purports to be the cure." He cites the classic experiment of wiring the muscles of the forehead with electrodes. When faced with situations of fear or pressure, the patient's muscles tighten; but when exposed to "thoughts of a peaceful lake at sunset," the needle on the dial drops sharply as tension disappears.

Well, we wish we could have wired Dr. Singer into the forehead of a Manhattan angler who recently told us about *his* last fishing trip. In fact, he has a weekend place just a couple of long casts from New Haven, and it was a shame Dr. Singer wasn't along to see the needle break off.

EDGAR CULLMAN HAD BEEN fishing the Restigouche for twenty-five years out of his lodge, Runnymede. He had picked Deeside Pool that day last year, June 15th it was, and had just begun working the water with medium casts of about thirty-five or forty feet when a great gray-brown back swirled about his fly and disappeared.

"I rested the big fish for a few minutes, because I could tell by the coloration that it would be worth the wait. Then I cast again—the same swirl, the same result. Then the fish moved astern of the canoe."

Cullman held a strategic council with his guide, Lee Marshall, and after the manner of seasoned anglers, decided that they had the right fish but the wrong fly. "We changed from a #4 Rusty Rat to a #4 Green Highlander, and I blind-cast to the fish's lie. Another pass, but no contact."

Then it was back to the Rats, but this time a Silver Rat, a #2. "By this time I was getting nervous," Cullman admitted, "and my heart was palpitating. I didn't know what would happen next."

Cullman had reason to be nervous. After twenty-five years, he knew what a big salmon looked like. For the same period of time he had been looking at a "monster" of forty-one pounds hanging back in the lodge, taken back in 1940. And this ghostly apparition before him looked like a twin.

"I cast out again and watched the line sweep around. There was a great swoop, the fly was in the salmon's mouth— and my heart was in mine."

They pulled anchor, moved to the middle of the river, toward the Quebec side, and the fish turned downstream—the beginning of the classic and traditional battle. By now, Dr. Singer's meter needle would have been starting to click from unwanted tensions.

"I started to take in slack," Cullman continued, "but the

line jammed on the reel as soon as I began my retrieve. The line would run out, but I couldn't bring it in very far.

"I was in luck, though, because the big fish lay dormant—temporarily. I told the fish, in no uncertain language, to stay that way, because I had seen something like this happen before."

Cullman knew then that he would have to cut the line section off of his other rod, then attach the line from his jammed reel to the backing on his other reel.

The line was cut, then tied to the spare reel's backing with three quick square knots. "The fish suddenly took off with a zing and a zang," Cullman recalled, "as if he knew our repair work was done. He took the usual runs, pulls and shakes, and after another forty-five minutes I brought him to net—about half of him, that is, because his big tail was still unconfined, and we knew we had another monster."

By that time, any wires in Ed Cullman's forehead would have shorted out from hard sweat, of course, and Dr. Singer's anomalistic test results would unfortunately not have been recorded. Stress, strain and tension would have had a field day.

Because the fish, almost lost because of the line-change in midstream, scaled out at forty-five pounds, the greatest fish logged at Runnymede Lodge since they started keeping records back in 1895. Four pounds over the resident "monster."

And then there was Joe Cullman, Ed's "big brother" and lifetime fishing companion. If Ed hadn't pulled this off, how embarrassing—and stressful—it would have been to explain to Joe, who is also president of the Atlantic Salmon Foundation.

"Joe and I had fished this water for twenty-five years," Cullman told us. "It just happened that I was in the right place at the right time with the right fly. Fisherman's luck, I guess."

"Back at camp a holiday atmosphere prevailed, and we all exchanged cigars," Ed remembered—which was easy for him, because both brothers are in the tobacco game and probably get them wholesale.

NOT JUST ANOTHER "Me and Joe" story, Dr. Singer, just a typical tale of stress astream, another day in the life of a fly-rodder.

We fly fishermen can't really relate to your "drifting and dreaming," nice as it sounds.

With us it's rather a matter of "tension transference." Our peculiar calling doesn't usually do much to relieve the tensions of today's frenetic life, but Doc, it *is* one hell of a counter-irritant!

Lest Ye Marry, Gentlemen
(1971)

SOME MONTHS AGO we rejected a piece of advertising—along with several stink baits, a bobber that rang a bell and several other devices too sordid for publication—which we have since had second thoughts about.

The advertisement we have in mind, and we haven't been able to get it off, was that of a marriage broker who guaranteed to arrange a happy marriage or your money back. Our first reaction was that such services were inappropriate to our pages, but we now wonder if we weren't precipitous. Perhaps there is a need for someone who can assist younger fly fishermen in marrying well. It is a very complex decision, and no immature angler—under 60, at least—is competent to make a proper choice. One's mental state and body chemistry is not usually in balance at such times. Marriages made in heaven can be quickly unmade in the hell of a militant streamside confrontation between man and wife.

It is probably fortuitous that most wives do not make it to the stream, but do their damage before the angler leaves home—if he leaves at all. One wife we know, rather well, in fact, found solace in the early stages of her husband's piscomania through a blissfully conjured vision of her husband perpetuating the flame of fly fishing first lighted in the family by her late father. Daddy had fished two or three times a year, and didn't bring back many fish.

Then, when her husband began to increase his trips to several times a month, with new equipment for each trip, the eternal flame began to flicker. The angler soon learned that, although Allah might not deduct from the hours spent in angling, wives do! Some of them, like the other utilities, even install meters.

The old saw, "If you can't beat them, join them," is not always applicable. We were just recently reminded of the potential for evil in this philosophy while reading Van Dyke's classic, *Fisherman's Luck*. He records the plight of a weekend widower who finally tricked his wife, through a low scheme, into learning to fly fish. She soon became an expert, as she was in everything else she essayed, and the poor fellow was last seen, rodless but carrying a landing net and a creel, following her along the banks of the Beaverkill. And this was many years before Women's Suffrage, let alone Women's Lib.

We wonder if our marriage broker friend has an inventory of beautiful young women whose beauty is marred only by a slight paralysis of the right wrist; who demonstrate an early allergy to mosquitos or other flying insects; who love to clean, cook and eat fish; who would not arise before 7:30 A.M. to put out a fire in the baby's crib; and who, ideally, are deaf, dumb and blind?

However, we doubt if such a paragon has ever existed—if she had, Theodore Gordon, a life-long bachelor, would have married her.

But—it's all academic, for we have lost the name of the marriage broker. The best that *Fly Fisherman* can do, we suppose, is to ensnare and train young men in the art of fly fishing in their early, formative years. Then, by the time they are of marriageable age, no woman would want them.

Meanwhile, we will hie ourselves off to bed, curl up with a copy of Dame Juliana Berners' tome, and wish ourselves happy dreams.

· · ·

The Art of Sly-Fishing
(1978)

THE FLY FISHERMAN's high season approacheth, that moment in time when our hopes re-hatch along with the mayflies and we sashay with renewed abandon into angling's midstream. Personally, I dread it.

Supposedly, it is the mark of growing intelligence to realize one's limitations, but such growth can be fatally impaired when the boundaries of one's abilities become delineated by high barbed-wire fences and large signs reading "Beware of the Clod." One keeps mumbling to oneself, "Every day in every way I'm getting klutzier and klutzier." Angling is supposed to be a cathartic that flushes the soul, but if your need for catharsis lies elsewhere, the only thing you'll get out of fly-fishing is yourself.

I will confess, and have before, that I once had such hang-ups. While fishing alone, I could handle them, both those in the trees behind me and those in the psyche within me. "Angling is a solitary vice," I explained to myself satisfactorily, for I had long before passed through the stage of acne. It was only when angling became a social experience to be shared with a group of piscatorial peers—and especially when my profession as recorder-of-deeds of angling derring-do gradually upgraded my choice of increasingly peerless angling companions—it was only then that I began to see myself as others saw me. Through a martini glass—darkly.

It wasn't all in my imagination. One has only to return from a long day at the casting pools and find his arms a mass of contusions where he had been "zapped" for not "zic-ing" by the late dean of fly-casters, Charles Ritz, to sense one's delinquencies. Or to fall glumpily into a vile bog on one's first cast to a Great White Brook Trout at "Uncle's," Robert Traver's Holy Water. Or to see Schwiebert blush—on any occasion, but especially as an unwilling accomplice in my grand fishing felonies. Nor does one easily forget the pained wince and stammered

53

mutterings of Arnold Gingrich on presenting him with a gross and gaudy construction which purported to be a #8 Adams. "Where do you fish?" he finally asked. Before he had a chance to follow up on that straightline, I beat him to it. "The Mississippi," I answered quickly, and then changed the subject before the other TGF-ers at the table could decide whether I were a wit or a bumbling idiot. No final decision was recorded.

BUT ALL THIS SPEAKS of a darker age. Not only have I learned to live with the bomb, I have actually developed a limited but militant and burgeoning cult. We have learned to play the game of "Hang-upmanship"—we've become experts in "the Art of Sly-Fishing."

There are no basic rules to the game, no cant or specific jargon to our art. It requires only an attitude, a frame of mind, plus a natural aptitude for none of the required skills of fly-fishing other than those of sloth, lust, greed and the capacity for high deceit. Armed with these, one need only allow the natural animal reflexes, already honed by years of exposure to derision and jibe, to flow unfettered through one's veins.

For example, the Sly-Fisherman rounds a bend in the stream, only to be confronted with his club's two top dry-fly anglers enjoying the evening vespers at Church Pool. The water is heavy with fly, and they invite him to become a fellow-celebrant.

Now, the Sly-Fisherman can't tell one fly from another. They all look alike to him, even when he can see them, which is not now. He refuses to expose himself, however.

"Thanks, chappies," he calls out from the far bank. "Three's a crowd on Church Pool, I've found over the years." He squints across-stream, then asks, "What are you using?"

"Number eighteen Hendricksons," one calls out between casts.

The Sly-Fisherman flashes a friendly "V-for-Victory" sign to him, then replies, "Any port in a storm, eh?" Suddenly his hand flashes out into the growing dusk, clutches a piece of mist, examines it, then calls out a knowing "Ah-hah!" For our Sly-Fisherman is about to invent a hatch, and the other anglers turn expectantly. They are not to be disappointed.

"Just as I thought," he reveals in a hoarse stage-whisper.

"*Parasticus ucablandus* duns." The two anglers both stiffen as one, their lines dragging limply in the current.

"Usually follow the Hendricksons this time of the year." The Sly-Fisher fumbles momentarily in his vest pocket, then turns to his auditors. "Happen to have any #28 hooks on you?" They nod in disbelief, then start to wade over to our Sly-Fisherman. He of course expected this, and before they arrive, he has whip-finished, for the ninth time in the case of this particular #22 Darbee Midge, a crude head.

The anglers were impressed. "Never seen anyone tie up a little midge like that on-stream without a hand-vise. Not in thirty seconds. What do you call it?"

"The Big-Headed Bastard. Tied palmer."

"Fantastic."

"Yes, things haven't been the same since the Big-Headed Bastard came along."

The Sly-Angler goes on to tell them that it's the only thing for the *ucablandus* hatch—which is probably going on right now upstream, must get up there, good luck with your—"what were they, #18 Hendricksons??" he chuckles—"never fish them before early June, myself," then disappears into the upstream mists to "kick a few riffle rocks around!"

And so saying, he did, knowing that such knowledgeable activity would not only impress the two experts further but silt the hell out of their pool.

BACK IN THE CLUBHOUSE, over the communion bowl, the Sly-Angler's name could already be heard punctuating the buzz of *après*-hatch apologia when he stomped into the room. It had been dark for an hour.

The group turned to him expectantly. "Just flew in from the Barn Run. Boy, are my arms tired!"

"Stirred up some action, eh?" one of his dupes asked.

"On that *Parasticus ucablandus* midge?" the other queried, his voice unable to contain his admiration.

"Yep," the Sly-Angler allowed. "Tied palmer, of course."

The two anglers sidled up to him "Couldn't tie up a few for us, could you?"

The Sly-Angler smiled mystically. "Sorry. Used up my last hackle on that #22 I tied out there. Right from Darbee's brood stock, too. Even Elsie can't get any. Harry sits out there by the pens with a 12-gauge every night."

One of the other club members moved in, a bit belligerently. "Couple of us checked this *Parasticus ucablandus* hatch out. Schwiebert doesn't mention it anywhere."

Any other fly fisherman would have blanched under this ultimate accusation. But the reflexes of the Sly-Fisherman had encountered raw truth before and not been found wanting.

"True," he admitted. "I've always found Ernie interesting, but occasionally a bit uneven. And of course he's always taken a dim view of Rhead."

A hush fell over the room. *"Louis* Rhead?" the now not-so-belligerent angler muttered as if stunned. "You picked up this *Parasticus ucablandus* thing from *Rhead?* Never found anything like that in *his* stuff."

"That's understandable," the Sly-Fisherman condescended. "It's only in the Dog-Eared Press first-edition. Mary Orvis Marbury picked it up much later, but only in the original manuscript. You should take a shot at it." He reached for another cup of good-fellowship, trying to figure out a way to get out of this. Help soon came.

One of his Church Pool colleagues spoke up. "We both heard a big splash just after you went up to Barn Run. We stopped fishing by then. Water was getting a bit roily for some reason. That your fish we heard?"

The Sly-Angler downed a heady draught. "You probably heard the take. The bastard dove like a jack crevalle after that. Wasn't really much fun."

"He must have been a monster."

"Don't really know. Too dark to see. Too tired to weigh him." A fleeting smile crosssed his face as he stood up and started to walk to the door. "Stopped carrying yardsticks with me years ago. But he was a good eight pounds, I suppose."

Even after he stepped out onto the porch of the clubhouse, it was still quiet inside. So quiet that he had to pour the water out of his waders and into the bushes so they wouldn't find out that he was soaked through to his credit cards. He reminded himself to stay away from those damn ledges along the Barn Run at night.

Of course, it's the curse of the Sly-Fisherman that he must

always encore—or else improve, or stop fishing altogether. Unthinkable alternatives.

But he smiled confidently to himself. He knew he would be ready. There were more fish where that "eight-pounder" came from.

After all, he thought, misquoting his old fishing pal, Lee Wulff—"Oh yeah, I try to get up to his little camp on the Miramichi at least once a year"—a big lie is too good to be used only once!

To Hell with Scurrilous Discourse!
(1974)

OUR FATHER WALTON would not have expressed it in such a coarse manner."

I turned on my stool at the long mahogany bar of the Antrim Lodge to identify the source of the thin but cultivated little voice that had suddenly sliced through the soaring decibles of anglers reporting the triumphs and frustrations of their day on the Beaverkill and the Willowemoc.

I had found solace in the words of a nearby angler as he told his companions of a particularly uncouth spincaster who had violated the waters of Junction Pool with a Lazy Ike obviously designed for pike or tarpon, putting down a finer fish the angler had been working for over an hour. His friends chortled appreciatively as he recounted the rather bizarre and anatomically challenging instructions he had called out to the interloper as he finally surrendered the water to him.

The owner of the voice was himself equally thin and little, with a pink, wizened face sharpened by a full head of white hair and a pair of steely gray eyes slightly misted from drink. He did not appear to be real.

"Pity," he muttered as I acknowledged his presence to his satisfaction. "Our brothers of the angle today have lost the grace of language and thought that our great mentor both cherished and bequeathed us."

"That's true," I allowed, with the wisdom of many years spent on bar stools next to blithering idiots. If you're too agreeable, however, they eventually pull out pictures of their first wife or their last salmon, and this requires equally balanced measures. "But you heard what he said about the big Lazy Ike. The bast—"

He waved a tiny finger at me. "Ah-ah-ah! Walton hears you. I commiserate with the poor fellow, but not with his language. Father Walton spoke to us all when he laid down his thoughts upon sacrilegious and lascivious language and jests. 'A Brother of the Angle,' he had Piscator tell Corydon, 'that is cheerful and free from swearing and scurrilous discourse is worth gold.'"

He paused to make communion with Father Walton by taking a rather large gulp from his slowly withering martini, and I also reflected on Izaak's warning about not trusting "men warmed by drink." But he quickly resumed with his Waltonian vesper service.

"'Give me,' Father Walton said, 'a companion who feasts the company with wit and mirth and leaves out the sin which is usually mixed with them.'" He paused for a quick communion, then continued.

"A sylvan trout stream is, of course, a cathedral of the spirit. I too have encountered frustration and hooliganism upon the stream, but I have also managed to chastise the offender without profaning the sacred air about me."

I had begun to shape my lips to ask "How?" when I realized that he was going to tell me anyway, so I used the convenient aperture to pour down a slug of medicinal scotch and listened.

"I recall the time that I took a week's fishing on the Miramichi. It was greased-line casting with a dry fly over a productive yet shallow hold. A most boorish type whom I cannot dignify by the word 'gentleman' had the affrontery to cross the run no more than twenty feet above me. When I glared at him, he cursed me roundly, but I did not lower myself to his level. I became excessively worked up over this, I admit, and climbed from the water, but not before I looked back over my shoulder angrily and cried out, "Spawn of an empty redd!' I believe even he understood my reference, and I was able to sublimate my anger in a most satisfactory and Christian manner."

I was suddenly impressed. There was a certain fire in his pale eyes as he repeated his mild curse. Father Walton would have approved.

His eyes took on a sparkle. "And I was not found wanting that day on the West Branch of the Ausable when I found a young man perched precariously on a large boulder in midstream. He remained there for two hours, dominating the pool and flailing the water in all directions. I finally left, but not before I was able to deliver a parting shot."

I leaned forward eagerly. "Which was?"

"May your next cast, sir, be plaster!"

I rested my hand on his shoulder, which served to steady us both. "Sir, you have opened up a new world of invective for me and for that angling fraternity of which we are all members." I had already moved into his tranquil world, and besides, I thought Walton might really be listening.

Then I told him of the shocking encounter with an inebriated worm fisherman on the Pere Marquette who had challenged me to a fishing contest for money. We had quite a confrontation, exchanged many coarse words, and almost came to blows—the only thing that kept me from thrashing him was the fact that he was at least six-and-a-half feet tall.

How much more satisfying it would have been had I merely said, quietly and calmly, "May your fate be that of the Tups Indispensable!"

I spoke of this with my new mentor and he chuckled roundly. "Splendid, splendid," he cried. "You will find many more now that you have found the true Waltonian spirit." Then he further confided in me. "I have always found this one to be most satisfactory in reprimanding wayward fishermen." He leaned over confidentially and whispered, "Your grandmother fishes riffles!"

The high frivolity that this recollection engendered caused a mild seizure, during which he teetered drunkenly on the edge of the stool and fell into a paroxysm of coughing and laughter. He found the fresh martini placed in front of him an effective antidote, giving me time to think this all out.

Unseen vistas suddenly lay exposed before me. That time on the Upper Peninsula while fishing the Black River, when I found another fisherman chumming a particularly attractive pool with the innards of a recently cleaned fish. How appropriate it would have been in Hemingway country to have drawn upon the words of the master by sneering at him, "I spit on the silk of your Muddler!"

· · ·

OH, THE COUNTLESS TIMES I could have dignified the occasion with the appropriate invective, satisfying both to self and to the memory of dear Izaak.

"Your father was a worm rancher!"

Or . . . "May you go penniless to a Catskill fee pond!"

One could even direct one's ire toward a fish that had thrown the hook; more than one poor salmonid had been the target of my profane curses. Instead, why not "You son of a grilse!" Or, "May you develop gout in your adipose fin." At once creative, yet recreative, a catharsis to flush the soul and the mind of sinful thoughts and gutter jargon.

The possibilities are infinite. "May your next hatch be in your fly box!" I was just relishing "May Ed Zern defame you in his next book!" when I glanced back at my friend to see him slowly and majestically sliding from his perch like a small piece of silly putty.

I reached out to steady him, but in so doing I knocked his drink over, olive and all, drenching his shirt front and waking him suddenly from his shaky reverie. He cried out in alarm, bringing the bartender over to ask what had happened.

He pointed his trembling little finger at me, his face maroon with anger, and screamed unbelievably—"This sonofabitch spilled my goddam martini all over me!"

I rose from my stool, shocked and disappointed. Then, reflexively, I countered him with a terrible oath, gleaned possibly from an earlier encounter with an icthyological glossary.

"Male catostomidae!"

He turned to me with a stunned look,—hoist, so to speak, by his own petard—then marched unsteadily out of the bar and upstairs to his room.

I smiled and hoped he looked it up.

Brothers of the Angle
(1979)

SADLER (Walter Dendy). — Thursday.

JUST A FEW DAYS AGO during a business trip to Manhattan, I found a spare hour to spend at the Museum of Modern Art's Matisse Exhibition. As one who cannot even draw a crooked line, I usually stand in awe of artists—as long as they are dead.

Alive, they are usually illiterate, overpaid and incapable of coherent thought, and I say this even though some of my best friends are artists—which clearly delineates the low estate of my companionship over the years.

But I doubt if Matisse fished, because he certainly doesn't draw fish very well, but I don't require that in artists, except, of course, for those who work for the magazine, and the hour with the masterful Henri at the Museum was well spent.

Back in Vermont, safe once again from the pagan lures of Manhattan, I managed to locate a small reproduction of a painting from the Tate Gallery in London, a loan from the collection of angling apocrypha belonging to Phil Wright, keeper of the Big Hole in Wise River, Montana. Illustrated here, the painting is photographic in its representation, and requires of one only that a sensitive soul and searching eye exert every effort to determine just what the hell is going on.

The data below the painting gives us little satisfaction; Walter Dendy, the artist, obviously wanted us to participate in the event pictured, and only tells us that this is "Sadler," and then adds cryptically that it is "Thursday." After that we are on our own.

We see before us an order of fishing monks frolicking in the water meadows just outside the walls of the abbey. This is classic chalkstream water, probably in England's Hampshire district, and quite possibly near Winchester, where many holy orders cluster about.

Dating the painting is another matter, owing partly to the changeless manner of dress of the brothers. The rods, obviously pre-Hardy, are our only clue, and they suggest the seventeenth century at the latest. And then, there's the chair. The empty chair.

Many of you will be viewing this painting during the Christmas season, and some, after determining that there are twelve monks in the composition, could be deluded into reading a deeper religious significance into the empty chair. As rendered by the artist Dendy, the work demonstrates a certain distinct, though controlled frivolity which would approach the sacrilegious if the scene were viewed on another level.

The chair itself has a classic simplicity that nullifies any effort to assign a design period to it. We checked it out with a local Vermont antique dealer of some authority, and she agreed that it would be difficult to place it in any one period (she did add, however, that she could easily move it for 500 bills during the October foliage season).

We would like to think that the empty chair only recently bore the superior posterior of the famed Dame Juliana Berners, who early on had liberated the streams of England and who had already taken her limit and hastened back to her Abbey at Sopwell for evening vespers and a candlelight fly-tying clinic. Such an interpretation is heightened by the lecherous sulk on the face of the seated Abbot, well-read in Chaucer and frustrated in his plans to continue his devotions that evening in his quarters with Dame Juliana over a vintage claret.

BUT, ON TO THE ACTION. The artist has forced our eye to the grouping at center, where a brown trout of substantial proportions is about to be landed. Brother Theodore, the successful piscator, is being warned by his companion to "keep a tight horsehair," while his gillie's face carries a look of mystical exultation as he holds his net at ready. Perhaps he is fresh from his scriptures and had, only a moment before, advised his brother of the angle to "cast to the right" rather than the left. Dendy has given us much to ponder.

Much of the charm of classical art lies in the nicely turned detail of the artist's compositions, and here we are not disappointed. Dendy teases us. Through his art he leads us into unintended identifications. It is, of course, only we who see, in the dour figure behind the seated Abbot, the cowled visage of a Lee Wulff, at first glance seemingly involved in telling his beads but actually in the act of tying a fly to match the hatch, possibly the title of the yet-unnamed work of Brother Ernest who lies in moody abandon at his feet.

Our imagination is further piqued as we watch the two dissidents in the left background, Brothers Swisher and Richards, as they decry the excessive and worldly use of hackle to decorate their brothers' artificials. We cannot dwell on this pair for long, because our eyes are drawn to the seated brother in the distance, who is either watching a spinner fall or in a deep stupor. The angler beyond him also has his eyes raised, oblivious to the penance of the novitiate brother, Nicholas, who has been sent a sensible distance downwind, not to say his "Hail Marys" but to clean the fish.

For, of course, this is not an Anglican, but a Roman Order. Dendy himself has told us that it is Thursday. There will be fish at table on Friday!

A Fly Fisher's Etymology

$\mathbf{N}$OT TO BE CONFUSED with *The Fly Fisher's Entomology*, by A. J. Ronalds, another scholarly work published 150 years ago, my magnum opus, *A Fly Fisher's Etymology*, is an on-going and yet-unpublished tome defining the terms of angling for newcomers to our pages and streams.

First begun nearly a decade ago, this continuing series immediately was accepted without dissent by all readers—documented by the fact that not one person in nearly a decade has even mentioned it. Not even Mr. Al Goldstein, publisher of *Screw* magazine and a tireless defender of the First Amendment right to freedom of speech and expression.

As I write these introductory words, Mr. Goldstein is being questioned by the audience of the "Phil Donahue Show" and has just been queried by a woman as to "why we need magazines devoted to sex." Goldstein shrugs and replies, "I like to fish so I read *Fly Fisherman* magazine."

This is not a juxtaposition I would have chosen were I planting a plug on national television for *Fly Fisherman*, a publication for persons not interested in sex. Thus, it is even more important that we "define our terms."

angler's log: a section of fallen tree, usually found near the far bank of a stream and easily located by the fly fisherman. The angler often leaves a souvenir fly in the log to record his presence.

backing: something without which no angling writer would leave on a fishing trip; usually obtained from tackle manufacturers or editors of angling magazines in writing before leaving town. In a secondary usage, it can refer to a 100-yard-plus length of braided line affixed to the reel core before adding the fly line. All writers use this type of backing to suggest that they expect to catch a very large fish (hence the expression used by unsuccessful fishing scribes, ". . . and then I ran out of backing." They then become angling editors.)

chalkstream: certain rivers in Hampshire and other south counties of England that have been chemically doctored by landowners and syndicates to counteract acid rain.

Croydon hand vice: Originally an adolescence problem in a British public school, but now refering to a rather chauvinistic device marketed in England and America for hand-tying flies at streamside.

dry fly code: a philosophy of angling deriving from *A Modern Dry-Fly Code*, encrypted by Vincent Marinaro in 1950 and understood only by Ernest Schwiebert and a few others at the Princeton Institute for Advanced Studies. The code was recently broken by Soviet intelligence, signaling a collapse of East-West detente.

grayling: A fingerling that has matured and become superannuated.

Idaho cutthroats: affectionate term applied by clients to fishing outfitters in the Henry's Fork area of the Snake River drainage; subspecies may often be found in West Yellowstone and Livingston, Montana, with additional unconfirmed reports from Colorado and Wyoming.

impoundments: large areas of water surrounded by bass anglers; used by the U.S. Corps of Engineers to store water stolen by them from free-flowing streams.

International Fario Club: A loose-hung organization of frivolous, if not gay, fly anglers who fished with the legendary Charles Ritz—but who could not out-cast him. Until Ritz's death a decade ago, they met each year in November at the Hotel Ritz in Paris during a period of low room-bookings to watch Charles cast, after which he would sell them Pezon et Michel "Fario Club" rods.

Izaak Walton League: Derived from a Sherlock Holmes/Conan Doyle story, "The Red-Headed League," in which a storekeeper is hired elsewhere to copy out the contents of the *Encyclopedia Britannica* while the bank next to his shop is tunneled into and robbed. Members of the Izaak Walton League, primarily hunters and spin fishermen, are made to copy out the contents of *The Compleat Angler,* thus keeping them off the streams for much of the season. It should be supported by all readers.

S-cast: a useful casting technique when a drag-free downstream cast is required; the rod tip is raised as the line straightens out and then supposedly falls in a sinuous curve onto the surface. Anglers frequently announce this difficult type of cast when completed by crying "s...!"—thus "S-cast."

salmon rods: various specialized rod-and-line combinations used by wealthy retired Atlantic salmon fishermen with stiff butts and deep bellies.

split cane: the direct result of using split-shot with a bamboo rod.

TGF: a club organized a number of years ago by several Manhattan-based anglers of too low a character to get seats at the New York Angler's Club. They originally met on the last day of the work week to plan their weekend fishing trips, thus the initials T.G.F., standing for "Thank God it's Friday." Later, as the members became more respectable they found that most of their colleagues had already left to go fishing by Friday. They moved their luncheons to Tuesday, but found nothing to give praise to the Deity about over *that,* so they changed their name. Now the group enjoys almost total respectability and acceptance in the fly-fishing fraternity under the name of the "Theodore Gordon Flyfishers." Reportedly they saved several hundred dollars by not having to redesign their bumper stickers.

tippets: a scientifically tapered series of hand-tied segments of monofilament connecting the fly hook with the fly line and designed to protect the rod by breaking when a fish larger than nine inches takes the fly.

trout: A word formerly used to denote members of the *salmonid* family of fish, but now copyrighted by Ernest Schwiebert (1978). He published a two-volume set of books under this title, primarily an extensive listing of the rivers he has fished and the various anglers who have watched him, but also preceded by 1577 pages telling you more than you thought you wanted to know about trout.

wading staff: a group of people employed by Orvis to test fishing boots. Older members of the group often use long sticks to steady themselves during testing, thus bringing the term "wading staff" into common usage by anglers. Younger members are called "hip waders."

water-testing kits: Glass containers holding a dark brown distillate, usually imported from Scotland or Kentucky, and used by anglers after a day of fishing to analyze their lack of success on the water. Results often point to a case of serious pollution.

dry martini: an olive-bodied concoction that is highly thought of by anglers, especially along many of the Eastern streams, where they are taken with relish, or even an onion, especially in the early evening hours. The offer of one along a Catskill stream, specifically at the end of a heavy hatch of Cahills, is bound to draw a quick rise.

Ernest G. Schwiebert, Jr: a house-name (such as "Betty Crocker") owned by several New York City publishing firms. They use this name below the "Introduction" to new angling books when they can't get Joe Brooks to write it. More than a decade ago a book was written that was so revolutionary that *no one* would sign his name to it—thus the name "Ernest G. Schwiebert, Jr." came into broad usage. Only a few publishing houses can afford to use this name which, we now understand, is being contested in litigation by an itinerant angler-artist-architect of the same name who lives in New Jersey or Norway or Patagonia.

keeper: there are several meanings to the word "keeper."

    keeper (1) is a small ring or hook tied to the butt section of the fly rod. This was originally intended to hold the fly when the rod was not in use, but today many beginning fly rodders use it to thread their fly line through. It is thus called a keeper because it keeps beginners from shooting their line and double-hauling during the early stages of their casting development.

    keeper (2): The manager of a quality stretch of private trout or salmon water; e.g., the fabled Mr. William Lunn, keeper of the Test for the venerable Houghton Club in England.

    Interestingly enough, Lunn, the most exacting of purists, reportedly threw himself into the River Test upon seeing a new member threading his fly line through the *keeper*

(1) of his rod. This incident spawned a famous British fly. A passing member who saw the rather sordid incident, after retrieving Lunn from the water with a sharp roll cast, was asked by another Houghton Club angler as to the identity of the fly on which he landed Lunn. "I used," he replied thoughtfully, "that little dry fly he tied up for me just this morning. Took it beautifully. Couldn't use just *anything* on the old boy, Lunn's particular, y'know." Thus was born, through a misunderstanding the famous Lunn's Particular.

Lunn recovered, happily, to live a long and productive life, although the Houghton Club members kept him from the river's edge by means of a long line threaded through a loose ring attached to his butt section.

keeper (3): A fish of a size that you would not have kept if you had caught it earlier in the morning. Usually a fish of nine or ten inches minimum, but this is a relative criterion. E.G., the Houghton Club angler did not throw Lunn back because he was a keeper (2,3).

Four Stars—But They Water the Martinis
(1980)

WHEN WRITERS ASK US if we publish fiction in *Fly Fisherman*, our standard response has always been: "No more than creeps into *any* fishing story." My generation, standing on the felonious shoulders of those before us, has learned to accept the Big Lie with grace, if not downright enthusiasm, perhaps because one good lie deserves another and we were equal to the task.

But now, ten years after the magazine left the spawning bed, a new generation of young turks has arisen who don't Just Fish. They are Into Fishing. They've Got It All Together and, accomplishing that, they then Let It All Hang Out. If such heresy weren't enough, they proceed to Tell It Like It Is!

Of course, this is alien to everything angling represents. Older heads know that truth only exposes, while the polished lie sustains and nourishes. They also know that fly-fishing is not a democratic sport. Regardless of their political leanings, these wiser types know full well that the great fly waters of Europe thrived under such beneficent despots as Hitler and Franco, and piscatorially, if not politically, they tend to think fascist. But—they will be sitting back listening to their waders harden during the next decade or so, and we must bridge the gap between them and the burgeoning under-30 generation who will soon take over. They suspect that the truth is not in us.

However, through clean living I have managed to maintain my youthful good looks, and unlike so many others who share my epoch in time, I occasionally find acceptance among younger people—which is about all there seems to be left. My credentials are close to impeccable: I have met Jerry Garcia, lead guitar of the Grateful Dead, and I have seen the Beatles naked in their shower. If more is required, I regale the youngsters with the fact that I once shared a stick of pot with one of Count

70

Basie's sidemen (some thirty-five years ago; there was a war on, and I suspected I might not come back).

All of this is by the way of setting up new "Truth in Angling" policy for *Fly Fisherman* writers and editors, one that will not only lend a new credibility to our magazine but also to the brief tale I am about to recount. . . .

TRUTHFUL FROM THE BEGINNING, I must confess that the trip had been troutless. If that's not Letting It All Hang Out, I will go even further and Tell It Like It Was—that it was actually a business trip to Boston. I had arrived in Brattleboro, Vermont, and was on my way to Manchester, Vermont, the sprawling metropolitan area of some 3,000 inhabitants of which I live in a distant suburb. The stretch is the longest forty-seven miles in the coterminous United States, and in winter can be compared favorably with a crossing of the Donner Pass—although it is not necessary to eat people, as there are several fine restaurants along the way, as there are in Manchester itself if you ever get there.

I had stopped in the falling dusk to admire the strange waters of the West River which parallels the road, waters that I hold so sacred that I have never fished them except in my dreams, in which I have stocked the upper stretches with brownies, the lower with smallmouth. By the time I got back into the car, it was martini time, and I knew that I had to have at least one because I had to drive.

I also knew that there was a place just up the road that held trout in some quantity namely the Four Columns Inn in Newfane known far and wide and to local farmer-economist John Galbraith as the source of the most delectable blue trout (or at those prices, *truite au bleu*). This storied inn, our family's first touch of Vermont so many years ago, raised its own trout in a nearby pond, moving them as required into holding waters at the entrance to the dining room, actually a six-foot-long glass structure that we assume at one time held hyperthyroid goldfish. I informed the *maitre d'*, after he had seated me at a small table on the opposite side of the dining-room archway from the trout tank, that I was extremely dry and would feel much more comfortable if I had a martini in the same condition.

I then went to the trout holding-water and selected the

smaller of the two, a female, I believe, with the knowledge that, in eating trout as in many things, small is beautiful. I commended it to the ministrations of chef René Chardain, knowing that his trained reflexes would drop it into the vinegar solution at the proper moment in this most testy of culinary challenges.

René's innate sense of timing had allowed for a second martini before the savory odor of imminent blue trout penetrated the warm, mellow haze about me. There it was, in gallant repose, with just a tinge of blue to give a hint of piquant things to come. But that which came was less than piquant.

THERE WAS THE FLASH of a leaping shadow on the wall, followed by a great tidal wave that totally engulfed me. The guests turned as one to see me choke on my first bite of blue trout, soaked from waist to head in water. Rivulets ran down the back of my shirt, and my hair was a mass of damp ringlets. Not only was the tablecloth soaked, but the foreign liquid had actually entered my half-empty martini glass, nearly filling it to the brim.

It had been one of the greatest trout rises the West River had ever witnessed, in dream or in reality. In its soaring leap the bereaved trout had nearly reached the ceiling, a nearby diner later calculated, before it dropped back to the tank with a flap of its tail that would have cowed Captain Ahab.

The *maitre d'* and waitress ran to me with towels and apologies, soaking up with one what they couldn't negotiate with the other. Meanwhile, the Great Trout bounced from one corner of the tank to the other in an orgy of anger.

"Are you all right, sir?" the *maitre d'* inquired.

"Yes," I admitted, "but if I haven't broken up a happy home, I at least have the feeling I'm eating someone's dear friend!"

The *Mobilgas Guide* for the Northeastern states gives the Four Columns a 3-star "Excellent" rating, and includes the information that "guests choose own trout . . . jacket at dinner." Next year there will be a footnote, if my advice is heeded, recommending the scampi as being safer, but if blue trout is chosen, that waterproof jackets are required.

And that the trout water the martinis.

· III ·

Casting About

Taking the Waters

IT IS THE NATURE OF THE WILD TROUT AND OTHER FLY-
rod gamefish to live in nice places—and the curse of most
anglers not to. But half the joy of angling is, as the Cunard
Line used to herald, getting there, and the algae always
looks greener on the other side of the stream, the state, the
country or the world.

The other joyous half is talking about it after one gets
back. Any joy in between is a bonus.

The Catskills, Britain, the Florida Keys and Colorado are
just a few spas that evolve in the off-beat ramblings in this
section. In my role as a self-styled recorder of deeds
piscatorial, I have had an unusual opportunity to get
skunked on most of the great waters of the world, including the Mississippi.

More than once I have been accused of being a "stream-
dropper" by jealous readers, but such will not be the case
here. Rather, I would like to think of these twisted little
essays as "stream-droppings."

· · ·

The Catskills Raffia Mafia
(1975)

WE WERE AMUSED, and for their sake, relieved, to hear on the television news tht the Mafia, which had apparently been doing extensive market research in New York State's Catskill Mountains, had decided against attempting to move in on the Catskills and stick with the safer and more socially acceptable activities such as dope smuggling and organized vice.

Quite possibly, and with a little luck, the Mafia could soon control the handle on the ladies' lounge mah-jongg game at Grossinger's, but the Roscoe-Livingston Manor territory at the confluence of the Beaverkill and the Willowemoc is another matter. This is angling's Little Sicily, and anyone with ideas of muscling in would have a contract out on him before the evening Blue-Wing Olive hatch and would probably end up in Junction Pool fitted for cement waders.

As anyone who has fished the area knows, the territory is rather clearly divided. The action *north* of the rivers belongs to Walt "The Dubber" Dette (though rumors have it that Winnie runs the Family).

South of the rivers, the Overlord of the Livingston Manor Family is indisputably Harry "The Hackle" Darbee and his moll, Elsie. Family councils are held at Darbee's every Saturday night, at which time Darbee and his wife take bets on illicit gamecock fights. Reports are that the handle is considerable.

Dette operates a bookie wire service for in-crowd anglers, who can call a private number any time in-season for the latest odds.

Both Dette and Darbee share in the olive and pretzel concessions at the Antrim Lodge in Roscoe.

Reliable sources say that a prominent Manhattan fly tier, some time back in the '30s, moved into Roscoe to case the action, but quickly thought better of it when he woke the first morning in his room at Antrim Lodge to find the remains of an Andalusian Blue Dun gamecock at the foot of his bed. He was last seen in Livingston, Montana (not Manor), where he has trained a number of women to perform various vise-connected activities.

All-powerful in their realms as are Darbee and Dette, nevertheless the entire operation is fingered—or Black-Handed—from the Wall Street district of Lower Manhattan. Long ago the mantle of power in the Catskills Raffia Mafia passed from the late and lamented Don Theodoro, and it now rests firmly on the broad shoulders of a venerable but coldly efficient gentleman of many aliases, but known as The God-father—Don Alfredo—to members of the Family.

Beyond this we cannot go, except to warn anyone seen using weighted Muddlers in Cairn's Pool. Especially if a big, broad-shouldered and venerable gentleman, sparse and grey of hackle, comes up and, with cold efficiency, kisses him on the cheek. Back in Manhattan on Third Avenue that could mean one thing, but on Route 17 along the Beaverkill, it's the kiss of death.

Overswill on the Beaverkill?
(1981)

During the period preceding this column, real estate de-
velopers were seeking permission to dump effluent into the
Beaverkill River in New York's Catskills, and rumors of
Mafia infiltration of the same area were rampant. Intense
activity by the Catskill Waters group of anglers has discour-
aged, if not eliminated, the former threat; the latter migra-
tion was re-directed by the second coming of Atlantic City,
where there is no limit to the kill.—D.D.Z.

LAST NIGHT I dreamed that I went back to the Beaverkill
again. I had gone there to do an article on the entomology of
the Beaverkill—and was stunned to learn that there wasn't any!

I don't know just what triggered such a nightmare. I have
learned in recent years that beer and pizza don't go down as
easily after midnight as they used to, but more likely it was
something I had read, because I often read things, and occasionally write things, that are equally indigestible. But never
after midnight.

No, I think it was probably the conversation with a fly-fishing friend of mine—a splinter-group angling agnostic who recently confessed to me that he doesn't really believe that rivers
have a life of their own, that they speak to you in voices loud
and soft, and that they should be approached as shrines. He
tossed off the Itchen, the Madison, a couple of "Ausables," and
then proceeded to revile the Beaverkill itself.

I immediately straight-armed him with a Lady Beaverkill
tied by the late Elsie Darbee, and he recoiled, of course, but not

before he admitted that he could not accept the divinity of Theodore Gordon, George LaBranche or Edward R. Hewitt—although he did look on them as great teachers. I'll never attend
streamside evening vespers with that fellow again!

No, I am a true believer. For a while I struggled against the
required suspension of disbelief, but eventually succumbed to
the scriptural writings of Haig-Brown, Gingrich and Schwiebert. Except perhaps in very hot weather, I don't remove my
waders before entering any of these Holy Waters of Angling,
but I do believe that they consist of more than just water running downhill. I hear voices on these streams, lovely sirenlike
tinklings and guttural murmurs that beckon me on. Often they
are accompanied by shimmering mirages of rising trout, mirages that seem to keep moving upstream and around the next
bend. But the voices tell me otherwise, that I should keep moving, that the fish are there and that I am almost there myself.

Sometimes they speak in accents of other times, of other
lands. It's rather like listening to three evening network news-
casts—you can never remember anything specific, but you continue to get the definite impression that something has
happened. And at no place, on no American river have things
been happening longer than on the Beaverkill in New York's
Catskills.

I suspect that the first artificial fly was launched over a
Beaverkill riffle in the smaller years of the eighteenth century,
and since then its fish have dodged the artful offerings of fly-
fishing's best. I am a strong believer in ancestral memory, as
well as conditioned reflex, and trout that have been fished over
by the likes of Gordon, Steenrod and Hewitt can't have had
things too easy. You can't tell me that, after an especially daring
rise, Mama didn't tell her fingerlings not to accept goodies from
strange men when the school broke up. I can even envision
little signs over the spawning beds—"Beware of the Blue Dun"
and "Here Comes Gordon; Pass it On!"

I have never met a stupid trout in my limited days on the
Beaverkill. Only stupid anglers.

I DREAMED last night of my return to the Beaverkill, but it soon
became a nightmare. I was bumper-to-bumper for an hour

along the Thruway, and when I finally turned off at Roscoe and looked for old Route 17 that ran along the river, I found that it had been turned into a skateboard path. As I pulled up at Junction Pool, I noticed quite a bit of surface action, primarily by water-skiers.

Pulling myself together, I drove over to what had been the Roscoe Diner for some hot coffee, but the old landmark was now stuffed to the gills with slot machines, just a minor tourist trap on the low-rent end of the garish new Roscoe Strip.

There was no place to go except the rambling old Antrim Lodge, since I had long ago surrendered my Playboy Club key. The ancient structure, since days too dim for me to know the off-duty headquarters of Beaverkill and Willowemoc anglers, was still there, although dripping in neon and a bit frowzy in its new coat of pink paint. But as I drove up I was consoled by a big "Opening Day" poster by the entrance. I was home again.

I was—until I learned that the "Opening Day" poster announced the arrival of Shecky Greene, fresh from long runs in Las Vegas and Atlantic City. As I stumbled dazedly into the long, low Antrim Lodge bar-and-grill room, a panorama of roulette wheels, gaming tables and slots spread out before me. The great mahogany bar that could administer medicinal martinis to forty anglers or eight horses was still there, but the bartender was now pushing Harvey Wallbangers to conventioneers and sales-contest winners. Trophy trout no longer decorated the walls of the great hall, but had been replaced with black-and-white glossies of Joan Rivers, Frankie Avalon and Rich Little. These were highlighted by a large blow-up of Frank Sinatra, posing in the spirit of good fellowship with Legs Diamond, Lucky Luciano and Nancy Reagan.

It was just not the same, somehow. For a moment I caught the eye of the *maitre d'*, but he quickly turned away after a flicker of recognition. Except for the sallow, drawn face and the clouded eyes, it could have been the double of Doug Bury, the longtime proprietor of the old Antrim Lodge—but of course that would have been ridiculous.

I was turning to leave, for just where I don't know, when I saw an old familiar face at the far end of the bar. Years before we had consoled each other after particularly unrewarding excursions astream. It was a warm reunion for both of us, and

after I explained to the fuzzy-faced young bartender how to
make a dry martini, my friend filled me in on developments.

"SAD, VERY SAD," he began. "It all started with that new thou-
sand-unit motel that opened up a while back. Then came the
golf course and the trailer park. By the time the place was finished, they were dumping a half-million gallons of sewage into
the Beaverkill, right near Junction Pool."

He gummed his olive, then shook his head. "Somebody's
out there squeezing hell out of the Charmin!"

I was stunned. "How do you fish the river?"

He smiled a humorless grin. "Very seldom. And with lead-
core fluorescent lines. There's still a few bottom-feeding
brownies around who learned not to inhale."

I shook my head in disbelief. "I suppose all the hatches are
gone."

He nodded. "First to go. Big streamers worked for a while.
Then the terrestrials, but even those gave out."

"What do you use now?" I asked.

"Fellow came up with a new one. Got one here, in fact." He
reached in his vest. "We call 'em 'Effluentials'."

My friend pulled out a vile construction tied on a number
six hook. It looked like a hyperthyroid housefly, and my companion confirmed it. "It's called 'matching the hatch,' my
friend." He guzzled the dregs of his drink, then added, "You
ever see any Hendricksons around a backyard privy?"

I shook my head. "Good Lord, man! Didn't anyone do anything about this?"

"Oh, sure, Trout Unlimited, the Federation of Fly Fishermen, the Theodore Gordon Flyfishers, the Catskill Waters
people—they tried. But you know, you just can't get anglers
upset. Just mention anti-gun laws, the NRA plugs in its com-
puters and twenty-four hours later half of Congress is down on
its knees. But you tell the average fly fisherman that a stretch is
crapped out, he just smiles at you and walks upstream a little
farther. Weird!" He signaled for another drink, but I wasn't
ready to give up.

"Well," I said as I stood up and paid the tab, "I'm not going
to give up, old buddy. I'm going out and wet a line while there's
still light. But it's a hell of a way to start the 1981 season."

He suddenly turned and stared at me. "1981?" He pointed behind the bar. "What do you think that calendar back there says? This is 1984, pal."

I BARELY RECALL leaving the Antrim Lodge during a Shecky Greene monologue and fumbling my way down to Junction Pool. I remember crawling into my waders and making my way deeper and deeper into the dark brown waters of the Beaverkill. The smell was enough to give you a deathwish, and the last thing I remember was standing in the middle of the current, the water lapping at my chin, and muttering to the water-skiers through tight lips—"Don't make waves."

I don't think they heard me. But then I woke up, gradually and gratefully, but I could still hear that hapless angler in the middle of a dying Beaverkill, still crying out: "Don't make waves, don't make waves."

The Nether Wallop Caper
(1979)

Spring's first hatch usually arrives in February or March in the form of the "Early-Season Catalogs"—followed closely in April by the "Black Duns" from the various tackle firms trying to collect the money they have legally extracted from us in that period of extreme vulnerability.

There is, of course, the catalog from Orvis, guilty of one of the earliest and most heinous assaults on our minds, souls and budgets. And there is Dan Bailey, mild-mannered ex-Brooklyn physics teacher, warning us of the dangers that lurk beneath the surface of Western streams and offering slick devices designed to fend them off. Then there is the Fly Fishermen's Bookcase and Tackle Service catalog, nearly as long as its name; Kaufmann's Streamborn Flies and its juicy presentations; the select and expanded presentations from Thomas & Thomas—where does one stop in recording these major contributors to our delicious delinquencies?

And where does one begin to explain to today's fly rodder the vacuum in which the first issue of *Fly Fisherman* was published ten years ago this month? Fly-fishing was in the deepest of doldrums, and the pervasive click of the spinning-reel bail was heard in the land. Even such neolithic types as Robert Traver took up spinning for a time, his last unexplored vice—but under the name of John Voelker, happily. One had to be a card-carrying member of the angling elite to discover that there were specialized fly-tackle shops in Manhattan, nooked away in the spires of the Chrysler Building or in the shadow of City Hall; tiny custom fly-rod shops tucked into the foothills of the Catskills and the Sierra; back-street addresses where a proper knock and a knowing wink might lead to a gut leader or a silk line. A careful reading of the bait ads in the classified sections of the outdoor magazines could occasionally expose the source of custom-tied flies to the masses, but even this was iffy.

The arrival of *Fly Fisherman* on the angling scene, a quiet event celebrated at first by a few thousand readers, then ten thousands, eventually hundreds of thousands (some cheat and read over subscribers' shoulders), served as a rallying flag for these disenfranchised fly rodders—and soon after for that underground network of purveyors to the fly fisher. As in a mass debarkation from Noah's Ark, out they came from the closets, from cracks in the walls, from under rocks after the manner of nymphs—the custom rodmakers and the specialized fly-tiers, the vendors of exotic fly lines and fashioners of bench-made fly reels, publishers of fly-fishing books and the designers of waders, angling clothing and those other vital accessories without which few of us could wet a line today.

And now, through these suppliers and their copious catalogs, America has at last brought fly fishing to the people. No longer the fiefdom of the British angling establishment, encrusted in its own tradition and withered through inbreeding, fly fishing has been liberated by good old American know-how, progressive marketing techniques and hard-sell ad copy. Today's tackle catalogs tell you everything there is to know about fly-fishing tackle, right? All the information you require, everything that can be said about our recreation, can be found in the pages of the American tackle catalogs, right? It could only happen in America! Right?

Wrong. It would be nice to think so, but it just ain't true, and thereby hangs a tale. In fact, a tale of two cities. . . .

IN ST. LOUIS, whose soaring Gateway Arch holds a promise of the "Biggest Mac" ever, the 44-year-old public relations director for The Seven-Up Company stared from his window and contemplated his achievements of the past year. Primarily, he had managed to do minor but lasting violence to Anglo-American relations. With the able assistance of the firm's advertising agency, J. Walter Thompson, he had dragged the Earl of Sandwich to the New York World's Fair to promote the company's International Sandwich Gardens. Flushed with this victory, the combine then proceeded to obtain, through auction in London, the legal title to "Lord of the Manor of Wormley," a small tract of nothing on the outskirts of London, and then awarded it, along with a trip to survey the manorial domain, to a Nashville telephone company executive as first prize in a national sweepstakes contest. (After his Lordship visited his Manor, he happily renounced his title and returned it to the crushed but impecunious former holder.)

His only accomplishment of note during the past year had been to achieve a certain tentative competency as a fly fisherman. Otherwise, there was no place to go but up. He had also begun to suspect that life was a terminal disease, more and more reaching epidemic proportions each year, and that if there was a Final Expiration Notice out there with his name on it, by God he was going to take a few trout and bass with him.

His evangelism soon took the form of starting a magazine on fly fishing.

MEANWHILE, IN LONDON, a 44-year-old British advertising man sat in the London office of J. Walter Thompson and stared across Berkeley Square. But the nightingales no longer sang there for Dermot Wilson. He recounted darkly the various heresies and outright treasonable acts he had committed during the past year in the name of his firm's international soft drink client. It was already the fall of 1968, and of him, he suspected, if he didn't get out of all this and go fishing. And so, as someone once said, he rose to a Dry Martini and was never heard from again.

As a director and board member of J. Walter Thompson, Dermot Wilson was too smart to start a magazine on fly fishing, but too neurotic to engineer a successful bank job. Instead, he devised a clever way to heist money from fly fishermen, by the pound sterling.

He would take his family back to the streams of his youth in the lovely water meadows of Hampshire. They would find a picturesque old mill, preferably one listed in the Domesday Book ("They just aren't building nowadays like they did before 1066"), and through the enticements of hiring angling on the choicest waters and a tackle catalog overflowing with disarming copy, they would soon separate thousands of fly fishermen from their discretionary incomes. Afterward they would ride off into the sunset.

Dermot soon acquired his hide-out—The Mill at Nether Wallop, which is just south of Middle Wallop, itself bounded on the north by Upper Wallop. The British like to be orderly about these things.

Before the arrival of Dermot, the Wallop's main claim to fame lay in having long been the source of England's best cricket bats, much as Louisville's "Sluggers" are to baseball. Good cover. Then, through purchase, lease and unspeakable chicanery, Wilson acquired prime stretches of the Test and Itchen rivers. In celebration of his new-found freedom, he would make these available to the angling rabble of his shores and ours for daily fees that viewed whole, tend to appear usurious, but once analyzed, turn out to be one of today's greatest angling bargains.

To complete the Nether Wallop caper, and to bring a tight military precision to the operation, Wilson brought in several of his wartime British Army buddies from the 50th Rifles Regiment. (This gave the operation an immediate let-up on larceny, for the 50th Rifles bears the distinction of being the only British military unit originally raised in the American Colonies.) Thus did Phil Pardoe, former British military attaché in Washington, and Bobby Morrison, gentleman farmer, join the ranks of Wilson's Whiz Kids—with the added front of Ian, Lord Lesiie, now the Earl of Rothe, financial adviser and part-time angling-clothing fitter. (Dermot claims not to take his advice in either area of expertise.)

And then, in March of 1969—just as the first issue of *Fly Fisherman* was published in the United States—the first annual catalog from Nether Wallop was unleashed in England. The initial effect, both among fly-fishing Britons and angling Loyalists here in the Colonies, was roughly comparable to the simultaneous announcement of the arrival of the Spanish Armada, the abdication of King Edward to marry a commoner and the enactment of the Stamp Act.

It is easy to believe the stories of mass resignations at the London Flyfishers Club, and even the heart attacks suffered by older members. For the 1969 "A Choice of Tackle" contained not only cartoons lampooning fly fishermen but also frivolous commentary such as the "Report from Dermot Wilson's Psychiatrist."

Later issues of the Nether Wallop catalog actually showed Wilson, not celebrated for his physique, wading the Itchen in nothing but a modified bikini. Things did not improve with the addition to the catalog of a statuesque female model of Viking proportions. Then, in a following issue of the catalog, Wilson announced the appointment of an "Acting Board Chairman" to his organization.

Here was a suggestion of normalcy which would have been received with relief by the angling establishment—had not the "Acting Chairman" turned out to be a chimpanzee! The Chairman became a regular feature of the catalogs until he eventually had to be discharged to that Great Banana Tree in the Sky after running amok in a girl's school and attacking the inmates. He still appears regularly, in memoriam, but maintaining the solid continuity of harmless insanity that pervades this Nether Wallop compendium.

For behind its college humor magazine facade, the Nether Wallop catalog and its racy prose cunningly conceals much of the angling-tool-and-technique wisdom of the world. For Dermot Wilson, consummate copywriter and canny con man that he is, is also considered England's premier dry-fly fisherman, and his knowledge of fishing tackle and its selection and use is unparalleled.

Dermot, and the fishing at Nether Wallop, have attracted the fly-fishing greats of the world to the little Hampshire village. With due modesty, I must admit that I myself have made the pilgrimage more than once, in the hope that Dermot would introduce me to some of them.

A FEW WEEKS BEFORE this writing, Dermot and I shared an eventful evening of reunion and good fellowship at the Algonquin Hotel in Manhattan after his trip here to address the annual Theodore Gordon Flyfishers banquet in New York and the United Fly Tiers dinner in Boston. After toasting our tenth anniversaries as hosts of two of fly-fishing's longest-running floating con games, observed that his has been the ultimate success. Anyone can pull off a job on the Bank of England. Only Dermot Wilson could pull it off on the bank of the Itchen.

The Loch Ness Monster Sinks the Cutty Sark
(1972)

WE HAD READ in the local paper with more than passing interest last year that a Scottish distillery had offered a reward of one million pounds-sterling for the landing of the Loch Ness monster. It was early April, and we were doing our income tax at the time. A rapid calculation (H. & R. Block lists nothing in its index under "Monsters") showed us that we could still hold onto a considerable hunk of the $2,400,000 this reward represented if we were able to beach old Nessie.

Our blood began to stir. But eventually lethargy triumphed, and it wasn't until a few weeks ago that we encountered the A.P clipping (in the H. & R. Block tax book from last year under "Legitimate Business Deductions"), reminding us that the year of the contest would be up on April 30, 1972.

Now, we had heard nothing out of England about any such event—we checked the "Reports from the Rivers" section of *Trout & Salmon* magazine rather carefully—so we began to think about it more seriously. After some research and planning, we contacted a representative of the firm in London. We have excerpted below from this letter, in which we outlined our plan and sought their cooperation in putting it properly into action.

"Early last spring we read with interest that your distillery announced a year-long contest to motivate anglers and other low types to derrick the Loch Ness Monster up from the depths in which he lurks. This was done, one presumes, in the spirit of good sportsmanship and conservation. The thought of Nessie finding a female monster is appalling; it would certainly do the Loch Ness waters no good.

"Nor did we overlook the fact that your distillery, in a burst of magnanimity, had offered an honorarium of one million pounds sterling. Based on estimates of Nessie's weight, this is roughly a pound-for-pound (sterling-avoirdupois) relationship and certainly most adequate compensation.

"After reading the article last spring, we admit that we did think more than once about the possibilities of taking Nessie on a fly rod, but we discarded the idea after realizing how pushy this might seem to our British friends. However, our people in Great Britain have informed us that the Monster has not yet been landed, let alone risen to any man-made lure, and we thought that it might be acceptable to push ahead on the matter. If, on the last day of the contest—April 30, we believe—the Monster has not been taken, we would like very much to take a crack at it with a small fly rod and specially devised fly.

"It is our opinion, and that of our advisors, that the monster has not been approached with the proper delicacy of presentation—which of course only the fly rod affords. We fully realize that there is no insect hatch on Loch Ness offering proper fare to get a rise out of the Monster; however, the Monster quite possibly dates back to prehistoric times, and we have devised a fly-rod lure more likely to attract him. In essence, it imitates the fledgling pterodactyl. We have high hopes for it.

"We would be most interested in hearing your evaluation of this project."

Well, we had just about perfected the midge pterodactyl fly, and had even interested a network TV news department in covering it, when we received a letter from a director of the distillery, from which we excerpt the significant passage that follows:

"We have read your letter with interest, but we regret to advise you that we are not able to co-operate with your project. The writer is of the opinion that the existence of the Loch Ness Monster is a myth, and in the circumstances we feel that you would be wasting your valuable time in coming to Scotland with a view to capturing it!
      We are, dear Sir,
      Yours faithfully,"
      (Signature)

We were stunned, and imagined their stockholders would be, too, when they found that their directors had authorized the firm to take out an insurance policy with Lloyd's of London to cover the possibility of Nessie being landed. Most Scotsmen would judge it frivolous to spend that kind of money insuring a myth.

We won't be fishing for Old Nessie on April 30, but we'll be sitting back and sipping someone else's product (our distillery friend will remain anonymous; in fact, neither the product nor its name will ever cross our lips again!), and having the last laugh.

Because we are, dear sir, sending you a telegram in the early morning hours of the night of April 30. It will arrive, through an intermediary, from Loch Ness, and will read as follows:

"Landed Nessie tonight on midge pterodactyl fly. Returned him in best tradition of fly fishing. Monsters are too valuable to use only once."
"Yours faithfully,
dear sir, et cetera."

Fishing the Epilimnion at Lake Megayuk
(1980)

NEARLY TEN YEARS AGO the U.S. Department of Commerce announced its recommendations for a "ten-year changeover period," at the end of which the United States would be "predominantly, but not exclusively," on the metric system.

This leaves anglers one more season to go before the proposed 1981 deadline for predominant, if not exclusive, conversion to the metric system. In the chance that not all readers have already adapted comfortably to this logical and universal method of weights and measures, I have briefly recorded a recent fishing trip which I took with my old friend, Dr. Thurmond Klein, a Ph.D. fisheries biologist of enormous grasp. His friends call him "Thurmo."

WE WERE FISHING the shores of Lake Megayuk, where my companion had his wilderness fishing camp. The sun was dropping low in the west, a mist was beginning to sprawl on the far shore.

"Yep," commented Klein, "I've fished this little old resource since I was a kid." A shadow crossed his face for a moment. "Dad and I used to call it . . . 'God's Little Hectare.'"

I didn't trust myself to speak. I knew that he treasured this spot, for on the drive out from the city he confessed to me that he wouldn't take a megabuck for it if it were offered to him. And he would be right to refuse. Thurmo had been in charge of the electroshock crew just last season when they gigavolted these same waters—100 kilograms per hectare. It's hard to find fishing like that anymore. But my musings were cut short. My companion was already putting up his rod.

"I'm going to take the canoe and work the limnetic zone," he informed me. "Want to get down to the hypolimnion before oxygen depletion sets in."

I allowed that this was clear thinking and that sometimes

cold hunches like that can pay off. But I had other ideas. "Think I'm going to walk the shore and see if I can pick up any action."

Thurmo's eyes brightened. "You will. Usually fish that old littoral zone myself. But just to be on the safe side, take your waders along. About a kilometer down the trail there's a shallow spot where you can wade out a couple of hundred meters or so into the epilimnion. Then count to five to give your nymph a seventy-five centimeter-per-second sink down into that elodea and potamogeton. That's Diatom City, man!"

Thurmo is always generous with his little tips. He eyed my light rod as I slipped the reel into place. "Going to use the little old two-meter Payne, huh? Okay for the littoral zone, I guess, but I've got to work a lot of water out there in the limnetic zone, especially if I'm going to hit the hypolimnion before dark."

He flexed his big lunker rod. "Little on the heavy side, I guess, but it'll cast a country kilometer!"

I had neglected to bring my limnetic rod, let alone my spool of hypolimnion line or fluorescent streamers. I gave Thurmo an envious glance as I walked him down to the canoe, a light four-meter job that would get him out to the limnetic zone in a nanosecond.

As I pushed him off, he called back a final bit of advice. "If you're up to the hike, remember that aquifer outcrop near the north shore. Got up to 35 degrees Celsius in the shade this afternoon. Shallows might still be a little warm, so that cold water might pull 'em in."

I waved in agreement, even though Thurmo had forgotten that he had taken me there on my first trip here some ten years ago, while he was still working on his doctorate. I had fished that aquifer outcrop when it was a spring hole.

But no mind. I still had a kilometer hike ahead of me. Now that Thurmo was halfway to the middle of the lake, I could pull out my converter to multiply 5,280 by .61. I tried to pace it off in meters, the way Thurmo would have done it, but my old hernia was acting up.

Despite the looseness of my calculations, I found the shallows, clear and promising. Hectares of diatoms in my own backyard! I made a note to pass that one on to old Thurmo. He would like that.

THURMO WAS JUST a distant, shadowy outline when I heard the quiet dip of his paddle. Dusk had turned to darkness by the time I negotiated the kilometer back to camp. Thurmo was flushed with victory. True to his name, he had hit the thermocline, head-on.

"Not only that, boy," he effused. "I broke into the *profundal* zone. Caught myself one big lunker anomaly!"

I feigned surprise, but, truthfully, one could expect no less from the profundal zone. However, I wanted to share the glow of Thurmo's triumph with him.

"A largemouth, old buddy. Gamest fish that swims . . . centimeter for centimeter, kilogram for kilogram, of course," he qualified. "One of the biggest I've ever seen in these parts. Four kilos, give or take a few grams."

I gave him that much.

"The water must have warmed up too much over in the pads on the other side of the lake. The devil headed down like a depth bomb. Not an oxygen molecule per cubic centiliter down there."

I put my hand on his shoulder. "You saved him from a terrible death."

"There's a paper in this, friend. Never heard of a largemouth in the profundal zone. Cold, no oxygen, black as pitch. Had to reach it with a lead-core line. Thank God I had my Lucky Lefty Neon Flasher on or it never would have taken it down there."

I nodded in agreement. "You could call it the 'basso-profundo' zone."

We both got a good chuckle out of that. We always have a million laughs out at the old lake.

But our merriment was cut short by the arrival of a lean, bent figure—the old geezer I had seen fishing at the north end of the lake. He was staggering under the strain of a bulging creel, with a telltale overflow in the form of a tail the size of a funeral fan. Thurmo sidled over to him.

"Evening, mister. Looks like you got the pick of the litter there."

"Yep. Best rainbow I ever took. Should run two feet if she's an inch. Took it on a little black midge, 6X leader about fifteen foot long, down by that old spring hole yonder. It'll push ten pounds, I betcha."

Thurmo wasn't prepared for this arcane discourse. He looked at me with a puzzled, blank expression on his face. "What's he trying to say?"

My pocket metric slide-rule converter wasn't up to translating this one, but before Thurmo could react the old gentleman moved on toward the road, dragging his bounty along behind him.

Old Thurmo was beside himself. He gave a brief lecture on how his *salmo gairdneri* brood stock couldn't take pressure like this, that he had been pushing his luck on the high pH content of the water, even with the surface-to-water ratio of a eutrophic lake like this, and that the sonofabitch had probably vomer-hooked it, anyway. Then he shook his fist at the old geezer's wake. "What would you have if every bastard who fished this lake took out a fish like that?"

"One hell of a draw-down," I guessed, but happily Thurmo was wiping the froth from his lips and it didn't register. "Fish *my* aquifer outcrop, will he?" he muttered, and then I decided to change the subject while we packed up to head back to the car.

"I didn't have much luck. Waded out into the epilimnion, but there wasn't any action, Thurmo."

His brow beetled. "Can't understand that. You used a four-meter leader like I said?"

I nodded. "Give or take a coupla millimeters."

"How about your tippet?"

"Half a hectomicron, just like you told me."

"Hmmm." Then he brightened. "You use a little nymph?"

"Sure did. Number eighteen. My best epilimnion fly."

"But did you sink it exactly seventy-five centimeters per second, right into the elodea and potamogeton?"

"Right on."

This was even more puzzling to Thurmo. "You didn't pick up *anything?*"

I shook my head. "Just a little elodea and potamogeton." I've always figured that if you aren't picking up a little elodea and potamogeton, you aren't fishing.

"Well, old buddy, you should have improvised a bit and sunk it another half-meter down into the myriophyllum. Now that's habitat." He gave me a wry look. "Get with it, boy. I can't do *all* your thinking for you."

Thurmo had told me about the elodea and the potamogeton, but not about the myriophyllum. I felt cheated, but I decided not to go out on a hypolimnion because he would go into another thermocline.

But by then Thurmo's mind was on more temporal matters. "Got a bottle of Old Specimen back in the car. You ready?"

"Take me to your liter, Thurmo."

We were loading up the trunk when he finally noticed my less-than-flattened creel. "Hey, you've been holding out on me. What's that in there?"

"Well, I finally waded back into the shallows by the shore. Found this baby scraping around in the cattails like a beached submarine."

Thurmo stared in disbelief. "That's a kilogrammer if I ever saw one. He must of had a death-wish to come back into that shallow water along the shore!"

"That's what I thought, Thurmo." Then I smiled. "You might say I took him littorally."

That caught Thurmo where he lived. In his native habitat. He giggled insanely, then slapped me on the back. "That deserves a drink, old buddy." He reached for what I like to call "the fifth."

"Say when."

It had been a rough day, and my personal ecology had been sorely tested. "About half a dekafinger, Thurmo."

Thurmo bent double. "Half a dekafinger! You're a million laughs, buddy."

Of course, we always have a million laughs fishing out there. We don't call it "Lake Megayuk" for nothing.

Return to Esmerelda
(1982)

I OWE IT TO OUR READERS." I told my wife. "Those poor, sniffling souls trapped up in Denver and Chicago and Minneapolis and Boston . . . they'll want to know that there's a life after January."

She turned down the TV and stared at me. "And will they want to know that it's only 60 degrees in Vermont?"

She was in the final stages of cabin fever. "That's the reading on the living-room *thermostat*," I explained. "It's 50 degrees in our upstairs bathroom. With a wind-chill factor of 25 above when the vent fan is on. It happens that it's 18 below zero out there. You haven't been outside since a week before Christmas. That was the night you wanted to pour hot maple syrup on the carolers for rushing the season. If you don't get out of your hole the groundhog is going to beat you to it."

"This is the same song and dance you gave me three years ago this very second," she began, savoring each sibilant. "Weather reports on the hour and half hour. Medical bulletins on the state of your growing depression. Then the siren call of the saltwater flats and it was off again to Esmerelda while I shoveled snow and fended off the fuel bills."

How vile of her to bring that up. "Why do you keep calling it 'Esmerelda'—as if I were keeping a blonde somewhere? You know it's *Islamorada*. The heart of the Florida Keys. Sportfishing capital of the world. But *you* wouldn't go. You had to play midwife."

"And those bony fish and terrapins were more important than the birth of your first grandchild, I suppose. We had to dredge you out of the Everglades to let you know."

"Yes, and right in the middle of a creek tarpon—t-a-r-p-o-n—run," I recalled darkly. "How was I to know the kid was going to be early. First member of the family ever to get anywhere ahead of time." I was about to add that all babies look alike, like her father, pink, bald and toothless, and not half as

95

charming, but I didn't want to sweet-talk her. I wanted her to make the decision not to come with me on her own.

But such was not to be. Her cabin fever had reached the crisis point, and in her delirium she accepted. We were off to "Esmerelda."

I DIDN'T STAY AT "JACK'S SHACK" this time, the abandoned but tastefully renovated cobia cannery I usually called home in Islamorada. With the intuition ingrained after 33 years of marriage, I sensed a certain testiness on my wife's part. Instead, I went to the bank and arranged a loan large enough to cover a week in an ocean-side villa on the grounds of The Inn of the Seven Heavens—"one for each day of our stay," I later told her during one of the few light moments that were to follow.

On the night of our arrival in Islamorada, I quickly numbed her with drink, then phoned my long-time Islamorada fishing guide, Florida Flatts. He was the only one in the Keys with an unlisted number, a ploy encouraged by the Islamorada Fishing Guides Association but misinterpreted by Flatts as a move to make him less competitive with his rival colleagues. He claimed 10 years as a skipper, but at least half of these were spent as a chum-chopper on a Marathon party boat until a casually overheard "fish or cut bait" opened up a new world of opportunity for Flatts, if not for his future clients. It gave him, he once told me, a new sense of direction, but after one day in the back-country with him I suggested that a good compass would have been equally useful. It is legendary throughout the Keys that during his first year as a guide, Flatts became lost three times in the harbor of Bud 'n' Mary's Marina while trying to locate his slip.

The phone rang some 10 times before Mrs. Flatts answered. "This is a client of Mr. Flatts. I'd like to set up a trip tomorrow with him."

There was the usual pause while she reached for her script. "Capt. Flatts is booked for the next two weeks . . ." Then the very short pause before a live one could hang up. "But perhaps there might be a cancellation. If you'll give me your name and number . . ."

Capt. Flatts uses this device to write his phone bill off against advertising. The only time he's been booked for longer than a day at a time was back in 1979 when he was picked up by the Coast Guard during a marijuana raid off Key West. He was later released when he claimed that he thought he was buying box lunches. He even produced witnesses to testify that he had complained angrily about the unusually high prices.

"Just tell the Captain that 'Lefty' phoned and that I have every hope that there will be a cancellation. I'll be having coffee over at Papa Joe's at nine o'clock."

Perhaps I should explain the "Lefty" business. The only reason I ship out with Capt. Florida Flatts is that we both nurture each other's fantasies—I, that he is a competent saltwater fly-fishing guide, and he, that I am worthy of him. On our first trip he had been calling me "hey, guy," but eventually he asked what I would like to be called. At that time, some years ago, Keys angler Guy de Valdene was knocking off bonefish records every few months, and Flatts allowed as how that would be fine with him. But "Guy" didn't do so well that afternoon, so I changed over to Stu Apte the next day, and "Stu" did a bit better. On our last sortie I had been "Lefty" Kreh, my original saltwater mentor, and had actually performed rather well— when I was able to steer the Captain close enough to a fish.

AFTER A QUICK TOUR of the grounds of the Seven Heavens, during which I pointed out such unearthly delights as the heated swimming pool with adjoining bar, the luncheon veranda and the lighted shuffleboard court, my wife and I arrived at Papa Joe's for a quick sip of coffee before a raspy voice broke the silence.

"This is yore Captain speakin'," he yelled. "Let's scrub them scuppers fore and aft." With this leftover tidbit from an old Wallace Beery movie, my wife and Capt. Flatts became uncertain shipmates. We crossed Highway 1 to Bud 'n' Mary's and descended into Capt. Florida Flatts' "skiff," actually a patched-up World War II surplus Coast Guard dory. Flatts had added a personal touch with a crudely stenciled "Hackensack Whaler" on the bow. He had picked the name from a regional map which, unfortunately, did not include Massachusetts. He felt that it had a certain ring.

We reached the mouth of the marina harbor without incident, a fact which I did not read as a harbinger of good things to come. My wife was uneasy around any body of water larger than a hot-tub, and Capt. Flatts was already hop-skip-and-jumping down the outside of Lower Matecumbe Key looking for the school of bonefish he had spotted earlier that week— probably while driving his wife down to the laundromat in Marathon.

My wife's white knuckles were telling me something, but before I could phrase it clearly, Flatts cut the motor, yelling "Hit the deck . . . bandits at twelve o'clock!" Rod at ready, I went along with the gag, climbed up on the foredeck and, allowing that Flatts was usually on Pacific Time, I cast my Pink Shrimp about 40 feet out at nine o'clock.

"Right on," Flatts screamed. "Set the hook!" I saw only a fleeting little shadow, but my captain had spoken, and I gave my ghostly quarry a taste of steel. Well, it ended up at three o'clock, Eastern Time, well behind the boat, not a bonefish but a small yet familiar denizen, a preserved copy of which I had acquired as a young boy on a Caribbean freight steamer in a Barbados shop. I had hooked a cowfish. In the port udder.

"Nine inches if it's a foot," yelled Flatts rather cryptically as he reached for his gaff. By that time I had boated the poor thing and started to unhook and release it to graze again. But old Florida had other ideas. He pulled a Metro Miami Fishing Tournament brochure from his ice-chest and was already looking under "Cowfish."

"Keep the thing on and cut off your leader," he ordered. "If it tests under six pounds, yore in business. We'll enter it under 'General'—the Tournament just started and I ain't heard nothin' about no cowfish."

My wife was unable to contain herself. "So this is Esmerelda? Sportfishing capital of the world!" She looked down at the miserable little creature, then up at another one. "I'd rather be in Philadelphia." I promised to check the plane schedules, but then decided that a good run against a growing chop would settle her hash, and I signaled Capt. Flatts to hit the throttle back to the marina.

We planed all the way, the bow slapping the water smartly, and the bilge, bright with floating beer cans from a previous excursion, worked itself into a malty froth. My wife, color her green, endured it with tight lips, at least until we negotiated the slip. "One cruise aboard the Love Boat is enough," she hissed. "Get me out of here!"

I shoved the rental-car keys and a charge card into her sweaty palms, suggesting that if she didn't like Bud 'n' Mary's she'd probably love Irene & George's, Islamorada's quiet but clear answer to Saks Fifth Avenue. "Drape yourself properly," I urged her. "There are still Six Heavens to go," I added with bravado.

TO TELL YOU that the rest of our day was merely inauspicious would be sheer puffery. The water was clear, the air warm and windless. Flatts had tested the water temperature that morning, and as usual, it registered 88 degrees, for it was a rectal thermometer left behind by a Michigan doctor. Where, I can only guess.

Lord knows, the fellow tried. "Who are you today?" he finally asked. I thought for a moment, then replied, "Joe. Joe Brooks." This puzzled Capt. Flatts. "But—he's dead." "I know that, God rest his pure soul," I answered. "But I haven't got back to the hotel yet!"

From flat to reef to mangrove to hole we ran. On instructions from Flatts I cast to, and after a sterling cast nearly landed, a sunken channel marker. We ran aground chasing a mythical school of bonefish, but he climbed the exposed flat like a snowmobile, after which he overran a school of redfish and took two with his propeller. My only comfort lay in the fact that, after one more season, he would have enough money saved to have that cataract operation he'd always wanted.

At five-thirty, just off the harbor, we ran out of gas and had to wait until we drifted into poling depth. Immediately we were surrounded by a huge school of rolling tarpon, bronzed and glinting in the setting sun. Yelling hysterically from his Jerry-built flying bridge, the skipper snapped out orders. "One o'clock, two o'clock, three o'clock, shoot. . . ." None was within 100 yards, of course, but I kept shooting and Flatts kept pointing and boxing the clock. Together, encircled by leaping tarpon, we created a living tableau that, if commissioned to the proper artist, would have held its own on the back of any bar on the Keys.

Eventually we drifted into the shallows, and the Captain

poled us into the snug harbor of Bud 'n' Mary's and to an igno-
minious docking. A large crowd of tourists lined the wharf
area, my wife in the forefront. Ours was the last skiff in, and I
searched the slips for the sign of a record sailfish catch or a
huge marlin.

"Let's see it, fellows," someone called out. "The record
cowfish on a fly! Haul it out!" My wife had not spent the entire
afternoon at Irene & George's, that was clear. And Florida
Flatts was in his element. I tried to blend into the crowd as he
pulled the nine-inch cowfish out of the ice-chest, then tried to
break it up by drawing their attention to the large sign at the
entrance to the docks. It had always amused me, but now it
became utilitarian: "NO TRESPASSING AFTER SIX P.M.," it
read, and it was already five minutes after six. I didn't want to
take credit for the catch, just grabbed my grinning wife and
headed for the car. Eight hours of *legal* trespassing had been
enough for me.

LATER THAT EVENING, after we had made peace with each
other over several therapeutic martinis and the manna *du jour*
at The Seven Heavens, I took my wife for a drive up the Keys.
"It's a nice evening, and I thought you'd like to run up to Key
Largo and see the African Queen."

She looked stunned. "You mean we came all the way here
from Vermont to go to some drive-in theater? We've seen it five
times, and you've got the tape at home!"

"Aha!" I countered, after her own manner. "If you were
paying attention you would have noticed that I didn't put *The
African Queen* in quotation marks." I had just read that a Key
Largo businessman had just acquired the original *African Queen*
that week, and that it temporarily reposed on a flatbed truck at
the Holiday Inn.

I pulled into the parking lot, and there it was, sans Bogie
and Kate, to be sure, but otherwise authentic, its brass polished,
hull caulked, all shipshape and trim. I had finally impressed
her.

"Can you imagine," she began, admiring the thirty-foot little vessel with its single boiler, "two people trapped up on a
little boat like that for a whole week?"

"Yes," I answered softly. "Oh God, yes, I can!"

·IV·

A Better Class of People

After a Better Class of Fish

IF YOU'RE GOING TO STEAL A LINE, STEAL FROM THE best—then rephrase it. In fly angling, Arnold Gingrich once wrote, "you'll meet, if not a better class of people, a better class of fish." It was about the time of that epigram that I began to meet both and realized that Arnold was not totally infallible.

Early on in my angling career I began to realize that I had never met an angler I didn't like. I met a few who didn't like me, but that was understandable. On the whole, and on the stream, fly-fishing brings out the best in people. At home or at work, they very well might beat their children or scream at their colleagues, but on the stream they are pussycats. Once, in Michigan on the Au Sable river, a passing angler, undoubtedly moved by the creeping senility which led me to leave home without my waders, took his own off and gave them to me after noticing my out-of-state auto license. They leaked like a sieve.

However, the happenstances of my trade have afforded undeserved opportunities to meet, know and fish with (or a respectful distance behind) some anglers who proved to be a better class of people—both in and out of the water. Some have cropped up elsewhere in this book, and others were cropped out by time and space, but the crop included here is top-growth and beyond reproach.

Two Last Casts—Gingrich and Ritz
(1976)

THE DRUMS OF THE JUNGLE TELEGRAPH that links the tight little world of fly-fishing sounded with a muffled beat during that long and hot weekend in mid-July.

Sparse Grey Hackle, who lives a half-life as Alfred E. Miller, called Nick Lyons on Friday morning, July 9th, to tell him that Arnold Gingrich had just died quietly in his Ridgewood, New Jersey, home, after a brief illness. Then Nick phoned me. Only a few days before, Nick and I had compared notes on Arnold's condition, and the consensus had been that it was under control and that there was a good chance for recovery. Nick had been preparing a piece for a special issue of *Esquire*, of which Gingrich was founding editor, and both of us had been in regular contact with his office.

I was surprised and saddened by this news, but, oddly enough, my first practical thought among many muddled ones was to cable Charles Ritz. Friends for many years—they had fished together for nearly two decades—Arnold had written the introduction to the latest edition of Ritz's autobiography, *A Fly Fisher's Life*. I knew that he would want to know, and that he might wish to contribute some thoughts on Arnold Gingrich to this issue of *Fly Fisherman*.

But such would not be forthcoming from our European Editor (a job without a description for which he volunteered). Instead, on the following Tuesday, as I was reading over my Mailgram confirmation copy of my earlier cable to Ritz, my telephone rang. My eyes were still focused on the cable—"ARNOLD GINGRICH DIED QUIETLY YESTERDAY . . ."—as I heard the Western Union cable operator read back my earlier words, but with a slight change: "CHARLES RITZ DIED QUIETLY YESTERDAY. MY SINCEREST CONDOLENCES TO MRS. GINGRICH. MONIQUE RITZ."

My first thought was that a mistake had been made, not unheard of in today's electronic communications, and that I was hearing a verbal confirmation of my earlier cable *to* Charles. Then I asked the operator to repeat the message, and it was all true. I asked for a printed confirmation, and thanked her.

The sudden lump and moistness left as quickly as they came. Charles was a practical man, and it was again time for practical thoughts. I had planned to leave Vermont that morning to attend Arnold Gingrich's funeral services in Manhattan that afternoon, but car trouble had prevented the pilgrimage. I realized that many of Arnold's and Charles' mutual friends would be attending the services and should know of this second sadness. I phoned Nick Lyons, but he had already left for the funeral home, for he had been asked to deliver a eulogy—a request he honored hesitantly but, I am told, with the expected sensitivity and taste.

Then I thought of Len Wright, the prominent fly-fishing author who whiles away his days as a promotion executive for *The New York Times*. His office was near the funeral home, and I knew he would be going if business pressures allowed. Len was stunned, of course, but also practical, and one of his first thoughts was to make certain that the *Times* newsroom had picked up the story. Shortly after our conversation, a call from a *Times* reporter indicated that neither they nor their Paris bureau yet had the story. Answering the reporter's questions, I became an unwilling accomplice in filling in the existing *Times* obituary of Monsieur Charles César Ritz. So, within twenty-four hours the world of fly-fishing, and the world of affairs, lost two of their most distinguished citizens—Arnold Gingrich, at 72, and Charles Ritz, at 84. Each of them had made his ineradicable impress on both of these worlds.

Arnold Gingrich had taken a word from the dictionary and capitalized it into *Esquire,* one of the most original, creative, and influential magazines of its era.

Charles Ritz had taken his own name—and his father's— and placed it solidly into the dictionary in lower case.

But, in any case, both men were unique. Each was a skilled fly angler, but each had other talents—enthusiasm and an ability to communicate—that soared beyond his own expertise as a fly fisher. Both were close personal and fishing friends, and together, their sphere of angling influence spanned many continents and many decades.

Of course, the sadness felt by anyone who knew either Gingrich or Ritz—personally or through their books—at this loss is, first, for their wives, Jane Gingrich and Monique Ritz, and their families and immediate associates. But then the sadness descends upon us and the fact that these men are no longer to spice the angling scene—for we can hardly look back on the lives of Gingrich and Ritz and feel sadness for unfulfilled careers or unrealized potentials or frustrated dreams. Both of them lived long and full lives, died with little or no prolonged illnesses to color their last days, and left so many delightful memories that we can only envy the productivity of their combined 150-plus years and treasure the small personal claims we might have had, directly or indirectly, on a facet of their lives.

If there were a contest, which there isn't, Ritz and Gingrich could be described as ranking among the world's leading fly fishermen. Many other anglers have cast farther, have caught more fish, and have published more books covering advanced angling techniques and entomological studies. There are several who have certainly done all these things. Probably the very pre-eminence of these two men—through their lives, angling and otherwise, and through their books—lies in the fact that they showed us why all this isn't really important.

It is important for anyone who seriously pursues the fly fisher's recreation to know of these men, that they existed, and what they have meant to the world of fly-fishing. For the next few pages the author would like to take the liberty of running on for a few columns with some rather personal views of Arnold Gingrich and Charles Ritz. Both have had strong influences on his life and on *Fly Fisherman* magazine.

Arnold Gingrich, Esquire

Urbane. How many newspaper features and book dust jackets carried this cliché word in a capsule description of Arnold Gingrich, usually lumped in along with "sophisticated"? I once asked him about that, and after a reflexive wince, he told with delight of the annual banquet of a small trout group at which he had been introduced by the emcee, "reading apparently from an exceptionally dusty dust jacket," as the "sophisticated and urban" Arnold Gingrich.

"Urban," Arnold repeated, treasuring the malaprop. "That's the way I think of myself. Stuck in the damn city!"

But, like it or not, Arnold Gingrich had "stuck" himself there. Born on the banks of the Au Sable in Grayling, Michigan, in the smaller years of this century when there were still a few grayling to give credence to the town's name, the son of a fly fisherman, Gingrich never fished until he was well into his 20's—and then with a bait-casting outfit for bass, pike and pickerel on Wisconsin and Minnesota lakes. Early on he had moved his base of operation to Chicago, that toddling town where people still danced with their wives and which teemed with creativity in the arts, in journalism, in radio (and later in television programming), and even in advertising, for this was back in the days when many advertising people still realized they were just "drummers," albeit fast-traveling salesmen with a louder drum. And in Chicago, the beat was fast and the reverberations long-lasting.

And, among its brightest creations was the magazine *Esquire*, which Arnold founded eight years out of the University of Michigan. A spin-off of the magazine he had been editing, *Gentlemen's Quarterly*, (neé *Apparel Arts*), *Esquire* hung loosely on the hook of men's fashions but quickly became much more, an exciting and original amalgam of the literary and humor magazines of the 20s, but blazing with color, full-page cartoons and the bylines of writers who today comprise our literary anthologies—Hemingway, Fitzgerald, Faulkner, Dos Passos, Mencken, Lardner, O'Hara, Parker, Lewis, and on through the index. Whether Gingrich totally caught the spirit of the mid-30s Phoenix rising from the Depression depths or whether he helped create it is beyond the scope of this short piece, but alongside the earlier *New Yorker* and *Time*, and its 1933 cribmate, *Life, Esquire* was unquestionably among the most original creations of magazine journalism in the past half-century.

I still remember with the clarity of youthful eyes the days in the mid-30s that I found a pristine stack of *Esquire* magazines in my father's den. Dad was in advertising, and several of his clients had been early advertisers in *Apparel Arts* and *Esquire,* so he received *Esquire* regularly. The svelte Petty Girls and unique cartoons (a neighborhood friend told my shocked mother that he liked "the dirty roosters" best!) helped prepare me for meatier fare, for in an early issue Arnold had begun the results of a survey, made by whom I never learned, of how, when, where and at what time young ladies lost their virginity—an early Kinsey Report, naïve and reeking of innocence by today's standards, yet opening new horizons for a 12-year-old-boy. (I later confided in Arnold the fact that he had introduced me, through *Esquire* and through his book, *The Well-Tempered Angler,* to the separate but equally fascinating worlds of girls and fly-fishing; he hoped, he told me, that I had found both rewarding.)

He also introduced me to the exciting world of magazine journalism, and my early bouts with *Esquire* led me to begin a publication of my own—rejoicing in the name of the *Webster Flash*—in competition with the high-school newspaper, which wouldn't let me on the staff because I was too young. I also soon learned about free enterprise, because a year or two later, a smart aleck young freshman began a newspaper in competition with me—a skinny kid from another neighborhood, much too young. But the skinny kid kept it up, and after World War II ended up on *Esquire* as one of Arnold's top editors, where he spent nearly a decade until the *New York Herald-Tribune* folded and he bought out its new magazine section and built it into one of the most lively and controversial magazines of this decade, *New York,* and then annexed another, *The Village Voice.*

Clay Felker and I finally made peace with each other a number of years ago when I called his office and told his secretary to tell him this was the editor of the *Webster Flash* calling the editor of *Good Business*—for that was the inglorious but, for the late depression years, optimistic, title of skinny old Clay's first publication. Since then, business has obviously gotten even better.

I told Arnold about all this at lunch one day in New York when I revealed to him my plans for starting a magazine on fly-fishing, and he was fascinated to hear about the early days of one of his Young Turks. But he also confided that the Turks were getting younger all the time, or that he was getting to be an Old Turk, and he wistfully admitted that "I don't go back to the editorial department much anymore. I don't understand what they're talking about."

With his typical generosity and enthusiasm, Arnold encouraged me in my endeavor, thought it was a splendid idea, timed just right, and never let on that he was, that very month, putting out an early issue of that fine publication of the Federation of Fly Fishermen, *The Flyfisher,* of which he was editor at the time and the existence of which I had not known. However, he watched our earlier progress with an editor's jaundiced eye—and the myopic eye which I have detected among dozens of successful professional men, top industrialists and brilliant academics who, when sitting in committee on matters piscatorial, lose all of their orientation and genius and become fuddled and silly, totally happy but totally lacking in the judgment which carried them to their lofty levels.

In his book *The Joys of Trout,* Gingrich later wrote that he was a bit concerned about our first years: "Zahner got off to a rather wobbly start, a few years back, and the first few issues showed a rather elastic attitude toward what does or doesn't constitute fly-fishing than its most fanatical practitioners were quite ready to applaud, but he straightened up rather quickly and he's been flying right ever since."

Some of Arnold's concern—as founding director of Fanatical Fly-Fishing Practitioners—was centered on the fact that we frequently made mention of rods longer than six feet, of lines heavier than #4–5 carrying leaders as short as nine feet, of hulking flies of #14 and larger, and even ran articles covering developments which have occurred since the passing of Gordon, Skues and Halford. He was, of course, too much the gentleman even to discuss publicly our indecent exposure of information on fishing for bass and bluegill and unmentionable saltwater species.

I later told Arnold that, if he, creator of one of the country's liveliest and most contemporary magazines, had been allowed to select material for a new magazine on fly-fishing, the subscribers would instead, within a year, be reading Chapter

Twelve of the Bankruptcy Act. He supposed this was true, he said, and then made a mental note never to make a foray back into *our* editorial department either, even mismanaged as it was by an aging Turk. (This is certainly no commentary on Gingrich's kindest intentions and editorial genius, but *Fly Fisherman,* along with excessively long rods, #10 flies and smallmouth bass, still exists.)

Arnold did, however, have some basis for concern. As I sank further into the beckoning morass of fly-fishing in the early '60s, I was invited to sit with the Great Gentleman at the weekly luncheon of the Theodore Gordon Flyfishers at the Williams Club in New York. For some unknown reason I had a recently tied fly in my pocket, and when the conversation turned to fly-tying, I reflexively pulled it from my pocket and displayed it for all to see. The members recoiled as one at this deformed, ragged and hyperthyroid creation—as if I had suddenly thrust a gleaming crucifix into a clutch of vampires—and Arnold found it necessary to take a gulp from his drink before trusting himself to word a reply. But then, amid the groans, giggles and guffaws which my gesture deserved, he managed a typical Gingrich rejoinder.

"An authoritative lure. It should certainly catch fish, but I don't know what kind."

I didn't tie another fly for two years, and even that was too soon.

MY LAST CONVERSATION with Arnold was last winter at a meeting of the Museum of American Fly Fishing, of which he was president—held in Manchester, Vermont. That evening, after he had dispatched with "urbanity and sophistication" his duties as perennial toastmaster, we had a few minutes together. "The magazine," he allowed, "is even better than ever," meaning, of course, that it wasn't as bad as it used to be.

"But how about the articles on bass and bluegill?" I asked testily. He smiled, then stared into the fireplace for a moment. "Oh, I just don't read those anymore."

Shortly afterwards, his renewal subscription came in. For three years. But we—not the editorial but the piscatorial "we"—owe him much more than an unfulfilled subscription. He made certain that the traditions of Berners, Walton, Halford and Gordon burned brightly, through his own angling life, through his books, and through his continuing presence wherever a Company of Anglers gathered. For he was the Chairman of the Board.

Charles Ritz, the Un-Ritzy

Charles Ritz was exciting to be with. He always had new ideas, new opinions, new theories, and when he uttered them they carried the authority of a Papal Bull. Regardless of the scheme of the moment—whether it was the design for a new fly rod or for the lobby of the new Ritz in Chicago—you immediately hit the sawdust trail, ready to hoist by his own petard any blaspheming infidel who interfered with your quest for that particular day's Holy Grail.

It would often be hours, months, or sometimes years before you stopped to think about the viability of a rod made of plutonium alloy or a split-level bar overhanging the lobby. And was it *really* true that cervical manipulation, maintenance of the natural balance between the flexor and extensor muscles, red wine and carrots, and the instant availability of a top urologist form the secret of immortality? Not totally true, it sadly turns out—but I do remember the night in the Cambon Bar of the Paris Ritz when Charles held in thrall a French industrial magnate, a Belgian casting expert, Bertin, the bartender (Hemingway's old fishing friend), an American businessman, and the Princess von Quadt of Bavaria as he extolled these very virtues to all of us—all true believers, if not, later, faithful followers. A photograph records this moment of Charles' physiology seminar.

Charles carried that gift of instant intimacy. If you were more than a few years younger than he—and the odds were with you on that—a father-and-son relationship would quickly develop, with occasional role reversals as his youthful vitality and childlike freshness took over. I had known him for roughly two hours before he had learned of a recent prostatectomy in my family, had told me about his—"painless"—and then, as we later performed our ablutions that evening after a long communion with wine, commented admiringly from the adjoining stall, "Well, that's one operation *you* won't need!" Earthy, perhaps, but that was the true Charles César Ritz, separating as he so quickly did the myth from the man.

At breakfast one morning, while munching dry toast and coffee, he told me that he seldom ate large breakfasts anymore, not since he used to have to eat in the kitchen as a child. A certain sadness came over me on hearing of this lack of parental affection—until I realized that the kitchen was in the Ritz of the turn of the century, and that the chef was George Escoffier, who managed to whomp up some rather tasty dishes in his time. As the English hangman once said as he announced his retirement after dispatching a member of royalty, "After the silken cord, who can return to hemp?"

But anecdotes such as this can get a capsulizer of *la vie à la Ritz* in serious trouble, especially when read by someone who didn't know him personally or through the various editions of his book. Ritz the cosmopolite, the proprietor of the premiere hotel of that name, confidant of royalty, and the man who added an additional inflection to the word "Ritz," was not actually "ritzy."

Sent over to New York early in the century by his father as night manager of the Ritz-Carlton, Charles used the quieter hours at the Ritz to refurbish old fly rods he had picked up in local pawn shops and then sell them to Abercrombie & Fitch. This supplemented his modest salary and allowed him to spend time fishing in the North Country and set the pattern for his angling life.

Was Ritz "ritzy"? Grandson of a Swiss cowboy—he told me that in all seriousness—and wet-nursed by a gypsy, Charles was a sergeant in the U.S. Army in World War I. He owned and operated one of the first motion picture theaters in New Jersey, the progenitor of myriad others of the same name—"The Ritz"—and in between films held prizefights on stage. He eloped with a teen-age American girl in a brief earlier marriage, then went into the stock brokerage business, operated a shoe store in Paris in which he sold the *après-ski* shoe for which he held the original basic patent but which establishment was apparently a convenient "front" for angling friends to gather in and discuss more important matters. For many years he was rod designer for the fine old French firm of Pezon et Michel, where he created the "Parabolic" action (which that firm named—Charles called it "progressive" action). Happily, Pezon et Michel has risen again under sound and dedicated stewardship, and has just issued a beautiful new catalog in the United States full of Ritz "Parabolics"—a welcome and lasting, if not semantically correct, tribute to Charles Ritz.

For further details of this "fly fisher's life," angling and otherwise, we can heartily recommend his book of that name. It also details one of the highlights of his life, angling and otherwise—his meeting with and eventual marriage to the lovely Monique.

I hadn't seen Charles for nearly a year when he arrived in the States and we spent a weekend together. I asked how things were and he said, "Fine. I just got married."

"Charles," I exclaimed, "how splendid."

He pursed his lips, flicked the closest thing to a smile he could summon (any "smile" on Charles' face recorded on film can only be ascribed, as in babies, to gas pains), and added quietly: "Yes, I had to."

"Charles!" He then explained that the woman—Monique—was helping him redecorate the Paris Ritz, and that he thought it was foolish to drive her home in his auto every night when there was a perfectly good suite across the hall in the hotel. Her Gallic mother, however, had other views: "not unless he marries you!" Which he did. If the story is apocryphal, my apologies to Monique, but it came from a usually reliable source, and like anything he said, I believed it for a period of time which has not yet ended.

Joseph Wechsberg, writing a feature on Charles and the Ritz several years ago in *The New York Times,* spoke of his annual fly-fishermen's dinner party at the Ritz as being "the greatest social event in the fly-fishing world." Perhaps this is true, but no one has ever learned the exact requirements for membership in his Fario Club (a Latin word for "brown trout," which you were often required to explain to the unwashed), for it encompassed a motley crew pressed from the nooks and crannies of Charles' broad world. My wife, an admirer both of Ritz and his natural entrepreneurial inclinations, believes to this day that his International Fario Club banquet in November was a sales promotion scheme to fill out the Ritz guest list during a brief lull between seasons.

When his close friend, French casting champion Pierre Creusevaut, died recently, Charles disbanded the Fario Club, probably because Pierre handled the membership list and invitations and because Charles himself didn't know exactly who the hell were members and who weren't. Often the members didn't, either, from year to year.

Instead, he started a new club—the International Salmon Club—because he thought that trout were probably in better shape than salmon at this point; he held one meeting in Paris last spring.

Charles Ritz, among his many honors, should have received an honorary degree in engineering from MIT or the Sorbonne. Of course, he was already an engineer in the truest sense of the word, for he had a magnificent model railroad in his suite at the Ritz. He confessed that he had wished that he had earlier arranged a stretch of track to run across the corridor so he could send over lurid messages to his late friend and neighbor in the other suite, Coco Chanel.

Charles loved to design and invent—in fact, he held the original patent on the *après-ski* shoe—and no one was more intimate to the inner pulse and flexations of a fly rod than he. At the drop of a hint, Ritz would deface any tablecloth with penned diagrams of rod dynamics. The only napkin I have ever stolen was one from the restaurant of the Paris Ritz, in order to have source art for a modification of his parabolic-action rod designs—which he later recalled for further modification. As mentioned earlier, Charles never liked the name "Parabolic" which Pezon et Michel coined to describe his short butt/long tip rod design; "progressive action" was his terminology.

My last letter from Charles, sent earlier this last summer, acknowledged the fact that my wife and I were finally going to

ANGLISH SPOKEN HERE

· 114 ·

take our long-postponed trip to England later in the year and
he invited us to come to Paris and spend a weekend with him
and his lovely Monique—signed, "Your fly-swatting friends,
Charles and Monique."

One can argue that Paris is Paris, and changeless, but we
didn't visit Paris this fall. We decided not to test it so severely—
not this year.

On the Beach with Ernie's Army
(1974)

I̶T̶ I̶S̶ T̶I̶M̶E̶ to tell the truth about Ernie Schwiebert. We once printed in these columns that "Ernest Schwiebert" as an entity did not actually exist but was only a "house name" owned by a group of Manhattan publishers—like "Betty Crocker" or "Aunt Jemima." This is not true, for Ernie Schwiebert *does* exist, but even the truth is misleading when applied to Schwiebert. Unlike you and me, he puts on his waders both feet at once, not by ungainly acrobatics, but by leaping into them with one single and graceful motion, after the manner of Tom Mix levitating into his horse's saddle. It's beautiful to watch.

It's done with Vaseline. He greases the inside of his waders each night, not only to facilitate quick entry the next morning but to protect the special insulated lining of his custom waders. These waders are made up especially for him by NASA from experimental materials soon to be used as re-entry shields on space vehicles. To those anglers who do not know Schwiebert, such accoutrement might seem a bit pushy, but quickly accessible and well-insulated waders are among his most vital pieces of equipment.

At any moment the tranquillity of the Scandinavian dawn might be broken by a knock on the door of his little fishing inn—and it's the King of Transylvania announcing the arrival of a head of great sixty-five kilo salmon in the Smorgasbord Pool of the Aquavit. And you don't keep kings or sixty-five kilo salmon waiting while you fumble around in the dark trying to fit your contours to a semi-rigid iron maiden.

Besides, Schwiebert fishes the same places to which our boyhood hero, Don Sturdy, ventured in the picaresque novels by Victor Appleton (which *was* a house name)—"The Valley of Ten Thousand Smokes," "The Land of the Giants," and "The Sargasso Sea." He stalks his prey amid geysers, fumaroles, man-

115

eating denizens and great floes of breaking glacial ice. Siren winds come up and the shadows of legendary anglers walk the banks of the stream and the corridors of fishing inns he inhabits. He does exist, but not as you and I.

He finished his first book at thirteen (actually the first draft; he wisely polished it up a bit for the next decade until the maturity of twenty-three years gave it fuller credibility)—the first person ever to rhyme "match" and "hatch" and make it scan properly. He writes with sophistication, élan and, happily, great frequency, illustrating his own books with the consummate skill of a gifted artist and the draftsmanship of a trained architect, both of which he is. (Between trips to far-off lands—pausing only to wave at Henry Kissinger—Schwiebert designs airport complexes, builds planetariums, lays out college campuses and redesigns small cities, but his architectural activities are being phased down a bit now by Ernie as "distracting.")

Our first encounter with Ernie Schwiebert was a glancing blow, but sufficient to establish him, at least in our eyes, as more than just another weekend fisherman. It was about ten years ago, and we had managed to scrounge a day or two during a trip to New York to run up to Henryville Lodge in the Poconos for a go at those storied waters. While registering, our eyes fell on a crowded page of the guests' fishing log on the desk. "Well," we remarked to Mrs. Henry, "*that* party certainly did well this week." The ledger sheet was jammed with some sixty choice withdrawals and redeposits of Henryville trout, and well-annotated with detailed notes as to the method of capture, etc., all done in a cuneiform script that would have been instantly intelligible to any trained egyptologist. "How many days were they here?" I added.

"Oh?" Mrs. Henry queried, looking down at the log book. "That was Mr. Schwiebert's entry. He was just up here for the morning. I hope you do as well, Mr., er . . . ?"

"Mr. Smith," we replied anonymously as we filled in the name we decided to use for the occasion. "Mr. John Smith." And we paid in advance. No use starting out on the wrong foot at Henryville.

Several years later we had a better chance at Ernie. We had attended the spring banquet of the huge Colorado Chapter of Trout Unlimited and Ernie was the guest speaker. Our good friend Phil Wright had invited Ernie and us to spend a few days at his fishing cabin on the South Platte River in the 10,000-foot mountain-rimmed plateau lands of Colorado's South Park. Several dozen of the TU members and guests would be driving down to the South Park Sportsman's Club for a few days of early-season fishing for the king-size rainbows that infest that stretch of the South Platte. Phil and Ernie and I had spent an hour or so the evening before we left in solemn seminar at the Brown Hotel lounge, and Ernie announced that he would join us for the drive to South Park. Phil hastened to invite him.

The first morning of fishing at South Park began inauspiciously. We had quietly broken in earlier that morning on an isolated stretch of water before Phil and Ernie were in gear, but the intensity of our repeated presentations on one particular run had attracted the interest of the late TU president, Martin Bovey. Local chapters and other fishing hosts were in the habit of penning up huge fish at one end of a pool in advance of Martin's arrival, then leading him casually to that spot on the bank and into instant lunkerhood. We think that Martin had caught onto all this—known as the "Eisenhower Syndrome," Ben Schley once told us—and liked to get away on his own. Only seconds before he hove on the scene we discovered that we had been casting to some poisoned suckers, not trout—and we didn't want to add another one to our list. We told him they weren't taking, and that we'd better hurry and meet Ernie, Phil and the others upstream.

Ernie was walking along the bank, alternately casting and being interviewed by two newspaper outdoor editors—with a photographer at their sides. Behind him, at a respectful distance, gathered the first lines of what we like to call "Ernie's Army," the group of admirers in spite of whom he usually manages to catch fish. But this morning, neither Ernie nor his legions were doing any good. The writers by then had all the facts—now they wanted action. But Ernie had exhausted several entomological species from his voluminous fly box and was now relying totally on his natural charm to sign a quick "thirty" to the newspapermen's stories.

Then suddenly, the shaky arm that couldn't get a rise out of a sick sucker stiffened as the rod and line it held twanged into a large rainbow—in the exact spot Ernie had cast a minute before. In quick succession we raised another, caught one that broke off, and finally landed a beautiful eighteen-incher.

Then it happened.

Ernie stopped, obviously in desperation, turned back, and shouted against the growing wind: *"Zahner! What are you using?"* (As his loyal readers know, Ernie always talks in italics—as it is necessary to do for those wishing to communicate with him.) Here I was, being asked by Ernie Schwiebert himself what fly I was using—and I didn't even remember. Then I looked down and recalled that I had tied on one of Sam Slaymaker's little mini-streamers at the beginning of my sucker foray and had never removed it. I pointed down to the fly, which was still in the beached eighteen-incher's lip, and called out stupidly, but in italics: *"Just a Little Rainbow Trout!"* I later realized that the adjacency of the fly to the fish led him to believe that I was facetiously referring to the fish itself and not Sam's "Little Rainbow Trout" streamer. Our friendship strengthened in later years, but I never recall his once asking me again for streamside guidance.

BUT THAT AFTERNOON was a different story. Several club members had sidled up to Ernie at lunch to tell him about A Great Fish that had resisted the top anglers of the club for more than a year. It reposed under a half-sunken log on the far side of a stream that rushed down from a nearby red-rock mountain, fast but clear water, with no place to shield oneself from the eagle-eyed lunker that was reputed to be as selective as a gourmet diner who had stumbled into a hash-house. *"At least twenty-four inches,"* they muttered, *"and it must weigh at least six pounds!"*

"How much is that in kilos?" Ernie asked, but no one heard him, because they didn't understand italics.

Within an hour, Ernie's Army, nearly 100 strong, had established a beachhead near the stream where it raced down through the mountain draw. Ernie approached within twenty feet of the bank, then crawled on all fours in the manner of one who was about to take a machine-gun nest. Then, in a prone position, he reached behind him and, with a downward motion of the flat of his hand, signaled the troops to lie low. Phil and I had taken a position behind a small hummock, and as we glanced about us all was quiet and prevailed. Only the down-slope wind, as it whistled through the sage brush, broke the stillness, and the only motion came from a few tumbleweeds. The scene resembled a weird montage of "High Noon," Custer's Last Stand and Omaha Beach on D-Day.

And there it was. The lumbering rainbow was striking its insect prey with the regularity of Big Ben. Ernie risked a grab at a passing insect, inspected it and then his fly box. There were later rumors among the outriders that Ernie had rejected the total contents of his Pandora's box of flies, tied up an exact imitation on the spot, and then sketched it in pencil for his next book, but it would be irresponsible of us to inject that undocu-mented detail into the angling literature at this date.

The Great Fish was ascending in a sipping rise every forty-five seconds, and the current about the sunken log was as intri-cate as those in a whirlpool bath. A testy false-cast directly over the fish could have been fatal—but not to the fish—and the wind was rising higher by the minute. A low backcast would be necessary, but several stands of sage on the rise behind Ernie could easily interfere. And the heavy mid-stream current would belly the line in a few seconds. It was the ultimate chal-lenge, and one to be faced by the ultimate angler.

Schwiebert rolled on his side, bent on the fly of his choice, then rose to his knees. The scene was as exotic as an Easter sunrise service at Stonehenge, and as unreal.

But it was over in a minute . . . an upstream false-cast, then a backcast between the sage brush, followed by a shoot of line some sixty feet across the windswept surface and a delicate drop of the fly some ten inches above the huge rainbow. After a float of some two seconds, the fish took what was probably its first taste of steel. Ernie's Army descended on him at stream-side in a great cheer as he fought and brought to bank the most beautiful fish we had seen since we last visited Dan Bailey's "Wall of Fame" in Montana.

Talk about "angling pressure"—millimeter for millimeter and kilo for kilo, Schwiebert is the gamest fisherman there is. That night the Hartsel Hotel, which looks like something left over from the last horse opera made on the Universal lot, saw a great gathering of celebrants as toasts were raised to the con-quering hero. As the evening wore on, a great wind rose outside, for these Western anglers had at last found a man to match their mountains *and* their hatches. As the air thickened and hearts warmed, anglers could detect the presence of a Pantheon of legendary fly fishers gathered about them in spirit to commemorate the lofty deeds of the day.

And that night, as the mountain winds swept down from the rimming peaks of South Park, ghosts walked the corridors of the old Hartsel Hotel. This, of course, generally broke things up, because the Hartsel Hotel, under earlier and less worthy management, had been a house of ill repute, and no place to launch another legend.

· · ·

Angling's Dean Emeritus, John Voelker
(1977)

THE LATE ARNOLD GINGRICH, writing with his usual perception in *Joys of Trout,* nominated John Voelker as the next dean of American angling (for "angling," read "fly-fishing," for in Arnold's copybook the two are synonymous).

"It is as self-depicted in *Trout Madness* and *Anatomy of a Fisherman,*" Gingrich proclaimed, "that John Voelker earns my nomination, as he emerges from their pages as the curmudgeon's curmudgeon, the character's character, of the true trout-lover's world."

Gingrich reverently acknowledged in his segment on Voelker that the reigning dean is, of course, Sparse Grey Hackle, and commented further on the "nice coincidence" that Sparse's "obvious and logical ultimate successor to this unofficial title should also be the wearer of a *nom de plume"*—a reference to the pen name of "Robert Traver" under which John Voelker concocts his delightful felonies.

This use of aliases by angling writers is not new—I think of Britain's "Jock Scott" (Donald Rudd)—and it is possibly appropriate to the inherent deceit that lies at the core of this "confidence man's recreation" that we all pursue. We all live the lie that we are smarter than the fish, and continue to build in this fiction for the remainder of our lives. I would like to use an alias myself—but I would fish under it, not write under it.

First as a lawyer, then as a prosecuting attorney, and later as a Michigan Supreme Court Justice, John Voelker began writing books and publishing them under the name of "Robert Traver," placing him on the level with more than one of his clients or defendants who carried the "pen" name—quite literally—"a.k.a" (also known as . . .). Then, in 1958, Voelker published his famous *Anatomy of a Murder,* which spawned the movie of the same name, and which eventually led to the publication of *Anatomy of a Fisherman.*

It also led to the publication of yet another "Anatomy"— *The Anatomy of a Movie,* the story of the making of the motion-picture version of *Anatomy of a Murder,* and which was *not* written by Voelker, although it featured him along with the on-location Hollywood cast of characters including Jimmy Stewart, Lee Remick, Otto Preminger and a Boston lawyer named Joseph Welch who played the judge in the film almost as well as he played the key role in the real-life drama of the Army-McCarthy hearings on TV in the mid-'50s. (John and Joe Welch and their wives became close friends and went on a round-the-world cruise together.)

Practically the whole mining town of Marquette, Michigan, had walk-on parts in the movie, and for years they filled the local theater to overflowing every summer with an "Anatomy Festival" when everyone turned out to munch popcorn and laugh hilariously at themselves. Voelker, long a prominent figure on the Upper Peninsula, quickly became a folk hero, and his role in the legend has grown with the years. Once, in a tavern where John played cribbage, I was refused, not a drink, but payment for it, just because I mentioned I was looking for him. Another time I was moved to a larger suite in a local motel because I had "come to fish with Yonny."

Acceptance of this latter "perk" turned out to be fortuitous. We had spent our *aprés* fishing hours at his fishing shack in a seminar on the proper use of commas, one of which I had removed from a manuscript of John's—a venal sin—and two of which I had added—a mortal sin in the Voelker dogma. During this session I was forced to do penance by treading water for several hours in a bottomless Old-Fashioned of Homeric proportions. John, born leader that he is, would not ask his men to do anything that he wouldn't do, of course, so by the time we left for the demanding circumnavigation of the cedar swamps that isolated us from that civilization that is Marquette, neither of us was, as they say, "feeling any pain."

In fact, after the manner of the lawyer, John insisted on proving this, by proceeding to fall heavily into a dark gulch by the side of the road. Still feeling no pain, but convinced that something was amiss because of the peculiar changes that had taken place in his extremely vulnerable nose after he had wiped the blood from it, Voelker suggested, with an animal cunning developed over years of familial living, that "we not bother dear old Grace" at this time of night and that he should stay at my motel. After a fitful night, rent with John's dark curses, I insisted that we drop over to the hospital, where the entire staff seemed to converge upon its Johnny Voelker and bring a new level of dedication to the term "intensive care." Various specialists fought over their diagnoses. I remember one calling for an iron lung. Concerns were quickly dispelled, however, when they learned that it was only a fractured nose and a few cracked ribs—much less serious than a displaced comma. I've never touched one of his commas again, nor have I offered him one.

ALTHOUGH FAME IS NOT TRANSITORY on the Upper Peninsula of Michigan, it is less than fleeting in the New York publishing world. We called the publishers of *Anatomy of a Murder* to get more accurate information about the best-seller status of *Anatomy* in 1958. After several most accommodating conversations with members of the staff—all of whom were pleased to hear that they had had a bestseller, but would I spell the name for them and repeat the name of the book—they finally explained that they didn't keep records on books "published so long ago." They would probably have been even more pleased to know, as we were when we learned from the reference department of the New York Public Library, that *Anatomy of a Murder* was the number two best-selling novel of that year, beaten out only by *Dr. Zhivago*. It was quite possibly still paying part of their salaries.

It's understandable that they didn't keep any records on *Anatomy of a Fisherman,* because it was never advertised to fishermen or really to anyone else. It was given sufficient time off the press for the ink to dry, then remaindered, and an entire generation of fly fishermen has been deprived of some of John

Voelker's best writing. Few writers give such a true picture of themselves in their books as does Voelker-Traver, but this quality is even stronger in *Anatomy of a Fisherman* because of the enchanted camera work of Bob Kelley. The camera doesn't lie, and neither does John Voelker. As Arnold Gingrich said in his *Fishing in Print,* "when better fishing books are written, Robert Traver will write them."

The Man Who Kept a River
(1980)

NO PEOPLE have toyed with the works of Nature more, and in the doing harmed them less, than the British. Few are the acres of that tight little island that have not been gracefully manicured over the centuries, giving the living land that perpetual care that we too often reserve for our cemeteries.

Disorder of any sort—except in the House of Commons—makes the British edgy. Not only do they take pleasure in their trees, their flowers, their birds and their butterflies, but by the nineteenth century they had also classified and cataloged them—just to make certain of their total pleasure. They even cataloged the heavens, then out of reach.

They liked what they had, and they wanted to keep it that way. Even their highways and byways flowed with the terrain—until the recent onslaught of the threatening M-1-and-upward dual motorways that sound to many like the dangerous weapons that they are. A twentieth-century English poet once raised his glass in an ode "to that rolling English drunkard who laid out those rolling English roads."

To maintain their houses as homes, they retained housekeepers. To keep a proper garden and park, they had groundskeepers. Gamekeepers for stag and grouse. Then, as keepers of the kept, even gatekeepers to further secure things. And eventually, it was for the British to devise the ultimate in the art of maintenance—the river keeper.

Now, the name itself could easily be misinterpreted—as it has from time to time by our American "river keepers," whom we call "the Corps of Engineers." To keep a river from doing what it is supposed to do would be noxious to the British, as it is to many anglers. And as it had always been to Frank Sawyer, the late keeper of the Avon.

FRANK SAWYER, keeper of the River Avon in Wiltshire, died this spring on the banks of his river, in fact, on the very stretch,

Choulston Hatches, where he played midwife to hatching autumn olives and transplanted them for their growth into matu-
ring nymphs the next spring.

This loss of a life is ours, not his. For a half-century Sawyer
moved to the rhythm of this meandering South Country chalkstream, keeping the river as he found it—possibly with the addition of a few, if not divine, secular revelations—and finally
turning it over to posterity this April.

To be able to say, today, that you left your own little slice of
world as you found it would automatically make you a can-
didate for eventual beautification. But Sawyer did that, and
more, for his life carried far beyond the River Avon, bringing
fly-fishing to British youngsters through junior courses spon-
sored by the Salmon and Trout Association, and then to many
more through his classic book, *Nymphs and the Trout,* which
alone, many feel, positions him firmly with Halford, Skues and
Dunne in the long ranks of British angling literature.

However, few American anglers realize that Frank Sawyer
had become a popular BBC radio and television personality,
speaking not only of fishing but of the care of rivers and their
valleys. In fact, the first time I met Frank, I soon wondered how
he had escaped the clutch of the film studios of Ealing and
Pinewood. The fine head of white hair, the aquiline nose well-
placed on a pink-cheeked face, the controlled, rich South
Country voice, lean and rangy, a man warm and rich in his
mien but with the dignified reserve of the country gentleman
Sawyer was. Central Casting's loss was our gain. For us, he lives
on other more permanent emulsions.

I MET SAWYER against an auspicious backdrop, although little
of this was reflected in the encounter itself. It was the annual
banquet, at the Ritz in Paris in 1972, of Charles Ritz' International Fario Club. This was a loose-hung federation of some ten
dozen of Charles' most intimate angling friends, a term that
could be defined as "anyone who believed more than half of the
things Ritz told him." Each year these worthies were sum-
moned by M. Charles from various parts of the world as witness
to the latest revelations and to pursue established rituals.

We had all reeled in from the earlier cocktail party in a

nearby lounge to find our place-cards and confront the fish course, *salmo salar fumé*. I had fallen into conversation with the American gentleman to my left, Ben Fontaine, president of the International Casting Association, then living in Brussels, and we had passed the fish course and were well into the fowl (*dindonneau farci I.F.C.*) when I first turned to acknowledge the presence of my other companion.

I looked into this bright, pink, handsomely drawn face, and before I could speak my companion said, "I'm Frank Sawyer. You must be Don Zahner." I acknowledged the accuracy of both statements, although, after my abominable habit of "killing off" old movie stars, I had somehow thought that Frank Sawyer had died, lumping him in, I suppose, with Halford and Skues, who definitely and irrevocably had.

He then offered a hearty handshake while I tried to summon a fitting rejoinder to this serendipitous occasion of meeting a born-again Sawyer. But the best I could come up with was, "I like your nymphs."

Sawyer beamed and said how nice it was of me to say so. I should have left it at that, leaving both of us to ponder whether I was referring to his book, which Nick Lyons had just published in America a few years before, or his classic copper-clad imitations.

Instead, prototype of the bumbling American in Paris, I fell into the role of groupie, and thrusting my gold-crested Fario Club souvenir menu toward him, asked him if he would autograph it. Now, no one has ever been insulted by such a request, but even the gracious Sawyer could have taken understandable offense with my follow-up, in which I anointed the menu, his jacket and his shirt-cuff with my ration of Chateau Ducru-Beaucaillou.

I made guttural sounds of intense shame while Sawyer blotted away. "Not to worry," he smiled. "The '62 was a very good year."

Only a blot on his clothing, perhaps, but a lasting one on my angling career. My mind flew back to the fish course. "I wish it could have been the Gewurztraminer," I added wistfully. But, it wasn't, and I still have the menu to document it, spattered in red but still bearing Sawyer's slightly shaky signature.

We soon fell into the more relaxed conversation that can only develop between two men who have shared a great wine, and he talked of many things, of his nymphs, of his river, and with much affection of Charles Ritz, who kept interrupting us to give and receive long toasts in several languages. The next day, during the called-for pilgrimage to the Bois-de-Boulogne for the annual blessing of the waters by Monseigneur Charles, Frank Sawyer took me aside, bent on a Sawyer nymph to the line of my recently acquired Ritz Fario Club rod, and proceeded to give me personal and in-depth instruction in casting and fishing it. In Paris. In November. In a misty rain. Sawyer again wet and soggy.

FRANK SAWYER was equally at ease in Paris with princes and fools (documented), or in London clubs with angling doyens and attending pilgrims (observed). But he was only truly at home on Wiltshire's Avon, opening a weir, transplanting a hatch board, dipping a nymph, or, on those long winter nights, devising devilish new artifices for the season ahead.

Isn't it splendid that Frank Sawyer was among us for so long? For even though the need was so strong, we couldn't have invented him. How nice to know that he was there, even managing to leave his imprint, if not literally on the flowing waters in the valley of the Avon, at least on the mainstream of British—and American—angling.

At the close of his book, *Nymphs and the Trout,* he even stands with us on a high reach and points down to his little Wiltshire world, speaking with the fluency of the Avon and, perhaps, with a touch of the genius of that river's earlier upstream Bard:

"Perhaps from some hill or other you can overlook the valley where the little villages and their farms huddle together as though for warmth. In winter, after the bleakness of the downs the view brings a warm glow to the heart and in spring and summer comes that feeling of everlasting freshness, that of gazing at something new. Unconsciously, one's footsteps hasten down the hill eager to be there—eager to see more of what Nature has created in this hollow and enjoy to the full this heritage we possess. To the fisherman comes an even greater urge. He absorbs the scenery at a glance, for to him such sights are frequent. These river valleys are his life and immediately his thoughts go to what may be hidden beneath the surface of that shining strip he seeks, snaking away in the distance."

La Plume de Smith "Rouge"
(*1977*)

JUST BOUGHT A PAIR of the new wading shoes developed by Creative Sports out in Walnut Creek, California, and I'm still wondering if they're as good as they look—light, all-over double-leather construction to prevent rotting, hard toe and, of all things, speed laces to shorten that agonizing process that can so quickly dissipate any remaining illusions of one's immortality.

I couldn't try them out, though, because I found that my old stocking-foot waders, unused for a season or two, were also suffering from a case of terminal mortality. Any attempts at repair would have crippled the Akron rubber industry.

Andy Puyans of Creative Sports is also shipping a pair of their new and unusual "dry suit" waders of the stocking-foot persuasion as soon as he can customize a pair that conforms to my various deformities, but I needed an interim pair so I drove down the road to Perkins' Pole and Bait Shop in Manchester. They're pushing a new latex stocking-footer this season, black all over, and I was immediately reminded of a story that "Sparse Grey Hackle" wrote for us a few years ago.

I had wanted to say something about Sparse's most recent honor, conferred by the Theodore Gordon Flyfishers in mid-March in the form of the first annual Arnold Gingrich Angling Heritage Award for his "significant contributions to angling literature." I had spent the day of this signal event with Sparse, Mrs. Hackle (more affectionately and appropriately known as "Lady Beaverkill"; even for a man of his unquestioned stature, I must say that he certainly married well, possibly even "above his station"), and Nick Lyons, who was to present the award at the annual TGF banquet later that evening in a rambling seminar on matters angling, horticultural and otherwise. We later drove over to the hotel near Rye for the banquet, but not before the "conversation" devolved upon the Mexican Border

War of 1916, its strategies, tactics and eventual termination despite the very real if uneven presence of Alfred Miller, Sparse's real-life alias. These were meaty hours which held promise of a fascinating essay on the "real" Sparse Grey Hackle. Then, yesterday the newspaper arrives.

Damn that "Red" Smith! I suppose it is appropriate for the dean of sportswriters to comment upon the dean of angling writers, but there is no one around today who would knowingly try to upstage "Red" Smith, classical essayist who usually ends up on the sports pages because no other writers want to be within 100 picas of him. Not only did he take the wind out of my sails, his story, "La Plume de Sparse Grey Hackle," scuttled me in the most ironic fashion—by quoting the very story of the black waders, originally published in this magazine.

One of the major deprivations of World War II on the homefront was the shortage of waders. Sparse was piscatorially paralyzed until Dana Lamb came up with the idea of checking the religious supply houses catering to "immersionist Baptists," where he finally found a ready supply of pre-blessed clerical-black waders!

Sparse even added a second level to the article by recounting the tale of the fishing reverend who had hung his boot-footed chest waders in the belfry, as I recall, so they would be at ready when Sunday services had been rendered. All went well until the verger climbed the steps on an errand, saw the lower half of the dangling waders and ran terror-stricken through the church, fully believing that the good reverend had taken his own life!

So—if you missed Red Smith's column of April 27th or thereabouts in one of its several hundred syndicated appearances, you'll just have to read *Fishless Days, Angling Nights* or one of Sparse's other "too sparsely" published works, in one of which he himself asks the question, "Who is Sparse Grey Hackle?" Sparse has already been "done" by the master, and you're not going to catch me getting any further into it at this point. I'll wait a few years. Maybe Sparse will start to mellow as he gets a little older.

Because he certainly hasn't yet. That night at the TGF banquet, after Nick Lyons introduced him and presented the Gingrich Award, the man who was just warming up in the bull-pen during our seminar of that afternoon proceeded to lecture in depth on accurate reporting and taut prose, two laxities which he deemed most visible in much being written today. Outdoor writers and editors, probably attracted to the event by the cheap drinks, squirmed in their chairs for nearly an hour before class was ended and they were free to leave and consider other forms of employment.

For years Sparse was an unquenchable fount of wisdom in his regular communications with Smith and countless other recorders of the angling life, but this eventually ended, Smith observes sadly at the end of his article, "when Sparse found that there were editors and publishers willing to pay him for writing."

I agree with Red's final comment on that dreadful eventuality, and I further apply it to Red Smith's arrival on the scene. "It was," he commented, "a dark day for columnists."

Winter Memories, Summer Thoughts
(1982)

THE FISHERMAN'S WINTER in Vermont is a time to sit back in front of a cozy fire with a tall glass of scotch close at hand and watch the paranoia set in. In November and December one can sustain life by leaning on the nostalgia of picture-postcard New England, but by January nostalgia undergoes an early thaw. I once stopped by a "snowy woods" and couldn't get started again. Robert Frost was not around to help push me out.

Six months of snow cover, almost continuous, can cloud men's minds, and you find yourself living, not by the calendar but by the barometer and the thermometer. For a month or so, you find a certain solace in watching the icy inundations of your hometown and other old stomping grounds on the evening television news, but this electronic gloat does not last forever. The Midwestern thaws eventually come, bringing floods, but your glazed eyes do not see the tragedy and loss, only the heavy moving waters and men in waders, and this is sufficient to conjure agonizing thoughts of a sometime spring.

Even a stolen week on the Florida Keys in late January turns out to be a hollow victory. Air temperatures in the upper 70s, the delight of southering "snow birds," do not impress bonefish and permit, who do not subscribe to the Miami *Herald*. Rather, and no pun intended, they recall that footage on the evening news about the Florida freeze that gave you your jollies, and they are off to their comfy condos in the offshore deeps.

Nor does return to your home carry with it a rebirth of the spirit. The airport runway has been cleared but not the parking lot, and unless you are on intimate terms with your automobile aerial the location and eventual liberation of your car, while dressed in Hush-Puppies and Dacron slacks, can be a cruel and abrupt transition. The long haul to the homestead carries you along some of those little streams of summer that you've always planned to fish, now seemingly frozen in midriffle and devoid of life as you would like to know it. But all this is disciplinary, especially if you arrive home to the good news that your daughter's houseguests had failed in their attempt to burn the house down.

As in the case of any normal, aging American angler, your first impulse is to banish yourself to your little playroom in the attic and inventory tackle. There is much to do. Decisions must be made. Only veteran anglers such as you can sense the true importance of advance planning—making certain, for example, that you arrive streamside with both rod *and* reel, that the reel has a line on it, and the line a leader. Even the leader must be checked. You know personally of someone who arrived for the evening hatch of Hendricksons on the Battenkill with his little Payne rod at the ready, only to find that the sole leader in his wallet was most recently used for tarpon, complete with shock tippet. Friends consoled him by insisting that this would be no handicap.

EVEN AS YOU, I found myself moving into February with the full confidence that there would actually be another spring. I had mustered my mothball fleet of tackle for renovation and review, and had sent the dangerous daughter back to college after her sabbatical-of-convenience. By now, the nuclear family had split, but fallout was still a problem, and I've found that the family still has a half-life of its own. My sons were now playing magazine elsewhere in Vermont, my other daughter was now a book editor in San Francisco and quite harmless, but the news from my Dad was not good, and I soon found myself in other and sadder inventories.

If you believe the cant of archaeologists and anthropologists—that our trash will, in later ages, be the ultimate toll of our presence here—history will not record that my Father even existed. For exactly 75 years, the dapper little man had thrown away nothing but Kleenex. A church bulletin from 1907 documents that "young Oscar Adolphus Zahner will present a program of prestidigitation and occult magic at next Wednesday's church-night supper." This was the fountainhead of a stream of letters, documents, business cards, organizational publications, photographs, advertising copy (from 1916 on), old banquet menus, newspaper clippings, convention badges, dozens of personalized ashtrays and lighters, and 84 plaques and framed certifications of his existence. Don't count them, I did. There was even the residue of a protracted correspondence with the Jefferson Memorial Museum in St. Louis in his effort to donate all of his memorabilia to that institution. The last letter in this ten-year exchange gently informed him that the directors had explained that the acceptance of his generous offer would require the removal of the Jefferson Memorial's Lindbergh "Spirit of St. Louis" Trophy wing exhibit and that they had voted in favor of its retention.

Dad had spent some five years here in Vermont, maintaining an office in nearby Manchester in his capacity as Special Services Director of *Fly Fisherman*, but the nearby mountains, the crude roads and the long winter snows made him uneasy, and after the sale of the magazine to Ziff-Davis Publishing in 1978 he returned, with mixed feelings, to St. Louis and the ignominy, at 82, of early retirement. Among his effects was the remainder of the box of magazines announcing the sale of *Fly Fisherman;* he had asked us to ship them to him in St. Louis so that he could explain to his friends why he wasn't working anymore.

Although Dad was not an angler—at least in the most literal sense of the word—he was quick to adapt to his environment. One of his first moves on his earlier arrival in Vermont, after opening up his pre-shipped box of "roughing-it clothes"—which included his World War I uniform, complete with puttees and gas mask—was to enroll in the Orvis Fly Fishing School. I must confess that this was not because of a long-stifled urge to become at one with the natural stream ecology— he never totally understood fly-fishing, even after graduation, although his proudly framed proficiency certificate, along with his little fishing vest and rod and reel, turned up in inventory— but rather the natural reflexes of the primal ad man which he was. "I want to get a feel for this market," he explained. And he did. To him, the Orvis school certificate licensed him to open up instant and unilateral relations with the magazine's advertisers.

I just recently uncovered a note of a telephone conversation Dad had had with Dan Bailey, a most unlikely communication if it hadn't been for his function as coordinator of tackle-shop sales of *Fly Fisherman*. Dad was trying to up the number of copies Dan ordered each issue for his Livingston, Montana, tackle emporium, but apparently there was more to the conversation than this. I cringed as I read a final entry: "Gave fellow hell over that catalog cover," and recalled that Dad had complained to me about the lack of imagination in the selection of Dan Bailey's annual tackle catalog. I explained to him that Dan felt the twenty-year use of Ernie Bauer's splendid photograph of a Royal Coachman dry fly on his catalog gave it instant recognition, but Dad immediately gave me five reasons why "this fellow" was wrong and was "asking for a lot of trouble, boy!"

I HAD JUST READ this memo, confident that Dan's indiscretion had been revealed to him in depth during this 1976 conversation, when the 1982 Bailey catalog arrived, Royal Coachman and all. I made a note to inquire about all of this with Dan, but a week later I learned that it had been a long winter in Montana, too, and that Dan Bailey had died at the age of 78 in late May of complications following a heart attack.

Dan, of course, was one of the folk heroes of American fly-fishing. Trained as a physicist at The Citadel and Lehigh, he taught physics at the prestigious Brooklyn Polytechnic Institute while working on his doctorate at New York University. He had already gained a reputation as a fly-tier and teacher of the art by the mid-1930s, and for two years practiced his artistry on summer vacations from a trailer along the Yellowstone in Montana. Then, in 1938, with all of his graduate work completed except for the submission of his doctor's dissertation, common sense prevailed and Dan, with his wife Helen, moved to Montana to become a full-time commercial fly-tier. The first decade was more or less typical of any beginning venture such as this, but the outdoor boom of the post-war years found Dan ready and willing to supply the world with flies. Still the teacher, Dan trained local ladies to tie flies with the Bailey touch, and anyone who stepped into the store for the first time was immediately struck with this well-lighted gallery of typing benches peopled by women of the town, the walls of the store covered with plaques (Dad would have *approved* of this!) denoting trout of four pounds or over captured by his customers (and his ladies' flies), and finally Dan himself, at least back in 1967 on my first visit, ensconced regally on a raised and railed dais *cum* office, surveying his mighty domain from beneath those dark, bushy eyebrows that could have well been the inspiration for his Woolly Worms or Muddler Minnows.

In a conversation with John McDonald, the editor, writer and Gordon scholar and a longtime friend of Bailey's, John suggested to me that, if Dan had kept and mounted all the trout over four pounds that he had caught through the years, there would have been no room for the triumphs of his clientele. Dan carried his own "Wall of Fame" in his memories, and there were some good ones.

My few personal memories of Dan Bailey are also good. A group of us were fishing the Big Hole in Montana, at the proposed site of the Reichle Dam, in fact, and Dan broke away to take me upstream with him. He planted me in a good spot, then moved around the bend in the growing grayness of a mustering Big Sky line storm. I took a big one a few minutes later, which by some dark alchemy turned into a sizable mountain whitefish on closer inspection, and was about to return it when I heard a frantic yelp from upstream, followed by a terrifying splash. I shouldn't have let the poor old fellow fish alone, I muttered as I stumbled upstream to rescue him. I then fell sprawling into the stiff current, but a strong hand reached out from the bank and righted me, and I soon found that the poor old fellow had just been announcing his temporary involvement with a "nice brownie." "Oh?" he responded. "I guess it was 26 or 28 inches." My God, I had children smaller than that.

The thunderstorm hit, as they only can in Montana, and we retired to André Puyan's van for shelter and sustenance, the latter in the form of highballs all around and served by me because I had the obvious desire and the closest seat to the freezer. Later, my tongue loosened by drink, I proposed my long-gestating idea of beginning a magazine on fly-fishing. My lucid presentation of the project, plus the authoritative nature of my backseat libations, brought enthusiastic replies from André, Dan, Phil Wright and Ben Schley. Each of these gentleman-anglers were key supporters of *Fly Fisherman* from its inception. Three of them sent manuscripts, but one of them, tackle shop proprietor Dan Bailey, sent money—year after year. One of those ads he ran last spring brought more re-sponses than the magazine had subscribers after the first year.

Dan Bailey is and was unique. More will be said about him, here and elsewhere.

BUT—WINTER MEMORIES BRING summer thoughts. Although in early May I stepped into a vestigial bank of snow while fish-ing a Green Mountain stream here in Vermont, suggestions of spring mix with hints of summer on this first day of June. I am continually surprised to find once again trout, and a good head of them this year, in our little village stream. The winter kill was low, despite the record snows, and I've done fairly well astream. But no trash, not even any plaques on anyone's wall, to prove it.

Angling's Second Spring
(1969)

IF THE MONTH OF AUGUST does not offer the best of angling to the fly fisherman, it certainly requires it of him. The fly fisherman cannot complain, however, for he scarcely chose the discipline of angling with the fly for its lack of obstacles and challenges. The soft, heavy air of August lies oppressively across late summer streams, putting down both the water and the fish. Those fish not lurking in the dark spring holes quickly become the most discriminating of feeders, frequently reserving their prime repast for the stylishly late hours of the night. It is a time of test for both fish and fisherman, and whichever wins his duel in the sun gains a fleeting immortality.

But August does not bring down the final curtain on this little drama. For years the rich tradition of our angling legacy had led us to break down our rods in late summer and move into an early hibernation. But tradition can bind us as well as enrich us, and traditions that do not find their counterpart in nature can become shackles. If we keep our eyes only on the stream, we will see the first leaves of autumn floating the glides and bouncing in the eddies where mayflies formerly held their ephemeral court. But if we look along the banks, we see beavers a-building and chattering squirrels gathering their harvest of nuts. So it can be for the angler, for there is a store of fishing memories to be gathered before the final frosts send our quarry into their grey winter underworld.

To the anxious angler, autumn waters offer a second spring, fleeting, often cut short, but a definite season, a respite from the dog days of late summer, a firm yet fading foothold on eternity. The angler acutely conscious of the seasons, often takes on the cycle of nature, and autumn fishing allows him that luxury of renewal which the years enhance and appreciate in value. Ponds and lakes turn over, bringing the trout and the bass into topwater feeding grounds again, and streams cool,

bringing frenzied activity as the fish move again into aerated
waters and reap their final harvest before the winter ends it all.

It is not a time for subtlety. One does not match a hatch,
but a hunger. And big hungers bring big fish. The pressure of
heavy hands is off the streams in autumn and on the fish and
the angler. Both are hungry in their way, and both seek to
gorge themselves before the golden-browns of the fall backdrop turn to grey, then black, then white.

No fly fisherman knowingly makes a last cast or closes a
final season. Yet, as the seasons pile upon themselves, the angler who is at one with nature and part of its cycle does not
require the rebirth of spring to stir his blood; he will settle for
the brief renewal of the second spring, and the memories to be
stored against the grey nights ahead.

The young angler takes spring for granted, the middle-
aged angler takes it as it comes, but the wise angler takes no
chances. Spring lies on another calendar, but good fishing lies
immediately ahead.

We do not know if Dylan Thomas, the lyrical Welsh bard,
was a fly fisherman, but he had many of the angler's attributes.
He was talking of other matters, of course, but his words give a
reason to autumn angling. "Do not go gentle unto that good
night . . . rage, rage against the dying of the light."

On Angling Presidents
(1981)

WHILE ONE CAN HARDLY SAY that fishing is the sport of Presidents, it has certainly been a Presidential sport. With the rise of the campaign publicist during the past half-century, every United States President has been publicly documented as having fished, after kissing his quota of babies, of course. Certainly F.D.R. was a deep-sea fisherman in his more robust years, both before and after being stricken with polio. Harry S. Truman was an habitué of the sportfishing docks at Key West, his winter White House, and both Presidents Nixon and Ford, perhaps posed by p.r. men, have been photographed in fishing ragalia (although the thought of the slice-prone Jerry Ford unleashed on a crowded trout stream gives one a certain valid concern).

But serious fly fishermen in the White House have been as scarce as Blue Dun hackle. There is a published picture of Cal Coolidge gingerly holding two trout on a South Dakota trout stream, of course, but there is also a photo of him in an Indian war bonnet, and you would have a hard time proving to his old neighbors up the road from us in Plymouth, Vermont, that Cal was a Sioux. However, there is no question as to Herbert Hoover's fly-fishing credentials—he wrote a book on his experiences on the Brule River and elsewhere called *Fishing for Fun*. And certainly "Ike" Eisenhower, schooled during World War II and afterward by aide Gen. "Beetle" Smith, followed the sport with enthusiasm, occasionally venting his spleen at well-meaning fish and game officials who insisted on planting corralled lunkers wherever Ike went to fish.

But former President Jimmy Carter is unique in twentieth century White House angling annals. While he had fished and enjoyed other outdoor sports in his native Georgia, the revelation of angling in its ultimate form came to him during his early White House years, triggered, as he once told us, by a subscription to *Fly Fisherman*, a gift from his son "Chip." Soon afterward "leaks" from usually reliable sources in Washington told of a surreptitious trip by the President's daughter Amy to buy a fly vest for him at Christmas from Barry Serviente's Angler's Art tackle shop in D.C., followed by reports of later visits from his wife and White House associates bent on further suspicious purchases. Shortly there would be front-page photographs of President Carter fly-fishing in the nearby Catoctin Mountains of Maryland, then in Pennsylvania, and finally on to Idaho and Montana. (Just before his personal trip to China last summer, he called us to inquire about fly-fishing opportunities in Japan, where he would stop after his China visit; we turned him over to Leon Chandler of Cortland Line, who came up with a solid Japanese connection.)

But the depth of his immersion became clear as crystal when he confessed to us some two years ago that, in the early spring of 1979, while standing on the Madison portico of the White House with his wife, he had eyed wantonly a bushy-tailed squirrel on the lawn—not as a harbinger of Washington spring but as fodder for his newly installed fly-tying bench. After that, all of us here at *Fly Fisherman* magazine knew that there would be no turning back for Jimmy Carter.

In August of last year, along with many other anglers, he journeyed to West Yellowstone's developing fly-fishing shrine to attend the FFF International Conclave. In addressing a few informal words to attending anglers, Mr. Carter ended by saying, with warm conviction, "I am one of you." Well, that was very nice and appreciated by all, sir, but hardly necessary. As they say, it takes one to know one, and we sniffed you out long ago. Welcome to the fraternity.

Casting for Q in a Non-Q World
(1981)

AFTER SPENDING A DOZEN YEARS in this blue-chip company of anglers which gathers among the pages of *Fly Fisherman* in increasing numbers each issue, I still find myself asking the question—"just *why* are we here?"

Is fly-fishing an *escape* from the assorted drudgeries of our own little worlds—"a far, far better thing than we have done before"? Partly, I suppose, but most of the fly fishermen we have met over the past twenty years seem to lead personal and professional lives of more than the average satisfaction and fulfillment.

Or is it an opportunity to express our *individualism?* Fishing with the fly certainly offers this opportunity—show me two fly anglers who seem to agree on just how a certain aspect of fly-fishing should be accomplished and I will show you two co-authors of a book to be published the next spring.

I have read learned papers by psychologists and serious essays by qualified writers which suggest various *dark inner drives* and *reverse-macho hungers* as the source of this inherently unnatural act in which we participate with alarming regularity on the banks of streams and shores of lakes. Until reading these I had always thought that fly-fishing was just good, clean fun, and certainly not the cause of acne, but after absorbing such revealed wisdom I suppose that my only solace lies in the often-observed fact that I'm really not very good at it.

And then there is *snobbism*—that "eliter than thou" accusation we have all faced at one time or another with a certain discomfort. I say the hell with it! Accept the name and play the game, because I suspect that the ascent of fly-fishing today has a direct tie with the general decline of quality in American life. Equally suspicious about this decline is historian and twice-Pulitzer Prize winner Barbara W. Tuchman, and I didn't even have to warn her, because she has already published an essay on "The Decline of Quality" as the lead article in the Nov. 2, 1980 issue of *The New York Times Magazine.*

QUALITY, AS SHE SEES IT, "means investment of the best skill and effort possible to produce the finest and most admirable result possible." Ms. Tuchman is not a self-confessed fly fisher, but with a philosophy such as this she could soon learn to be. (Those "admirable results" so readily available to her would give more positive purpose to her threat to "leave for Alaska or perhaps Patagonia" the week her article was published to "reduce the hail of censure which is certain to greet it.")

She builds her case by pointing out the presence or absence of quality which "in some degree characterizes every manmade object, service, skilled or unskilled labor—laying bricks, painting a picture, ironing shirts, practicing medicine, shoemaking, scholarship or writing a book. You do it well or you do it half-well."

However, Tuchman does not suggest everything done well produces quality—that "admirable result." As she expands her essay, she borrows from the British writer Nancy Mitford, who herself walked a tight wire when she offered her tongue-in-cheek (or possibly foot-in-mouth) delineation of the British class system with the gimmicky introduction of "U" and "Non-U" speech and taste distinctions. ("Gents" was "Non-U", or lower-class, while "toilet" was "U", or upper-class.)

Under the clear focus of the Tuchman lens, the "Q" of quality becomes the public parks of London, the artistry of Fred Astaire, the enameled masterpieces of Cellini, and "Non-Q" labels such mass-market productions as Disneyland, Johnny Carson and plastic champagne glasses. Of course, one could argue that a certain skill, technique and utility lies within the design of Disneyland, the sustained cleverness of Carson, or the convenience of disposable champagne containers, but it is the essence of the question that success or skill or total effort is not the final criterion; the quality of the goal is still the test. Jumping seventeen automobiles on a motorcycle does not pass such a test.

Historian Tuchman, equally at home in the fourteenth

century as in the twentieth, admits to the passing of the "princely patron" who had the power and the wealth to commission the great works of art and architecture, and to the fact that his place has been taken by the common consumer—the patron is now the public, often with government or corporation as its agent.

BUT PERHAPS IT'S TIME to ask ourselves once again just why we fish with the fly. We are not to be ashamed of this, nor to make any concerted defense. As we become more conscious of the decline of quality—of craftsmanship, of life-style, of individual purpose and pride of performance—we begin to understand just why it is that we gather by the river each year with our supposedly arcane and flimsy tools to perform our minor deceptions.

Whether we are "escaping" from or to something, whether or not we are refueling the tiny flame of individualism within us, regardless of what black evils we might be exorcising in the process—isn't it really the pursuit of Q in a Non-Q world?

The fact that many of us are not now nor ever will be "top experts" does not really matter, even though the stark fact may fret us a bit. When we hear that a "leading" fly fisherman states this or that, some of us are a bit surprised to learn that we are in a race. Happily, dear old Barbara tells us that "quality can be attained without genius," the quoted passage being hers but the sharp underline in blue crayon on my copy of her article being *mine*. Quality is inherent in certain things, in certain products, and certain pursuits, and despite its increasingly fragile posture in the marketplace, she feels that "quality cannot be put down altogether." The recognition, appreciation and the pursuit of quality defines itself, and does not require modification or qualification.

In fact, I feel that the decline of quality was first signaled to us when the very word "quality" was accepted by lexicographers as an adjective as well as a noun, announcing to all of us that quality can be qualified. Ironically, and perhaps a bit nervously, the editors of Webster's Third International Dictionary buffer their rather weak position by quoting an example of such usage: ". . . this *quality* revolution in . . . buying habits"—a quote ascribed by them to *The New York Times*. (Readers of Tuchman's essay will also notice that the *Times* compositors and copy desk made their own Non-Q contribution by allowing two typographical errors to creep into an otherwise Q piece of writing.)

BUT—THE CONCERN HERE is Anglish, not English, and we must proceed to congratulate each other on our inherent good judgment, and then to question ourselves as to how it could have been otherwise that we have all ended up here on the stream together, pursuing our "unnatural act" in such a natural and satisfying way.

First, we saw the lovely water, winding through a green valley, far from the sounds of city. We wanted to become a part of this, but without defacing it.

We learned to look beneath the mirrored surface and saw more than ourselves, saw how brightness can live in a dark world, darting, silver and alive, and we wanted to touch it.

Then we found the way, older than the pages of books, to participate, techniques of sly chicanery and artful dodgery laid on us by older hands over the centuries and little-changed in the transition.

Neither casual voyeurs or militant interlopers in the wilderness world—acts we can understand or at least accept—we found we were privileged to take and return, or given the option of keeping our catch, to participate in the life cycle to which we would all eventually make our own direct and final contribution.

We soon found ourselves cast into a pool of excellence. Here and there at respectful distances were anglers who could read the water as we read a book, and then write magic in the air with graceful lines. The act of the search and the reach often became ends in themselves.

We met other fly fishers whose magic began at the tying bench, artists and naturalists who saw the underwater life as the fish see it and could bring to these lovely constructions a fleeting life of their own.

And our tools. We began to see how fortunate we are to have found hands, often turned from more lucrative and worldly efforts, which could spend the hours, days and weeks required to form the delicate instrument of subtle strengths which turns our early clumsiness into acts of grace.

Then there were the stream people, that company of anglers that helped turn us from the improbable-in-pursuit-of-the-impossible into the capable-in-pursuit-of-the achievable— the talkers, the teachers, the writers, and the tiers who helped lead us into the mainstream of fly-fishing.

Many of the names are legion, others only legend to those who have walked with them along the stream or talked with them in *aprés*-angling seminars at nearby watering places. Some are voices heard through books, and still others across the stream of time.

JUST RECENTLY we had word from England about such a voice. Robert Ince, a Hertfordshire angler, reported that a group of British fly fishers had met in pleasant ceremony to honor the memory of G.E.M. Skues, the London lawyer who flouted the laws of the British trout stream by suggesting, after years of study and experience, that the wet fly was a worthy supplement to the dry fly then in vogue, and later, that equal pleasure and challenge lay in fishing a nymph imitation under the surface— then, to British eyes, the province of enemy U-boats.

Skues lived into his nineties, and left us in 1949 with a liberating angling legacy so broad in its influence that its ripples are still felt on our shores and on our banks nearly a century after he began to fish. What a happy gathering of anglers it must have been on Skues's old stretch of Hampshire's River Itchen last August when the small group of fly fishers joined T. Donald Overfield, Roy Darlington and family member Keith Skues to dedicate the simple and utilitarian memorial to this grand old man—a stone seat along the banks of the Abbot's Barton fishery, with the words "In memory of G.E.M. Skues . . . who fished these waters from 1883-1938 . . . a man who had a way with a trout." We know that the American anglers who contributed to this memorial after the request passed on through these pages in 1979 will be pleased to know of the eventual "admirable result."

· · ·

BUT WORKS OF QUALITY need not stretch over decades. This was brought to our mind so starkly here at *Fly Fisherman* a few weeks ago when, while laying out the photographs by Jonathan Wright for an article on Yellowstone in our next issue, we heard the news of his sudden and tragic death in an avalanche while filming a mountain-climbing expedition in Tibet on assignment of ABC-TV's "American Sportsman" program. Jonathan's work had carried him throughout the world as well as onto the covers and pages of some of our most prestigious magazines. He was technically competent, of course, but it was an outdoor world as seen through his eyes and lens that enabled him, in his late twenties, to pass on a rich body of photographic art and an adventurer's view of what he saw.

Jonathan Wright was an avid angler and outdoorsman, as well he should have been, for he fished early on under two tough mentors, Ernest Schwiebert and his father, Philip Wright, my close personal friend and, with Andre Puyans, one of the key culprits in the conception of this magazine. I and his many other angling friends find it hard to express our sadness to Joan and Phil Wright and their family, but we know that Jonathan lived and worked as he died—at the heights.

WE TOO OFTEN RECOGNIZE quality after it is beyond our reach, or only when it becomes conspicuous by its absence. Such is not the case, however, in another passing made known to us only a few minutes ago. Field Editor Art Lee called to tell us that Elsie Darbee died yesterday, November 24th, 1981.

Elsie, one of the ultimate fly tiers of our time, was the Queen of the Catskills in the minds of countless fly fishers, as her husband Harry is the Dean. Legend has it that, at one time, she was "apprentice" to Harry, but he is always quick to say that she had outdistanced him many years ago—and there are many who believe everything that Harry Darbee says. In this case it is easy, for Elsie literally drew flies with her fingers—as well as streams of anglers who felt that the true confluence of the Willowemoc and the Beaverkill lay at the Darbee cottage, not down the road a mile or so. The old Darbee place at Livingston Manor saw her serve as tier, correspondent, hostess, cook and housemother to thousands of smelly but admiring anglers over a span of nearly half a century. Despite these many assignments, Elsie Darbee showed no decline in the quality of her flies—or her life. Harry's loss is irreplaceable, I know, but Elsie's many friends, and Harry's, will never let him be alone.

ARNOLD GINGRICH ONCE WROTE that in fly fishing "you will meet, if not a better class of people, a better class of fish." You and I, as did Gingrich when he removed his tongue from his cheek, see such quality at both ends of the rod-and-line. Let us continue to see it and honor it.

· V ·

Dates with an Angle

Times of Our Lives

IF THEIR MINDS WERE CLEAR AND MEMORIES SOUND, MOST
fly fishermen would never fish again. But there is always
that distant bend in the river, rich with promise, or that day
ahead, pregnant with possibility, that looms sufficiently
large to cloud their minds and send them stumbling off
into the clawing alder stands in search of the grail.

Days, dates and times claim a heavy toll on the lives of
anglers—opening days, first forays, the annual rites of the
great hatches, remembered triumphs astream—all of
which they manage to paint on a canvas with a selective
retention far beyond the skills of a Rembrandt or a Wins-
low Homer.

The true angling journalist suffers from total recall, and
dutifully records the angling life as it is lived, while the
creative journalist, unburdened by the yoke of fact, builds
myth with every cast, legend from every rise of a bare-
fanged brownie.

Yet, there are also those recorders of angling deeds
doomed to fish the never-never waters somewhere between
Scylla and Charybdis—two little-known trout towns south
of Phoenicia in the Catskills—forever casting between the
rocks and the hard places, never really certain of what he
has seen through the morning mists.

We will have none of that in this book!

Diary of an April Fool
(1983)

January 1, 1983 It's almost noontime and I'm beginning to feel better now. Wonder if someone has ever come up with a cure for the Bloody Mary? Or is it the disease of which it purports to be the cure? Paused briefly to confront the littered pantheon of years left behind; rejected them, as they did me. Everyone seems to be gaining on me.

5 P.M. Things *much* better now. Found eggnog takes sting from Bloodies. Have negotiated Sugar Bowl, Cotton Bowl and am making headway on Wassail Bowl. Rose Bowl beginning; wife thinks it's Super Bowl gone into overtime; how to explain about tomorrow? And tomorrow, and tomorrow?

Wonder if there is a Fish Bowl? If there is, I suspect I will play in it this year. *Farmer's Almanac* predicts unseasonably warm and dry winter for New England and early spring. May get jump on fishing season by going to Ozarks for opener March 1, my last publishable birthday. Then perhaps to the Smokies for some mountain brook trout. Back to Vermont for some early-season triumphs on the Battenkill before getting into the serious angling. Possibly the Henrys Fork to tone up the old reflexes before hitting Spring Creek. Must take brisk walks and do push-ups. More convinced than ever that my body is a temple giving eternal sanctuary to a great angling talent. I shall unleash it this year. But not today; today is a feast day. Where did she put the nutmeg?

January 15 I live at Ground Zero of the Great Snowstorm of '83. "Make Snow," the signs said, "Not Love." Vermont ski-lift operators prayed to a beneficent God and were answered by an angry Jehovah. Threw away my copy of *Farmer's Almanac*. Was 1972 edition. Two feet of snow in sheltered areas; drifts to tree-tops. The Mettawee, local stream that runs along our village road, has disappeared as has village road and much of village.

Was able to make it to our local store just as one gross DarDevl lures in blisterpacks arrived on shelves. Will take business elsewhere.

January 30 Cold and torrential rains are slowly dissolving Vermont. I now strongly suspect that I will never fish again. Wife has just seen check stubs from our Florida trip last February and she agrees with me. "Two thousand dollars to catch *one* cowfish? That's more than we paid for our first automobile!" I explain that fishing is my life; she tells me my life is over. I agree with her.

Daughter phones from Santa Barbara where she is college student. Only school in California where phone bill is higher than tuition. Gave her a SPRINT card for Christmas. She explains Santa Barbara is being washed away by rain and tides and she needs money. Went to bank to deposit life's savings in her account. She must be buying a boat.

My tax man just phoned. Says IRS will not allow my 1982 Florida and Michigan fishing trips as unreimbursed business expenses. Asked him if he had shown them copies of the columns I had written about these trips. Says yes, that's why they disallowed them.

February 1 Desolation and disaster is all around me. But that's not all, says Irving R. Levine. Every night on the evening news he warns of terminal bankruptcy. The world is going to hell in a handbasket bought on easy credit. Wife suggests we take our daughter out of school and get her a job with the telephone company, but I don't even know where the damn telephone company *is* any more. Only way to solve today's economic problems—shoot Irving R. Levine.

February 2 Our National Groundhog in Punxsutawney, Pennsylvania, apparently did not see his shadow today, except that cast by television lights, but I don't fish in Punxsutawney. Our local groundhog did see his shadow, or perhaps Irving R. Levine, because he just got his nose out and went back in to leave us with six more years of winter or whatever it is.

Met a crazy Hungarian named Pozsonyi at local rod and gun shop later that day who had recently rolled an old widow for a Garrison rod and was selling it at a usurious profit to buy a Baby Catskill Leonard. Asked him if he had seen *his* shadow. No, but had seen a hatch that morning on the Battenkill. His face took on the glazed look of one of Robert Traver's fevered types, ready to "zoom to the moon, gaily negotiating seven cedar swamps along the way." Was a time when I would have dragged my informant along behind me, but my only reaction was to fob the fellow off on that ultimate crazy Hungarian, Sylvester Nemes, who early on detected a certain urgency in the soft-hackled fly. He would like Pozsonyi. They're bright and inspired, but both a bit soft in the hackles.

February 8 Son of Great Snowstorm of '83. Snowing for two days without let-up. Sought solace in angling books. Can remember times when serendipitous encounter in dentist's office with a *Scientific American* article on spawning habits of the Arctic sheefish could send me into pre-season cardiac arrest. But this is over now. After a few pages, even Haig-Brown and Schwiebert, Lamb and Walden, Gingrich and Traver pall. Can see through it all now; a cunningly conceived publishing plot, now sustained primarily by Nick Lyons Books and others of that ilk, to cloud our minds to The Obvious Truth. They write or publish these books to make some sense of their desolate and wasted lives. Lyons greatest offender; he goes both ways. If I never fish again, I hope it will be with him.

February 10 Went to village library to donate my angling books. Librarian rejected offer; said her fiction shelves were already overstocked. Homeward through drifts to Bleak House. Light burning in living-room window turns out to be TV; we are now in sixth day and thirteenth hour of a television miniseries. Snow is now over two feet deep; and that's just on the TV screen.

February 21 First excursion beyond village. Ice Age is upon us. Passed large pond defiled by ice fishermen. Looked like some Arctic Hooverville. Little old men running in and out of their shanties. God knows what they do in there!

February 27 Decision never to fish again a sound one. Last vestige of hope for coming angling season dimming rapidly.

Found a pristine stream last fall hidden deep in the nearby Green Mountain National Forest. Made map and grand plans for this year. Now Secretary of the Ulterior Watt announces his own grand plans to open Green Mountain National Forest to oil exploration. How we miss Sitting Bull!

March 1 Prepared obituary. "Vermont Angling Editor and Writer, of Excesses . . ." Then faced fact of fifty-ninth birthday. How to celebrate the imminence of Social Security eligibility? Made note to be nicer to my children.

Went to post office. Bills and junk mail, plus several invitations. Last invitation received on birthday was in 1943 from F.D.R. First invitation today was to membership in American Association of Retired Persons. Nice of them but don't think I could pass physical. Other from old friend Rex Forester inviting me to spend a few weeks fishing with him during big April rainbow run. Would meet me at airport; all further expenses on him! Rex is head of fisheries for New Zealand. Unless daughter quits school his airport inaccessible.

March 10 Visited my upstairs playroom. Half-finished March Brown still in vise; begun during half-time of Rose Bowl telecast. Odd stirrings within caused me to finish it off. Rather scruffy looking, but just right for person not planning to fish again. Dusted off fly rods and varnished wraps. Getting them in shape to sell. Most of them, anyway.

March 15 Plans never to fish again re-confirmed today after hearing terrible rumor. Although New York State environmental officials are covering it up, a usually reliable source phoned to report that a munitions truck turned over at the DeBruce Fish Hatchery near Roscoe in the Catskills, dumping several tons of saltpeter into the trout chow!

March 16 To express anger over saltpeter spill refused two collect phone calls from daughter. With money saved bought lustrous Andalusian blue-dun cape from indigent type in local rod and gun shop. Don't know what I'll do with it now that I've quit fishing. Felt it was some kind of a statement.

March 31 Wonder of wonders! Woke this morning to hear drip, drip, drip from the eaves of house. Magic moment for Vermonters. Signifies beginning of mud season. Two golfers phoned by noontime. Word of defection from fishing getting around. Put them on hold.

April 1 Early phone call from Usually Reliable Source. Gist of message: "April Fool!" Saltpeter spill a scam. Catskill trout will have another roll in the redds.

Daughter phoned from college. Accepted call to express anger at Usually Reliable Source. Turns out daughter threatening to graduate this year. Cause for a double celebration: tomorrow is First Saturday in April, opening of trout season; first time in over twenty years have been released from this insane bondage.

5 P.M. Bit jumpy for some reason. Prescribed medicinal Martini. Off-taste in first one. Checked medicine dropper from vermouth bottle; dipped in Beefeater to sterilize. Second Martini still odd-tasting. By the third Martini all became clear to me. Acid rain in the ice cubes! Judas Priest, is nothing sacred?

11 P.M. Distilled water in ice-cube tray finally frozen. Still feeling a bit edgy. Took some Alka-Seltzer, then chased it with double Scotch. Eventually drifted off.

April 2 Awoke at dawn after fitful sleep. Had weird dream about acid rain. What if every fly fisherman in Northeast went to drugstore and bought case of Alka-Seltzer, then went to nearest trout stream and . . . but then I woke up.

6 A.M. Had coffee. Decided on a dramatic move. Would go down to Battenkill and savor experience of not fishing. Sight of all the resident weirdos up to their whizzle-strings in mud and ice would be catharsis to flush me of any residual guilt.

7 A.M. Arrived at Iron Bridge Pool. No anglers in sight. Went downstream toward Shushan. Parked, then slid down to stream. No anglers yet. Odd. Had brought along a rod to avoid looking conspicuous; for further realism had even tied on March Brown I finally finished.

8 A.M. Hint of a hatch. Haven't seen any anglers yet, but thought I did see a swirling rise on far side of stream. What the hell! As long as I'm here.

9 A.M. Fish & Game warden and I arrived at tackle shop to buy license, read fish and game laws to confirm Vermont opening day *Second* Saturday in April.

9:30 A.M. Rushed home after public humiliation. Message that my tax accountant had phoned; returned call. Questioned my inclusion of license fee as unreimbursed business expense. Explained IRS would accept deduction of fishing license fee "only if I received no pleasure from it." Told him to run it.

10 A.M. In disgust, went to upstairs playroom and tied up a few Quill Gordons to amortize my investment in blue dun cape. This would definitely be my last angling season. There's no fool like an April Fool.

On High Resolve in Low Pursuits

(1972)

THE MONTH OF JANUARY has little to recommend it, we suppose, especially to the winterbound angler. We have always assumed that the good Lord put it in the calendar—through the good offices of His man in the Vatican at that time, Pope Gregory—primarily to build character and to make us appreciate the other months of the year. That's about all there is to do in January, other than pay for excesses of the flesh and of the purse.

Unless, of course, you are the type that goes around making New Year's resolutions. The last one we made was not to make any more, and it is the only one on which we have ever followed through. But now we're going to break *that* one.

It has been a stimulating but uneven year for us on the stream, and after an agonizing reappraisal of our plenteous acts of commission and omission we shall, right here on this page, perform a few acts of contrition. We shall publicly debase and humiliate ourselves before the Ghost of Gordon and all in-force subscribers by confessing to onerous deeds astream, and shall further resolve never to repeat them—at least in front of anyone.

We must preface this exposé, however, with a plea for clemency. We lately find ourselves in the position of the house-painter in an early New Yorker cartoon by Charles Addams—having painted himself into a doorless corner, he plans suicide by hanging himself from a nearby light fixture. A depressing situation, we admit, even for January consumption, but not unlike the fishless moat we have dug for ourselves by publishing a magazine on fly-fishing. Initially we had planned to fish one month and put out the magazine the other month. We always get a good chuckle out of *that* one. We've had too many fishless months. Like that well-advertised "non-profit institution," we didn't plan it, it just turned out that way.

So, every fishing trip we manage to snatch from the jaws of omnipresent deadlines finds us approaching the stream bed like a bridegroom on his wedding night—eager in our anticipation but with great capacity for error. Allow us our few scattered and fleeting trips to waters near and far. Think, if you can, of the violence we might otherwise do to the manuscripts of anglers free to roam the mountains and valleys and return to tell tales of wisdom and derring do. We feel there is a need for the publication of a magazine on fly fishing and, like garbage collection, *someone* must do it.

Perhaps you will join us in high resolve as we, like the two-faced god Janus, look backward and forward across the adjacent 24 months.

1. We resolve to use longer leaders—longer. Now, understand, there's nothing wrong with 9-foot leaders—that another three to six feet won't cure. The only difference between a 9- and a 12-foot leader is the fact that the two-fathomer is more likely to have a fish on the end of it—which is why, brethren, we are gathered here by the river.

We often use a first-rate commercially made leader compounded of two tapered 5-foot segments. Certainly nothing bad about that. But, we also find ourselves changing flies like an Orvis field-tester and losing about two inches of tippet per switch. Programming that into our computer tells us that we are losing about 12 inches per hour—on a slow day—not only of leader length but also of tippet diameter. That 7X spider web we were using turns into a 1X hawser after a few hours, although we're still casting a #18 Light Cahill. Or, more accurately, leading it about on a leash.

Now, we probably won't stop changing our flies every few minutes—give us a few delinquencies to carry us through the next season—but we *will* change tippets and we *will* use 12- to 15-foot leaders wherever discretion is demanded. We need all the help we can get.

2. We resolve to shorten our casts— both in length and frequency. Unfortunately, we learned to cast when our eyesight was good. Nowadays we find ourselves overdriving our headlights, so to speak. Given the 20-1 odds that there is a catchable fish out there somewhere, we can usually summon enough strength to cast a fly line 75–80 feet. Now, this is pretty good cast, but we do occasionally find ourselves wishing that our leader and fly accompanied it. We wish we could say that we have never caught a freshwater fish at that distance (saltwater fly-casting is another matter), but unfortunately that would not be true. St. Peter himself was our gillie that day early in our career when we made one last, long cast to a sparkling riffle downstream—a measured 85 feet, before the witness of a neighbor and a young nephew. The fly was immediately taken by a hyperthyroid 15-inch rainbow, with Satan in his wake, and we were off to the races. Otherwise, I never recall taking a trout beyond 50 feet. Apparently trout just aren't impressed by the presentation of a trim backing knot.

The second part of this confession actually deserves an entire resolution unto itself. One of our last fishing trips of this season found us on Michigan's Upper Peninsula, fishing with a fairly well respected member of the community whose acumen and judgment, anytime before 5 or 6 P.M., had been considered to be sound by the finest legal minds in the state. "You cast," he muttered as I paused to let the froth settle, "like it was going out of style." If it had been after 5 or 6 P.M., he would have probably added that our style of casting was never *in*.

But it was true. Our eagerness to amortize our few hours on the stream found us intent on a search-and-destroy mission. Only a few useful casts can be made from any one position in or at the edge of a stream or pond without duplicating the effort—and giving aid and comfort to the unseen enemy. Trout are even dumber than fishermen, but they are eminently educable. Don't put your trout through college. Pick them off while they're still in kindergarten—with the first cast.

Next season we will ration our casts, or "hoard them," as the salty old judge phrased it in pronouncing our sentence. We've learned our lesson, and it cost us money, because he followed through with his threat to do an article for *Fly Fisherman* magazine on that very proposition. You'll find it as the lead article this issue, under one of his various aliases.

And you'll find us hoarding *our* casts next season.

3. We resolve to "fish out our fly." Early in the game we learned to fish out our cast—after catching, or losing, too many fish within spitting distance of our position in the stream. A bit later we began to realize that we were also, in our eagerness to keep the fly in the water (a sound basic tenet, since that's where the fish are), keeping the same fly on the leader for much longer than it took to prove its uselessness at that particular point in time and space.

But then, as we built up larger supplies from our own stock of flies, and fishing friends and fly tiers started sending us samples to test out, we found the pendulum swinging in the other direction. We were switching flies at the rate of a dozen an hour and not giving them a chance. Now let's face it, friends, there are only a few basic types of streamers, dry flies, wet flies and nymphs. If an obvious hatch is on, match it, natch, but next season we are going to be fishing out our fly as well as our cast.

Under general conditions, a change of flies every five or ten minutes is an angler's easiest crutch. Our problem, of course, couldn't stem from our reading of the water, or our presentation, or the style of our retrieve. Naturally, the wrong fly. True, if your #2 streamer sends your quarry racing to the next pool, or the trout are playing ping-pong with your drowning dry fly and rubbing their noses on your drifting nymph, it may be time to reach for the fly box and your leader clips.

But, assuming that the general type and size of fly fits the conditions existing at the time, there is usually more room for improvement at *our* end of the rod-and-line than at the fly's end. Even for such a polished angler as we.

4. We resolve to use fewer patterns of flies. Our current stock-box of fly patterns reads like the index to Schwiebert's *Matching the Hatch.* If it ever fell into the stream the fish-and-game people would have to hire fish psychiatrists instead of fish biologists— the fishies would all be schizoid.

NEXT SEASON, it's going to be different. About *six* patterns each of wets, dries, streamers and nymphs, but with a greater variation in sizes . . . at least *three* different sizes in each pattern. So, we'll hit the water with about a half dozen of each size, in each pattern, of each variety of feathery lure. The arithmetic of this is comparatively simple—our abacus tells us that this will amount to a stock of some 432 flies, streamers and nymphs, hardly "roughing it" under anyone's standards. Nor will this belt-tightening cause any heavy lay-offs in the fly-tying and fly-box industries. Professional fly tiers and supplier would much rather tie fewer patterns, anyway.

But, of course, when that rare *Flickus exotica* hatch hits, we may be forced to run back to the steamer trunk in the luggage compartment of the car.

5. We resolve to use the double fisherman's knot. Most of the fish we hook we manage to land—mainly for release. We do a little bragging here only to point up the many other errors of our ways. Nor have we had many problems with breakage of tippets in the struggle—even allowing for the fact that we haven't done much to clutter up Dan Bailey's "Wall of Fame." But lately we have been pulling in more than our share of curled-up tippets.

Most anglers today use the fisherman's knot, not the turle knot, and those who have used both for many years favor the former. Next season our fishing is going to take a turn for the better, we think, because we are going to take an extra turn of our tippet-point at the completion of our knot—bringing the point back through the loop of monofilament a second time before tightening up. This simple maneuver decreases the chances of slippage by a least 50 percent and takes an extra five seconds. We will also be certain to push the knot tightly to the eyelet with our fingernails, then test it with a slow but firm pull.

Remember, your leader is the cheapest part of your equipment. When you change flies—subject to all of the other resolutions made above—don't try to reuse the last fraction of an inch of monofilament. Inspect it for wear—abrasions, flatness, knicks, etc.—cut off any questionable section, and then add on a fresh tippet if you're running short.

The double fisherman's knot will be our last resolution for 1972, so, in keeping with the spirit of the New Year, we leave with the thought that, when you tie one on . . . make certain it's a double!

The Ephemeral Guttulata
(1982)

I DON'T THINK it was Cole Porter, but some idle songsmith once dittied-up a sprightly air loosely titled "I Wish Again to Fish Again in Michigan." Truthfully, I never learned the tune, but more than once did I compose my own music, usually a tuneless dirge of four notes, on my frequent and, I must add, Homeric, long-weekend excursions from St. Louis to Michigan's Lower Peninsula.

Throughout the decade of the '60s, all of my sorties to Michigan were targeted toward one end—a headlong confrontation with that Great Hatch that clouds not only men's minds but the sun, the moon and the opposite bank. I had read of this annual event in the learned journals of our sport, especially the convenient footnotes giving the exact dates on which the misnamed "Michigan Caddis" hatch was to flower. It was the beginning of my Ephemerella Guttulata Period, during which time I pursued a most clarifying collateral study on the true meaning of the Latin root word, *ephemera*. *The Oxford Dictionary*, a repository of truth unknown to American angling editors and writers of the '60s, defines *ephemera* as "a thing of short-lived usefulness," and derived from the Greek word meaning "lasting only a day."

For ten years I bracketed The Day. On my first trip, fortified with solid footnoting, I arrived on June 22 for a three-day foray into the Pere Marquette and the Little Manistee. My conception of the exact shape, size and coloration of the Michigan Caddis fly was apparently a bit hazy, for I had tied up a half-dozen lumbering beasts that resembled, if anything, stillborn pterodactyls. I had great confidence in them.

Although I averaged seventy miles per hour on my trip from St. Louis, I slowed to a safer pace during the last few miles just east of Ludington, Michigan, for I had been forewarned of the danger during the evening "caddis" hatch—when the insects mistakenly landed on the highways in armada-like swarms, causing errant motorists to skid crazily into roadside ditches. I soon found that I had been overly cautious, since the alleged hatch of *Ephemerella guttulata*, as reported to me later, arrived on the evening of June 25, coincident with my arrival back home in St. Louis. I had some nice takes on a #14 Adams, but there was never a sign of those big, swarmy things that go bump in the night.

Such was the general history of my later Michigan safaris. The next time I was told that the hatch was already over, although a knowledgeable bar-mate later that evening whispered that it had actually moved up from the Pere Marquette to the Boardman and the Black, just beyond the point of no return for this hurried trip.

On my third venture, that year on June 17, I was informed that I was "rushing the season a bit." The fourth time I took an outdoor writer with me, because everyone knows that they always arrive at the propitious moment—"Bill Garrison, the local fish-and-game officer, met me at the airport in his pickup, and by that familiar glint in his eye I knew we were off to the races at old Lunker Pool." I used the poor fellow after the manner of a wide-ranging bird dog, sending him splashing off upstream and down on three rivers and one highway—in the gathering dusk he had mistaken it for a fourth river—flushing an occasional fish of worthy size but not one sporadic "caddis." But he certainly did work the water, because he knew that, if he found the hatch, he would get an article assignment and perhaps an advance to get his carburetor fixed and drive to Montana where the local fish-and-game officer would meet him with a glint in his eye. But such was not to be. Rather sad about poor Old Tom. He started chasing rabbits. Had to shoot him.

THEN, ON THE LAST NIGHT of that particular trip, I ran into a friend, Sylvester Nemes, the Mad Hungarian who was, even then, pushing his soft-hackled flies. I was later to compound his felonies by writing a foreword to his book, *The Soft-Hackled Fly*. Despite the catchy title, Syl's book (Chatham Press, 1975) reopened the century-old case for that arcane creation and soon acquired many adherents, some of whom can be found in large airports selling soft-hackled flies. In acknowledgement of this "hooked generation," Nemes has published another book, this time privately but very nicely, titled *The Soft-Hackled Fly Addict*, in which he delves back in time to England and the original patterns and purposes of this unusual and eminently practical device.

But meanwhile, back at the "hatch"—it was the end of my fifth day and last, and Nemes and wife tried to console me. Over a dry martini, sparsely hackled, I explained that I had to be back in St. Louis the next day by noon or my employer would have my stripes. Nemes was certain the hatch was a little late this year, but it was now June 30th, and I had decided that the entire Michigan Caddis hatch by any other name would stink the same and that it was probably a commercial promotion of the Michigan Chamber of Commerce and that they weren't going to get any more of *my* business.

However, my personal boycott did not immediately extend to the bar of the bright little cafe in which we huddled, and while waiting for a third martini in the foot-on-rail position, I absorbed the wisdom of the back-bar inscriptions. One especially, printed in an hitherto unrecorded *platt-deutsch*, caught my eye and was recorded indelibly on the left frontal lobe of my brain: "Ve get," it propounded, "too soon Oldt und too late Schmardt!"

I have frequently encountered deeper wisdom such as this after three martinis in bars on several continents, but for a decade it burned, gemlike but latent, in that wayward lobe. I did record, however, some five years ago within these columns, that some day I would make a reservation for a date early in the period of this purported "hatch," then cancel out and make a later one under an assumed name. I would arrive anonymously on the week that I "shoulda been there," and I would once and for all either document or debunk this lingering Old Fishwives' Tale.

THEN IT HAPPENED, and fate turned into fact. I had a letter in early June of this year from the Jones boys, Buck and Ken. They had reserved their old three-bedroom cabin on the Au Sable, Middle Branch, just above Stefan Bridge, for five days at the projected height of the Michigan Caddis hatch, and could I join them.

Ah, ha! I had the old *Ephemerella guttulata* by the thorax

now. I couldn't do much about the "too soon Oldt" bit, but it wasn't too late to "get Schmardt." But I had to be rude, if not cruel. I told them that I would gladly abandon my grand-children to the wolves to join them, but "personal business" during that particular week forced me to beg off. "Of course," I added slyly, "if you could cancel the reservation and get an-other for, say, the first week of July . . . now, that would work out very well."

A few phone calls later they confirmed that they were able to take advantage of a last-minute cancellation—this very fact should have put me on my guard—and that they had a new reservation, in their name, for the first week in July.

The gods are good to those who believe. I was now the anonymous third man on a reservation made by two people named Jones! And they were twins! I was doubly indemnified!

I ARRIVED IN GRAYLING at dusk, and by ancestral memory found my way to Stefan Bridge—where, I recalled, I had fur-ther succumbed to the "Caddis" myth years ago when Cal Gates, whose Gates Au Sable Lodge lay just *below* the bridge from our cabin, had led me down the primrose stream-bed one dark night, occasionally throwing large rocks near the bank to suggest to me that these were great lunkers taking in a very hatch of "Caddis." I became further concerned after checking in across the road to learn that Cal's faith had dissipated some-what, and that he had just left to fish for tarpon in Florida. There were signs of deepening tragedy everywhere, had I only been able to read them.

But the reunion with Buck and Ken at nearby Edgewater-on-the-Au Sable was everything I had anticipated. A few years my senior, they were the shining idols of my youth. They were the first Cub Scouts in America, selected not only for their twin-ship but for their many good works. They taught me to shoot a .22 rifle. They slept in a huge attic dormitory room at their house, and they owned a bugle. I went to their graduation exer-cises, grammar school and high school. I spent Thanksgiving at their table in 1941 shortly before they returned from their as-signed year's Selective Service training, and our families cele-brated the fact that they would be mustered out "in early December of 1941!"

Then they were off to the Aleutians and early action there, but they stayed together throughout the war. After the war, when I had finished college and recently married, Buck—I had earlier regaled my friends with the fact that I knew personally the great cowboy star, Buck Jones—Buck, now the automobile salesman, sold me my first car, a massive green Packard. Packard had made tanks during the war, and had obviously not totally converted to peacetime design. He sold us this so that we could safely and regularly negotiate the thousand ruts that accompanied the approach to Thousand Oaks, the country resort he and his wife had just opened.

His conscience got the best of him after that, and he persuaded Ken, then a creative director in a large St. Louis advertising agency, to give me a job so that I could keep up the payments on the Packard. I had done a few scripting assignments for Ken, and if he had not detected a certain urgency in my prose he did see the imminent press of car payments, so for fifteen months, at ten bucks a blast, I wrote a seven-minute daily network "comedy segment" (quote/unquote, as in "Michigan Caddis") on a low-budget Lum 'n' Abner-type hillbilly music show for Mother's Best Flour. As I remember, that came out to about 25¢ a yuk, but Ken doesn't remember it that way— although he admits to recalling it as being rather yukky. But I never missed a payment on the car.

This flood of memories engulfed me as I sat with them at the window of our charming old cabin and looked out onto the tinkling waters of the Au Sable—and I didn't feel so bad about lousing up their vacation schedule. That night, after washing down a steak dinner, direct from Ken's farm near Hastings, Michigan, I dozed off to the unheard sound of great flapping wings hurtling up and down the Middle Branch. Visions of "caddis flies" danced in my head.

But the *guttulata* turned out to be as *ephemerella* as ever. By day and by night we stumbled our way upriver and down. Special regulations now prevailed, and trout between twelve and sixteen inches were "protected." Apparently Middle Branch brownies, like we, were undergoing a midlife crisis.

The most obvious surface activity came in the form of the fiberglass frigates of the Michigan navy, manned by crazed canoeists as they careened broadside across the most promising pools. On our last day we even fell victim to their radar, when several of them pointed down and yelled that there were "dozens of 'em right under our canoe." We waited patiently until their maneuvers ended, cast everything that would sink or float to this mother lode of trout, then moved in for a closer look at our quarry. Suckers! Below the water and above.

AT BREAKFAST ON THE MORNING of our departure—or rather, strategic retreat—we stared out onto the river in despair. Earlier we *had* noticed two gentlemen, recently arrived at the Edgewater, making their way upstream, one with an empty but available creel.

As we packed up, we saw them returning after taking several fish. I wondered just what learned journal they had gotten their information from, so we stopped them as they waded to the bank. They agreed that the "Michigan Caddis" had not yet "materialized"—notice how they resort to the jargon of the spiritualist in deep seance when describing the "hatch"—but added that they had picked up a few keepers that morning.

Dr. Bob Pinney of St. Clair Shores, Michigan, urged his companion, Leo Romzick, from neighboring Grosse Pointe Park, to show us his creel. As Leo turned around and displayed it proudly, I saw, emblazoned on the side of the creel, the words "FLY FISHERMAN MAGAZINE."

I quietly backed off, allowing Buck and Ken to carry the brunt of the conversation, and left, as I arrived, anonymously.

The Night of the Heavenly Hatch
(1978)

WE'VE JUST BUNDLED UP Associate Editor Craig Woods for a jaunt into the wilds of Michigan—that lower part still open to the Free World fly-rodder and not policed by Robert Traver and his troop of hardy Finns, loitering Laplanders and other low Upper Peninsula types. Woods will be working the Pere Marquette, Little Manistee, and finally the Au Sable, and we pinned a note to his vest announcing that "This man suffers from *dementia peacocks*—if found glazed of eye and comatose of body, please return to Fly Fisherman magazine, Dorset, Vermont."

For Woods, a young gentleman of sophistication and intellect who long ago rejected the existence of Santa Claus, the Easter Bunny and the Tooth Fairy, openly accepts the reality of the Michigan Caddis Hatch.

As an editor of several years' experience, he should not believe everything he reads, but man has always reached out for that which he cannot touch, ever willing to believe in the supernatural, the occult—and in the case of angling man, the Michigan Caddis Hatch.

MICHIGAN IS A LAND OF LIES. Hemingway's "Big Two-Hearted River," one of his finest stories and probably the most haunting angling tale ever told, has sent thousands of pilgrims to that Upper Michigan stream (at least before Traver's partisans mined the Mackinac Bridge) to cast in Papa's wake, never to realize that The Master included in that tale his one untrue sentence—for it was not the Two-Hearted River that he fished, but the Fox River, much lower on the Peninsula. Literary critics have tossed this off as poetic license, but we know that it is just plain old piscatorial guile. Hemingway had a good thing going and wasn't about to give it away. It was a good place and he knew that it was good and he wasn't going to let anyone else know that it was good.

The Michigan Caddis Hatch is another lie. I know, for I have gone to the well not once but six times. But it was not until the last time that I gleaned the whole truth. It came as a culture shock to me, as it will perhaps to our readers, to learn that the vaunted Michigan Caddis Hatch is not only not a hatch, but that it is also not a "caddis" hatch. It is actually a promotion of the Lower Michigan Chamber of Commerce. They had noticed a distinct drop-off in wurst-and-beer sales between the times of the Tulip Festival in Holland, Michigan, and the Grayling canoe races, and decided they had to whomp up something to wake up the lazy economy.

There had been rumors in the backwaters that angler Cal Gates, proprietor of the Au Sable Gates Lodge, had experienced a vision one night, a revelation in which he saw huge mayflies attacking him on the banks of the Au Sable. This was picked up by a Chamber p.r. man, then given a Latin name by a defrocked priest who had earlier been discovered attending more worldly vespers on the Little Manistee. To give the un-hatch credibility, the ex-cleric named it the *"Hexagenia limbata,"* which, roughly translated, means "going out on a limb to put a curse on your entire family."

The Chamber's p.r. man didn't know whether "mayfly" was one or two words, so he used "caddis" instead when he sent out the first news release. The rest is history, sordid as it may be.

The Chamber of Commerce even forced the JayCees—under threat of reduced portions of creamed chicken at their weekly luncheons—to run around each night in mid-June glueing drugged moths to the screens and neon signs of local juke joints to perpetuate the folk myth of the Michigan Caddis Hatch.

THE CURSE LAY HEAVILY upon my family, for each June I would sneak surreptitiously from my office in St. Louis on Friday noon and perform ten-hour feats of automotive derring-do that would have numbed A. J. Foyt. Arriving promptly on June 12th the first year ("going to be an early one this year," I was informed—"the lichens turned purple over Memorial Day"),

I found that the "caddis" had not yet revealed themselves. "Turned cold last night."

For five years I bracketed the hatch. Each year I returned to Grayling, or Ludington, or Muskegon, like a swallow to Capistrano, only to learn that the hatch had occurred a week before, or would not be developing until the 27th. One year I made a reservation for the 20th, but arrived on the 13th; however, my cunning undid me, because all lodges and motels were filled with True Believers, and by the time I found lodgings near Detroit I fell into a coma in my room and slept through the hatch.

On the last year of my pilgrimages, I decided to fish at the fountainhead. I went directly to Grayling, to the Au Sable Gates Lodge, to a High Priest of the "caddis" cult, Cal Gates himself. I even brought along a witness in the form of outdoor writer and Montana angling guide Tom Wendelburg. Cal would be busy during the day, we were informed, but he would consider it a high pleasure to take us out on the river that evening. The hatch, he told us, was on!

We got a late start, and by the time we reached The Pool it was pitch black. The Au Sable, especially as it runs by the Lodge, is the most humanely designed river for night fishing south of the River Styx. Firm bottomed, clear of dead heads and sudden drop-offs, one glides along with the gentle current, casting free of impediment into the inky black.

Cal had handed out great hulking flies to us, strange hyperthyroid creations purported to be of the *Hexagenia* persuasion. Cal kept hearing sounds that he identified as hatching *Hexagenia*, but to me they seemed more like bats. Occasionally we would hear loud thrashings in the distance that Cal ascribed to taking trout, but which I identified to my satisfaction as being the upstream presence of loner Tom Wendelburg, a most skillful angler whose wading techniques at 200 yards sound like a Mississippi sternwheeler hung up on a sand bar.

None of us caught a fish, but by midnight when we returned to the lodge for a late seminar I caught the magic fever of midsummer night fishing. No longer did I suffer from the knowledge that the Michigan Caddis Hatch is actually a local cottage industry, keeping thousands of good backwoods souls off the welfare lists by allowing them to furnish sustenance of various kinds to The Believers.

Wendelburg returned a week later, reportedly hit the hatch on the head, and did an article on it, but I knew that Tom needed a new carburetor to get back to Montana and would do anything to achieve that end. It's called editorial license.

AND ONE MONTH LATER, I came back. Back to fly-fish-by-night the friendly Au Sable near Grayling. I caught some fish, mainly on a plain old #18 Adams, and I wrapped myself in the dark August night and cruised the river like a canny old beaver. On my second night, however, I hit the Heavenly Hatch!

This is no concoction of the Lower Michigan Chamber of Commerce. I call for no editorial license. It was after midnight, and I knew I had a long upriver stretch to negotiate if I wanted to amortize my investment in a bed at Cal's Lodge. I lay back exhausted on a grassy bank at a wide stretch of the river, almost comatose, when suddenly I began to see great white streaks in the air above me. Three in less than a minute. A short wait, then another. Then another. Eerie.

Now, it is the curse of the gut-hooked fly angler, and part of the charm of his pursuit, that he quickly loses all sense of earthly involvement when he stalks the stream. Even I, of a scientific bent and an amateur of natural philosophy, had completely overlooked August's "Heavenly Hatch"—the Perseid meteor shower.

Spinners may not fall, but in mid-August, "stars" do. Like clockwork. Each year on about August 11th or 12th, the Earth in its orbit encounters a great clump of celestial flotsam, small pieces of stone and metal the average size of which approximates that of a #28 Midge.

As these particles strike the Earth's atmosphere, the friction of the encounter causes them to glow into incandescence, and, celestial *ephemera* that they are, they enjoy a brief but blazing life, lighting the sky for a fraction of a second in most cases, but in some instances cutting the starry heavens in half for many seconds and leaving a ghostly trail.

Most of the "shooting stars"—probably another promotion of the Chamber of Commerce, because they are members in good standing of our own solar system—seem to radiate from the constellation of Perseus, which rises in the northeastern skies shortly after midnight—and thus the name of this meteor shower. A few meteors may be seen in the evening hours, but after midnight (1 A.M. local daylight-saving time) they begin to reach a peak of nearly one per minute. At this time the dark side of the earth is moving directly into the swarm and collecting more meteors—just as we would collect more mayflies on the front grill of our car than on the back bumper when driving along a river during any hatch other than the Michigan Caddis Hatch.

The Perseid meteors are one of God's great gifts to nocturnal man, and we commend it to you. Dress warmly, sprawl comfortably on a lawn chair, and mark your calendar for the nights of Aug. 11-12 or 12-13. Assuming clear skies, the Perseid shower can be seen anywhere in the Northern Hemisphere. You may not catch a trout, but we can guarantee that you will catch a falling star.

And despite what Swisher, Richards, Schwiebert, Cal Gates or the Lower Michigan Chamber of Commerce might tell you, there's nothing to match this Heavenly Hatch!

April Is the Cruelest Month
(1973)

AFTER OUR MOVE TO VERMONT earlier this year we soon learned that the hard-hewn character of the state's inhabitants had been chiseled by more than its marble quarries, long winters, short funds and a steady diet of maple syrup. The ultimate test of character in a state of free-flowing rivers, fertile ponds and a preponderance of anglers is the long, agonizing wait for the opening day of the trout season.

The Fish & Game Department officials who set the seasons must fish the streams along Vermont's Canadian border, for both the fish and the fishermen are usually ready long before the season opens in the southern Green Mountain section of the state. The states to our south and our west, Massachusetts and New York, open their seasons a month earlier, and for anglers residing in the piscatorial cornucopia of Vermont, this is especially frustrating.

As we suggested, this is part of the Vermont character, but we cannot claim such hardiness at this early period of our citizenship. In the Ozark mountains of Missouri the trout season opened on our birthday, March 1st. We had always looked on this as an opportunity to take advantage of the ancient edict that Allah—or God, depending upon your affiliation—"does not deduct from the hours spent in fishing." Based on this, we were at once able to amass streamtime and knock off birthdays with calendar-like regularity.

SO, IF YOU CAN, HAVE SOME COMPASSION FOR US, worn and haggard after moving a family of six and a business some 1200 miles across the continent and arriving on the balmy, false-spring evening of February 28th. A quick check of the house and surrounding country acreage gave us our first hint of the exacting test of our moral fiber that was to confront us daily for the next two months. Even over the impatient groans and whines of a family without food, furniture or faith that either would arrive soon, we heard the rushing gurgle of the lovely trout stream that borders the north line of our modest acreage and that was quickly to become the conditioning Pavlovian reflex of our existence. Trout streams are nice places to visit, but one wouldn't want to live there—at least not out of season.

The following day signaled the beginning of our trials. We had scarcely had time to set our watch ahead to Eastern Standard Time, let alone adjust our personal calendar, and to us it was Opening Day.

It was the first day of March, a date that conjured up old memories of well-greased lines, vintage waders and the comforting smell of our kidney warmers. But against this haunting nostalgia our stream played a dissonant and agonizing counterpoint as we walked along it that first morning. Each day it became worse. If the month of March was bad, April, as another displaced St. Louisan once wrote, was "the cruelest month." Except for an occasional brief "sugar snow," the days of April were warm and friendly, but made even more cruel for us by the fact that the vagrant water we were watching would, within a few hours, enter New York, where its fish would be mauled by the worm-fishermen reputed to inhabit that state.

We were Adam in the Garden of Eden, and temptation did weigh heavy upon us. We even reasoned with our sons that it would be perfectly all right for them to accompany us to the stream carrying cameras, while we posed in full regalia, with rod, line and barbless hook—"for quick removal of a fish in case one should attempt suicide while I was posing for the photographs," I explained. I had even prepared in advance a lucid explanation to be delivered to anyone who might encounter us thus and misinterpret our actions.

"Warden," I would explain, "we realize this looks suspicious, but you must understand that we publish a magazine on fly-fishing and that we must, of necessity, work at least a month ahead. This tableau you observe before you is, of course, the cover for our next issue." But we finally rejected this ploy on the grounds that the warden might be a subscriber and not believe that we work even a month ahead.

Our shame became guilt, and fate sentenced us to a sixty-day term, without pardon or commutation or rod, in solitary confinement 150 yards from one of Vermont's better trout streams. The music of the gurgling waters had become a siren song, the stream a sinuous Lorelei beckoning our certain moral foundering. It was too much, too soon for a transplanted Midwestern angler for whom a day of good fishing required automotive acrobatics dwarfing the anguishing "Twelve Hours of Sebring" or the Monaco Grand Prix.

BUT WE SOON FOUND SOLACE AMONG NEW FRIENDS. We met them at the village post office and in the general store, and somehow, after the manner of dogs in heat, we managed to sniff each other out. Suddenly we would detect the lingering odor of rancid waders, or notice the silicone stains on their fingers. Perhaps they had spotted us that day of the first faint insect hatch in early April, as we stealthily sprayed emerging duns with a mild aphrodisiac.

Regardless, we found each other, and friends back home will be pleased to find that we have already organized a Vermont chapter of that loose-hung affiliation known as Anglers Anonymous, or AA. We have saved more than one angler from total oblivion by demonstrating how he can, without addiction to alcohol, manage to lose his job, his money, his friends and the affection of his family.

AS VERMONT'S OPENING DAY APPROACHED, we laid plans that brought a new and exotic dimension to the definition of "stream management." Vermont is an ecologically enlightened state; and in its laws there is no provision for private ownership of trout streams; we had to be especially creative. Our first measures were unimaginative and routine, but hopefully would be effective. Like moving the "Public Fishing Access" sign to an adjacent irrigation ditch and then posting a detailed map of the nearby Battenkill River in its place. But a move such as this would be diversionary at best. The dark thought of a descending army of wetback New York State worm-fishermen, reinforced by hardware merchants and thawed-out skiers, stirred us to new heights of ingenuity.

Why not, we asked ourselves after downing our nightly brace of martinis, merely mine the approaches to the main pools? Any state legislature that doesn't open its trout streams until the end of April can't be up-to-date enough to have provisions in its laws covering land mines. We could even have our little group send telegrams to the State House supporting such mining.

Or, what about dumping in several gallons of mercurochrome upstream each day and then spreading rumors about a "killing red tide"? Workable, and it would probably further enhance the appearance of the beautiful little pink-bellied native brookies that populate our stream.

IT WAS ONLY AFTER THE THIRD MARTINI that we began to see things clearly. Our thinking had been muddled, and the truth of our long-held premise that "fly-fishing brings out the best and the worst in man" was never more evident. How selfish and impatient we had been! We had connived to violate the fish and game laws, the state and federal laws, and the unwritten laws of mankind. What a low point of degradation we had reached! What low company we had fallen into!

But that is past. It is now nearly the eve of Opening Day, and we sit, like a guru who has found peace and truth in contemplation, on the hillside overlooking our lovely stream as it rolls its pool-stepped way down the mountainside to the highway and in a few hours reaches the New York boundary where Nature's nobleman, the worm-fisherman, is reputed to reside.

Our tranquillity is such that we may not even fish on Opening Day. It will be enough to watch the lucky worm fisherman who stumbles upon our isolated stretch of stream and plies his age-old trade along its banks. After a few dozen yards he will arrive at the shaded glen just below our favorite pool, and we will join him in spirit as he takes his ease for a moment on the crude little bench we have erected there.

The bench, placed for clear visibility at the edge of a soggy bank, bears the inscription "Fisherman's Rest . . . courtesy of the Vermont Chapter of Anglers Anonymous."

No, we probably won't fish that day at all, but will take our quiet pleasure vicariously. Besides, the forecast is for heavy rains. Our days lie ahead. This is a day for the worm fishermen.

George Washington Schlepped Here
(1976)

Earlier on we had firmly resolved to stake our claim on journalistic immortality by being the only magazine in the country *not* to do a special feature saluting the Bicentennial Year. However, the guilt of such un-American inactivity lay heavy upon us—and we finally succumbed.

After considerable research, however, we learned that little or nothing has been printed concerning angling at the time of the American Revolution—probably because all of our printers were busy publishing political broadsides. Arnold Gingrich, in his *Fishing in Print,* finds the same lack of angling information for that era of American angling history.

The only recorded mention of angling seems to come from General George Washington's diary. "Having lines," George relates, "we proceeded to the fishing banks, a little without the harbour and fished for Cod; but it not being a proper time of tide, we only caught two, with w'ch, about 1 o'clock, we returned to Town. Dined at Mr. Langdon's and drank Tea there, with a large circle of Ladies, and retired a little after seven o'clock." George slept a lot.

This report may be found to offer some "redeeming social value," but it's hardly guaranteed to stimulate a higher order of angler to grease up his lines. So rather than hang our researches on such a wispy tippet, we delved a bit further into the musty archives available to us—and serendipitously uncovered some heretofore unknown selections of angling arcana from a fishing publication of the Revolutionary War period. Readers will be amazed to learn that things haven't changed much since 1776.

. . .

From "Poor Swisher-Richards' Almanack" Ye Olde Streamwatcher's Logge

(Being a Survey of Angling with the Flye, circa 1776)

Of course, you've heard about the war; it's in all the broadsides. This has affected fishing opportunities a bit, but with a little effort, and a big assist from Ye Olde Streamwatcher, you should be able to find good fishing throughout the Colonies— or whatever they're calling them these days.

MASSACHUSETTS

BOSTON AREA Stream Reporter Samuel Adams is still pushing his new fly, but local anglers complain that they can't get it to sink. Sam tells us that fishing is slow in the Charles River, a situation made worse by the ever-growing disturbance caused by the shells of the Harvard crew. "The place was much better when it was still a seminary," comments Sam. "General Washington's press gangs should have taken them all when he took over the Continental troops in Cambridge last year."

Adams also touts the saltwater fly-angling opportunities in the Boston area, but suggests that you put in above the Boston Harbor at Nahant. "Fishing there has been off ever since that damned tea spill," he adds. "The stripers and bluefish are jumpy as hell, fly visibility is low, and you can't take them on anything but crumpets—and then only late in the afternoon."

Enemy naval traffic in the Harbor is also a hazard, Adams points out. To assist anglers in determining whether to fish the salt or the freshwater, Adams suggests that they check the belfry of the Old North Church in Boston each morning just before dawn. If one light is burning, fish the Harbor; two lights, fish inland.

LEXINGTON-CONCORD AREA Waters in "every Middlesex village and farm" are good to excellent, announces Stream Reporter Paul Revere, but he recommends night-fishing as the best approach. Paul's metalworking business has been slow lately, so at midnight he rides out along the Post Road to warn anglers of approaching British troops; the fellow really goes all out . . . let's hear it for old Paul!

Trout fishing on the Merrimac is good at this time in the lower reaches, Revere says, but warns that the upstream stretch is still under British control—so it's dry-fly-only all the way until further notice. Suggest you fish the Merrimac right up to the controlled stretch—but be sure to check the other anglers carefully for non-resident licenses.

Although the Concord is running heavy these days, Revere recommends the stretch just outside Concord village. "Fish it early to beat the Fourth of July crowds," Paul reminds us. He also recommends that anglers gain access to the Concord River at a point some 2.6 miles outside of Concord Village. "There's a rude bridge there that arches the flood," says Revere.

Paul says that it's necessary to fish deep in these heavy waters, but that considerable lead shot can be picked up along the banks there or on the Green at Lexington. He also favors felt waders in these heavy waters of the Concord, quoting as his authority someone named Paine—a local rodmaker?—who said recently that "these are times which try men's soles."

For overnight accommodations, Revere recommends the Old Tavern at Concord. "George Washington sleeps there all the time."

PENNSYLVANIA

PHILADELPHIA AREA Ever since the American patriots outlawed the Royal Coachman, the hot killer fly on the Schuylkill and other local streams has been, of course, the Betsy Ross streamer, but it's out of stock in most Philly shops these days because the lady tier who originated it is swamped with Government contracts. For those who would like to try this pattern, Stream Reporter Ben Franklin reminds them again of the tricky color combination—"red, white, and then blue."

If you should have trouble remembering this, Franklin suggests that you just think of the colors of the French flag. "A killing early-season pattern," advises Franklin. "Run this one up on your fishpole and see if anything salutes!"

VALLEY FORGE AND DELAWARE RIVER Reports Franklin: "The winter kill along the Delaware at Valley Forge was quite heavy this year; we lost many fish, too. Big news, though, is the new fly pattern developed at Valley Forge by a young aide on the staff of Baron von Steuben, the Prussian general assisting in training Continental troops here."

Franklin tells us that the young man caught some 100,000 kilos of trout with it during the long winter at Valley Forge—all the troops had to live on. "There were no ill effects from this singular diet," adds Franklin, "except that during the early spring shad run this year some of the younger soldiers displayed a tendency to swim upstream to spawn."

The young Prussian, Oberleutnant Ernst von Schwiebert by name, designed the fly to replace the outlawed Royal Coachman, Ben informed us.

He used peacock herl for the entire body and removed the red center-segment, replacing the white wings with a leaden-hued feather. Comments von Schwiebert: "Better lead than red! I call it der Leadving Coachman.'"

Franklin adds that he inquired as to the source of the wing material but that von Schwiebert cryptically replied that he had taken it from a feather he had found in the cap of a Colonial soldier riding into town on a pony!

"I asked him," Ben says, "if he couldn't have come up with a better idea than to name it after a lead-colored feather, but von Schwiebert just snorted: 'If you tink dot's bad, you should haff heard vot he called it! How vould you like to fish the Beaverkill Club vaters mit ein Macaroni Coachman?!'

Ben told us that von Schwiebert had enjoyed considerable success trolling the new Leadwing Coachman during wintertime float trips on the Delaware, especially at Trenton. "I vould haff done even better if General Washington vould not haff all der time shtood up in der boat!"

"He chust shtood dere holding his belly in und shouting 'Don't limit your kill . . . kill your limit!'

"Vot kind of crazy you got dere? You tink George the Third ist ein Schlumpfer? Chust vait till dis vun takes over. He's George der Last!"

When Franklin asked von Schwiebert what hatch the Leadwing Coachman was designed to imitate, the young Prussian shouted shrilly: "Vot match? Vot hatch? I haff not even invented 'matching der hatch' yet!"

For anglers planning to fish the Delaware at Valley Forge this season, Franklin recommends the Old Farmhouse Inn on Valley Road where the Continental Army officers made their headquarters. "Washington slept there," adds Franklin, "but not very well."

Franklin had to cut his report short because of an impending thunderstorm, during which he planned to discover "electricity," whatever that is. "Invest in it now," Ben hinted. "It's going to get expensive as hell."

Ben signed off with: "Early to bed and early to rise—is fine for the guys who don't tie their own flies."

MARYLAND

BALTIMORE-CATOCTIN MOUNTAIN AREA Third Lieutenant Olaf T. Krehbowski, a mercenary with the Polish platoon commanded by General Kosciuszko in the Baltimore area, reports a devastating fish kill on the productive Fishing Creek in the nearby Catoctin Mountains.

When asked for details, he told Almanack editors that "ve are using balls of gunpowder vich we are dying pink so are looking like salmon eggs. And are ve getting a rise out of dem!" We must, of course, allow for the language barrier in interpreting this disclosure. Krehbowski calls this lethal lure "The Olaf T's Deceiver."

THE WESTERN NEW HAMPSHIRE GRANTS

BATTENKILL-LAKE CHAMPLAIN REGION Colonel Ethan Allen of Bennington and his Green Mountain Boys (the mountains, not the boys), took off toward the end of the Hendrickson hatch on the Battenkill, he reports, and headed up to Lake Champlain for a week or so recently. "Fishing pressure was heavy, mainly because of the British troops we found billeted at Fort Ticonderoga," Allen reports, "but we managed to take a few hundred!"

MANHATTAN ISLAND

Our man in Manhattan, Nathaniel Lyons, reports that he's been too busy to get out of Manhattan so far this season, but adds that a quick check of local anglers indicates that the Hudson River is still choked with Atlantic salmon and other trash fish. Lyons predicts, however, that local residents will find ways to rid the Hudson and other rivers of this nuisance in the foreseeable future. (Reports have it that they are still prevalent in the Connecticut River and other major watersheds.)

Lyons also reports that Royalist forces are active in espionage and other intelligence activities in Manhattan and that rumors are that the British will soon try to occupy New York City. "They'll never find enough parking places," observes Lyons. He recently had lunch, he adds, with a local fishing writer who publishes under the pen name of "Shaggy Black Hackle," and Hackle disclosed that the Angler's Club had recently rented several of their Lower Manhattan rooms to a neighboring tavern-keeper named Fraunces.

"General Washington and his officers frequent the place," Hackle told Lyons. "The General is a first-rate fellow—for a cod fisherman—" he added, "but he keeps us up half the night with those damn farewells to his officers. I hate those long goodbyes."

Lyons says that there are no appropriate accommodations for anglers there—"Fraunces won't even let Washington sleep there because he snores," Lyons interjects—and adds, "in fact, there are no accommodations anywhere in New York because there's no reason to come here. It's a lousy enough place to visit; you certainly wouldn't want to live here!"

Reporter Lyons is not always dependable by mid-season. His report deteriorated toward the end, and the last desperate scribbling we could decipher seemed to tell something about "running up to Abercrombie and fish for grayling," but we couldn't locate the village of Abercrombie on our maps. Poor chap!

MAINE AND QUEBEC

Always dependable, however, have been our Stream Watcher reports from our roving Stream Reporter who sent those reports of big action at Brandywine Creek last season—well, he's now in Quebec after a long cross-country march through Maine and into Canada.

We questioned his reports of twenty-pound brook trout in Maine ponds which attack when hooked, but by the time he and his troops arrived in Quebec the man was raving about "the splendid salmon fishing," and even suggested that many of the locals actually eat these fish. He also tells us that the British troops are "exceeding friendly" and goes on to say that he and his aide, a Major Andre, have been doing some "angling of our own" with the British officers.

This is all difficult to believe—but after all, if you can't trust old Benedict Arnold, who can you trust?

Closing Remarks on
Opening Days
(1980)

BY NOW MOST OF US have undergone the discipline of Opening Day and are moving toward the relatively normal pursuit of the trout, the bass and those lovely little fish of the pan. Selective memory has already wiped out the indignities of weather, water and weakened flesh that usually accompany this recurring folk experience and color it a tattletale gray. May the rest of your season's days be balmy, your casts true and your waters gin-clear, with perhaps a touch of vermouth.

SEVERAL YEARS AGO in this column I dug into the archeologic past and recalled one of my first Opening Days—this particular one misspent at one of the Missouri "trout parks" near the headwaters of that storied Ozark float stream, the Current River. For some reason—possibly the fact that neither Mason nor Dixon wanted to negotiate a particular dismal stretch of swamp in what is known now as Missouri's "Bootheel" and allowed it to dangle loosely below their famous "Line"—Missourians feel that their state is southern, if not in sympathy, at least in climate. As a result, they have designated March 1 as the Opening Day of their trout season, and snow, sleet and icestorms have become integral factors in making Opening Day what it is—a minor, perhaps, but perennial apocalypse.

In this dark revelation I had spoken of standing in line at dawn in the concessionaire's store at Montauk State Park to purchase my trout tag, amid a frenzied crowd of desperate types bent on the purchase of bloody meat baits, assortments of pasteurized cheeses and various forms of kneaded dough—a situation that I likened to working the night shift in a pizza factory. I described the sudden low growl of the siren that signaled sunrise, rising to a piercing pitch matched only by the uncontrollable fervor of the inmates. I told how I had arrived at the riverbank to find the first wave already locked in combat, a thin gray line of humanity paralyzed by wind, sleet and sub-zero temperatures as March roared in like a lion. I even confessed to having foul-hooked a fat lady who had fallen into the stream while attempting to retrieve her jar of salmon eggs that had iced up and slipped into the swirling froth.

All this was again brought to my attention recently when a resident Missouri militant, writing under the name of "The Ill-Tempered Angler," sent me a hate letter from Montauk State Park on March 1st. "You reflected," I.T.A. began, "on your beginnings as a fly fisherman at Montauk, with references to hanging up your backcasts on the hatchery trucks, among other disparaging remarks. Such comments about a place that is the birthplace of the Woolly Worm, as well as the Velveeta Emerger, were not well received in many quarters here.

"Soon after that issue of *Fly Fisherman* hit the newsstands," he continued, "I made another trip to Montauk, and that evening after closing siren, small crowds gathered at the main campground muttering of violent acts. 'Zap Zahner' was the battle cry; the usually well-attended nature movies were cancelled. One fellow even suggested burning you in effigy, using back-issues of *Fly Fisherman* for the funeral pyre. Another asked for posters with a picture of you impaled on a fly-tying bodkin."

But then, after making an obscure literary reference to the work of an earlier Tom Wolfe, *You Can't Go Home Again,* Ill-tempered Angler seemed to mellow. "Now the tumult and shouting have subsided, and things have changed since your exodus to the East. We now have an automatic worm-dispenser in front of the main lodge. The headwaters of the Current River have been designated as 'trophy trout waters,' and the rabble with fly rods have returned to dunking their Woolly Worms while their families watch the nightly rabbit movies. Perhaps you can go home again, Mr. Zahner!"

To let Ill-Tempered Angler and the Fat Lady carve the mark of Zorro on my chest with a rusty bodkin? Certainly—right after I get delivery on my new Pinto and re-register for the military draft.

Such was the memory of one man's Opening Day.

· · ·

FOR YEARS I HAVE commiserated with myself over the vicissitudes of Opening Day—until I met a man who had no Opening Day.

Such was the case last month (March) one morning when I received a desperate letter from former subscriber H. A. Schubert, formerly of Montreal, but now being held hostage by his business firm in Saudi Arabia.

"I feel compelled to write to you about my personal predicament," he began. "Being a fly fisherman from head to toe, I am now deprived even of watching running water flow here in the Kingdom of Saudi Arabia, the only place in the world where there are no permanent rivers or water flows."

He went on to say that he had sought "psychological escape" by writing his fishing buddies in Montreal for solace and some back-issues of *Fly Fisherman*. They complied, although their solace took the form of an inhuman and vicious torture for which Mr. Schubert's already fevered mind was ripe.

"They told me that rains come to Saudi Arabia every twenty years, and that the eggs of small fish will hatch. They said that they had checked on this and found that I had arrived in the nineteenth year, and that this spring I will be able to fish here in the desert."

With the hot Saudi sun already beating down on him, Mr. Schubert made a last request. "Could you look into this and check a fishing calendar as to when this event is due?"

Well, the gentleman obviously needed an instant and massive dose of psychological salts. In a postscript to his letter he inquired as to the possibility of obtaining a subscription to *Fly Fisherman* while in Saudi Arabia.

Now, this was, if you recall, shortly after our gallant Canadian friends had managed the escape from Iran of several American Embassy officials, and his plaintive request called for unusual measures on our part. I personally recalled several years before when, during a partial embargo on U.S. magazines in Saudi Arabia, a highly placed member of the ruling family of that kingdom had made special arrangements for his subscription to *Fly Fisherman* to be intercepted at the docks and delivered to him personally. I decided that Mr. Schubert would be treated equally royally.

I phoned my daughter-in-law, a senior Pan American

flight attendant, who, through one of those inscrutable quirks of fate opportuning only to men of the highest purpose and nobility of cause, was leaving that afternoon on a flight to Daharan, Saudi Arabia! Yes, she had a copy of the "Spring Special" issue at home, as well as a plain brown mailing envelope, and yes, she would mail it to Mr. Schubert in nearby Riyadh, Saudi Arabia, upon arrival the next morning.

Some 48 hours after his letter arrived, a copy of the "Spring Special" was in our Canadian friend's hands. Hopefully, the sound wisdom and good counsel that pervades the pages of *Fly Fisherman* enabled Mr. Schubert to gain perspective on his situation and brought him back to normalcy—as we know it.

BUT A THIRD LETTER I received a few days later served to remind me that, in my heroics, I had failed Mr. Schubert in at least one of his requests.

The letter was from John Pierce, the managing editor of *Yankee* magazine, our neighbor across the border in New Hampshire. He was working on an article on stoneflies, of all things, and was looking for the source of some good transparencies of appropriate fly patterns.

However, even more to the point was the fact that they also publish the venerable and charming *Old Farmer's Almanac*, and were working on the 1981 edition—their 189th! Would we, Pierce asked, assist them in expanding the *Almanac's* section on "Best Fishing Days"?

I glanced at our copy of the 1980 edition, and found that this section contained a half-page of the soundest possible advice to expectant anglers, even including items of interest to the fly fisherman. I did suggest several possible contributors who might expand on this section to make it even more useful to their readers.

However, charity begins at home, and I began to think about this. Having spent well over a decade listening to the confessions of skunked fly-rodders, an equal amount of time publishing a journal for amateur astronomers, and several years as a weatherman with the Army Air Force, who could be more qualified than I to offer our own readers of *Fly Fisherman* the distilled wisdom of twenty-five years of water-, weather- and sky-watching?

Muttering under my breath, *"Yankee,* go home," I quickly turned my energies to the task of compiling the ultimate in angling prognostication—knowledge never before collected in one place . . . veritably the wisdom of Solomon, if he were an angler—which he was, of sorts.

Sol's Looney Tables

BEST TIMES TO GO FISHING:
- On the first full moon after pay-day if it falls on a three-day weekend.
- One week before or after the predicted peak of any big-name hatch.
- During a violent electrical storm; you will have the stream to yourself.
- On the cusp of a new moon when Mars is in the house of Aries and your wife is in the house of your mother-in-law.
- Thirty minutes after Nick Lyons has fished a particular stretch of water.
- During television rating week.
- Any time in 1980—there is an extra day because of Leap Year.

WORST TIMES TO GO FISHING:
- On Opening Day.
- For one month after you limited out.
- When the barometer is falling off the wall; too windy.
- During a line squall when the wind is blowing out of the northeast and your boat is blowing out of the water.
- During the week in which you made reservations for prize salmon water.
- When Ernie Schwiebert is going along with you.
- When there is a mackerel sky—unless you're fishing for mackerel.
- When the sun is in Aquarius, the moon is in conjunction with Venus and your wife is in opposition to the whole idea.

·VI·

Back Home

Wet Flies on Dry Creek

THERE COMES THAT UNCERTAIN AGE WHEN WE AGAIN RE-
turn in memory to our home waters—occasionally even to
our home before we were called to our non-sectarian min-
istry—to recollect, in that tranquillity legend has it that we
experience astream, the days of our beginnings, the time of
our novitiate in the piscatorial order of the angle.

We have all read, with varying degrees of gastric distress,
the memoirs of those Angling Greats who rolled gaily from
their cribs into the riffles of the Beaverkill, who were
weaned on Leonard rods and silken lines and diamond-
drawn gut, and who were throwing back sixteen-inch trout
from the Madison at an age at which most of us were still
throwing up from car sickness. Oh, those long, idyllic sum-
mers at uncle's salmon camp on the Whackapee where we
first blooded our salmon gaff. And remember how they
laughed when we fell into that dark pool after landing our
first three-pound grilse—hardly fair to a boy of four.

We stifle a wince. There are those of us to whom The
Truth came late in life, or in the back stacks of the public
library, or was revealed, in the case of a few, if not in the
gutter, in the Mississippi River, which is bigger and which
does not contain winos or little else.

And so, the memoirs of a self-made angler—obviously a
product of unskilled labor.

The Great Salmon-Egg Spill
(1977)

BACK IN MISSOURI it's Opening Day of the trout season, but I write this on the first day of March from behind the snowdrifts that obscure my view of wintertime Vermont, and the very thought of it gets me right here—or perhaps a bit lower.

Our former Vermont Governor gave us two weeks' leg-up a couple of years ago at the beginning and end of the Vermont season—with a name like Thomas Salmon what else could he do?—but a dampened line in mid-April doesn't wipe out your ancestral memories of those halcyon days of March 1. It's especially difficult when March 1 is also your birthday.

On my first Opening Day (piscatorial, not natal) I celebrated my birthday and then went fishing, but increasingly the dawn of middle age began to cast its light more directly on the angling and less on the forty-odd ripped-off calendar pages that still cluttered my subconscious. I soon concentrated on celebrating Opening Day and ignoring the birthdays.

Now—birthdays are easy to ignore or to forget totally, but opening days aren't, and I'm glad no one asked me about fishing. Each year, though, my Dad, who still subscribes to the St. Louis newspapers, invariably sends me clippings from the March 2nd papers reporting the glories, and some of the ignominies, of Opening Day in Missouri. Without suggesting that my stature as a card-carrying Missouri trout fisherman was a lofty one, I must admit that the reminiscences these clippings conjure are like a fall from a high place which causes me to relive each season-opener back on those Ozark streams.

SOMEHOW, THE GLORIES come harder in the recollection than the ignominies, which are etched on crystal and preserved in amber, and which the Museum of American Fly Fishing here in Manchester, Vermont, will probably wish to display in a back room after my death.

As anyone who has fished the Ozark streams can attest,

they are some of the most beautiful waters in the world. The warmer ones carry firm, deep-bellied smallmouth of a character mirroring the firm, deep-bellied Anglo-Saxon inhabitants of these still-isolated mountain valleys and ridges. The cold-water streams carry good heads of trout, most of them hatchery-bred but quick to adapt to the wily traits required of them.

However, no one seems to go to the storied waters of the Eleven Point, the Jack's Fork or the Current on Opening Day. Instead, all semi-ambulant anglers, and of the most bizarre persuasions, gather by several versions of what can only be described as the teeming Ganges of the "Show Me" state. In fact, you've *got* to be shown, because you wouldn't believe it.

I still recall sitting with the late Arnold Gingrich at a Theodore Gordon Flyfishers luncheon in Manhattan and watching him lean toward me, in the attitude of one who is about to unleash a particularly obscene anecdote, and with a nervous clearing of his throat, whisper softly; *"You're* from Missouri. Is it true that they have something called 'trout parks' there? And do they really sound a *siren"*—his voice cracked momentarily there—"to signal the beginning of fishing? And that as many as a thousand fishermen line *one bank* of a half-mile stretch? Is this true?"

Oh noble Arnold, who has walked with Father Walton down to the silvery Dove, born of Grayling brood stock on the gentle banks of Michigan's Au Sable and succored to angling maturity along the Neversink and the Beaverkill, how does one speak "truth"—at once profane and vile—to one whose sensitive ears can hear the gentle dip of a spinner laying its eggs, the quiet sipping of a great trout, fine and far off, or the soft wash of a rolling salmon up the stream? One lies, of course, through his teeth!

Chuckling hoarsely, I confessed that I had *also* heard of this, and had even read buried newspaper reports of these atrocities in one of our left-wing dailies, but that if our Department of Conservation people had in fact participated in such a crime against humanity they were only following orders. I reached for my TGF, Trout Unlimited and Federation membership cards to show him that my papers were all in order, but my answer seemed to placate him somewhat—although the burden of my half-truths obviously lay heavy upon him, as the world's sins upon a saint.

HAVE I SINNED? Let me count the ways. I reached for a medicinal sip from my martini, after which I fell precipitously from my high place next to Arnold Gingrich into the glare of the bare-bulbed "ready room" back at Montauk. Not the salt-water angling capital at the tip of Long Island, mind you, but Montauk State Park, eighty minutes from St. Louis and the meat-fishing capital of the northern Ozarks.

I was transported once again to the scene of the unspeakable crimes in which I had participated less than seventy-two hours before. I was in the concessionary store at dawn, standing in line for my "trout tag" that would for the length of my confinement dangle from my vest to brand me as a member of the mob. Others around me were making more exotic purchases— bloody meat-baits, domestic pasteurized cheeses, and various forms of kneaded dough. It smelled like dawn in a pizza factory—only the employees didn't appear to wash their hands afterward.

Suddenly, there was a siren, beginning as a low growl and then rising to a piercing pitch that aroused the inmates to uncontrollable fervor. Someone yelled "scramble!" and, as one, we ran to the waiting, revved-up river. But the first wave was already on the beach, locked in combat. Not to be bested, I secured a position between two other anglers. The young chap to my right had the glazed look of an unemployed drag-racer; he also had three fish, and had obviously beaten the siren by laying down a bit of rubber on U.S. 40 in the process. The old geezer to my right, reeking of stale Sterno, had obviously left the mission too late to get a seat in district court and was lurching heavily under the burden of his small grappling hook. Al McClane, who at that early period of my training was my prime and only literary mentor, had not told me about things like this. I'm certain that I was the only angler at Montauk using gut leaders (I had failed to check the edition-date of my well-thumbed library copy of his *Practical Fly Fisherman,* but I sensed that his chapter on gut leaders was definitive).

I finally managed a successful backcast—half the battle at

Montauk for a fly fisherman—and solidly hooked a hatchery truck, which I played for a moment and then broke off. In the next half-hour I managed to hook two small rainbow, a Rapala, and a fat lady whose jar of salmon eggs had iced up on her and slipped into the froth. In trying to retrieve them she had impaled herself on my weighted nymph, and she suddenly found herself in the midst of the greatest "hatch" Montauk has or ever will see again.

As she lurched about trying to pick up her eggs with her trout net, she fell heavily against me and dumped me into four feet of water. I was too involved in trying to recapture my trout—both of which had taken advantage of my submersion to swim from my deep-bagged net (McClane *had* told me about *that*)—to notice that the flashing lights about me came from a photographer with the right-wing daily who was recording the two heaviest catches of the opening-day event—hers and mine.

The woman had foul-hooked a 14½-pounder while trying to net her spilled salmon eggs, a creature scabrous and deformed but which the caption writer felt he must identify as "trophy fish (at left)," and the photo editor had judiciously cropped out my clumsy act of baptism (at left) when the photo appeared the next day.

Glories were fleeting that day, but my weighted nymph still reposed for posterity in the posterior of the other heavily weighted "nymph" in the photo.

And that's the way it was, Arnold. You would be happy to know that I have, ever since, rested that stream at Montauk.

The Day I Invented the Fly
(1971)

IT IS SADLY TRUE that I came from a piscatorially deprived family. Dad could, and can still, do fascinating magic tricks, and he owned one of the first motion picture cameras in town, with which he made a prize-winning documentary of the Ringling circus with me as the featured male lead when I was six. He took me to every sporting event ever held in St. Louis from the time I was five, and I include in this array of spectacles bowling tournaments, roller derbies, dance marathons and wrestling matches as well as the more obvious events such as prize fights, football games, baseball games and basketball tournaments.

He claims to have made several float trips on the Current River in the Ozarks between the early '20s and the mid '30s, but the coincidence of these dates with Prohibition, and my memories of mother's rather cool greetings upon his return from these leads me to believe that the angling done on these excursions was hardly of the piscatorial variety. Quite probably, he and his companions were more interested in catching a batch from the local stills than in matching a hatch on the then productive Current River, which lies deep in the Ozark mountains and beyond the bailiwick of any sane revenue officer.

Regardless of any claims, I had received no instruction in angling by the time I was a teenager. Perhaps he just hadn't gotten around to it—like our first discussion of sex, which occurred on the day I left for the Army. Of course, it's easier to pick up that information from the streets than instruction in presenting a dry fly, so I did manage to weather the evils of Army life in Europe and did manage to contract nothing more than a wife and four children a few years later, and in that order.

But, when angling historians come to measure the sum total of my angling career, they will find little or no precedent in my background to prepare them for the hard, cold fact, that, in July of 1937, I independently and dramatically invented the artificial fly.

IT WAS IN MY EARLY TEENS that I was invited to participate in a zoological expedition to South America with an old school friend of my father. I would assist him in manning my father's motion picture camera, through which I had been starkly documented since birth, and would care for the snakes, birds, and animals that we were to collect from the jungles of Dutch Guiana. To me, the prospect was a kaleidoscopic distillation of all the Don Sturdy adventure-series novels I had ever read, and the summer vacations couldn't arrive soon enough.

After our departure from New Orleans aboard a freight steamer, I soon made friends with the Norwegian first mate, a splendid fellow with a lilting Scandinavian accent and a cabin full of then-lurid pulp magazines. A further attraction was a fishing rod resting in a corner of the cabin. So, before we were more than twenty-four hours at sea, my education on several levels had begun. I had enjoyed, with varying degrees of enthusiasm, a sip or two of aquavit, had had a go at several of the more illuminating pulp stories and had received my first lesson in fishing. Thus, all of these low pursuits were, through parental default, learned in the gutter.

It was in Mobile Bay while we were taking on a cargo of lumber for the West Indies ports that I first wet a line with the full knowledge of what I was about. I was about, I decided, to catch a fish, which I did shortly after dipping the live bait from the fantail of the ship—a four-pound bass. And further, it was documented in full-color 16-mm motion picture footage, with First Mate Kulsing-Hansen beaming alongside. It was a heady moment, but one to pale in comparison to a later event on a South American jungle stream, the significance of which I realized only recently.

We had reached Paramaribo, the capital and main port of Dutch Guiana, and were steaming up river toward the bauxite ore mine of Moengo, some hundred miles inland. The Guiana streams are narrow but deep, and were navigable for nearly their entire length by oceangoing vessels. As we made meandering turns the bow and fantail alternately scrubbed the tropical foliage and bright flora along the banks, and occasional villages occupied by Arawak Indians or by Bush Negroes—the descendants of escaped or liberated slaves—loomed momentarily along the bauxite-tinted red banks of the Commewijne River.

A tropical rainstorm cut off all contact with even the minimal bit of civilization around us after our arrival at Moengo for the first day, but the following morning dawned clear and full of anticipation. My advance researches, primarily in old copies of *The National Geographic,* had prepared me in various ways for the tropical world. It was certainly my first encounter with extra-familial female bosoms and especially of the shade then segregated into the back-of-the-book segments of the *Geographic;* in fact, by the time I left the native villages of deepest Dutch Guiana, I proceeded to grow up fully expecting my wife to have a heavily tatooed torso. (It was with mixed emotions that I later found this not to be true, the only disappointment of my nuptial night.)

But more appropriate to my chronological age at the moment was my fascination with the "devil fish of the rain forest rivers," the piranha. Don Sturdy, I knew, had nearly been attacked by a school in *Up the Amazon;* intrepid National Geographic Society explorers, inured to brown bosoms, gave them wide berths; and then I had finally viewed, with a mixture of terror and anticipation, a film-short showing the decimation in three minutes of a 300-pound warthog by a school of ferocious piranha.

First Mate Hansen was ashore arranging for the loading of the bauxite ore, along with his mates, leaving me alone to my devices—which, it turned out, were rather crude. I had been sleeping in Hansen's cabin and eating with the crew for most of the trip, so I had picked up a bit of forecastle lore. I knew that the boatswain's mate's locker contained a variety of treasures, and among them, after a furtive search, I located several huge objects that appeared to be clothesline hooks. I sharpened the points of one with a coarse file and wrapped Hansen's fishing line around the threads of the screw-in section of the hooks.

Then came the problem of bait. Admittedly, the crew enjoyed a lesser table than the handful of expedition passengers, and the mate *had* informed me the night before, with a twinkle of his sky-blue eyes, that the stew, or "lobscotch" as they called it, was based on mule meat, but I couldn't believe that we had been feasting on warthog. So, I made a testy sortie to the galley, knowing that the cook was also ashore and that I might still have some rapport with the mess-boy. Although I was skinny to the point that I could have recently escaped from nearby Devil's Island, it was not because I didn't feed my face. I was a regular visitor to the galley in off hours, and was by now *persona non grata* there. I had conjured, without too much imagination, a picture of the cook, a dirty, gruff German, and the purser, a sinister Middle-European type whom I later identified, at least to my satisfaction, as appearing in several Sidney Greenstreet-Peter Lorre films, as partners in a smuggling venture, and perhaps with white slavery as a subsidiary activity (the latter corporate venture a spin-off of my recent encounters with the mate's pulps).

I was not in high repute with the mess-boy, either, and he regularly greeted my requests for food with his only English phrase: "Vot you tink, every day Christmas, mon?" I always countered with my only phrase of Norwegian, delivered as a foul curse: "Shibet slingrer voldsömt!" He had earlier seen me tippling from Hansen's bottle of *aquavit,* and by adding to this the fact that the Norwegian phrase actually meant "the ship rocks very much," I can only imagine that he and the cook were convinced that they had a budding teen-age alcoholic on their hands.

After establishing that it was not Christmas today and that it was my continuing impression that the ship was rocking very much, I left the galley baitless, with not even a choice cut of warthog to my name.

But I was up to this exigency. In a moment of divine revelation, I went to my cabin and unraveled a section of sweater with which Mother had seen fit to provision me on my tropical journeys. Wrapping it around the shank of the 10/0 grappling hook, I pricked my finger, drew what blood I could summon, and dabbed the wool body of my gigantic "fly" until, to my fevered mind, it resembled a bleeding warthog. Aunt Edna, who had knitted the sweater for me, would have dropped a stitch.

Since I wasn't totally familiar with the proper holding waters for piranha, I merely ran to the fantail of the ship and lowered my bloody, wool-shrouded anchor into the brown-stained waters of the Commewijne. The current carried the device no more than ten feet when an entire school of piranha suddenly declared recess.

The rod bowed mightily, the line twanged and the bait-casting reel shrieked frantically as the hook disappeared beneath the hull of the S.S. Sörvangen.

The longer the battle continued, the stronger and heavier the quarry seemed to grow. To say that I eventually *retrieved* the fish would be misleading, and not worthy of the exploit. Actually, I keel-hauled them in the best tradition of the Spanish Main. And I say "them" advisedly, for not only had I acquired two squirming, chomping piranha on my improvised fly, but each of these piranha had the jaws of another piranha firmly locked to its tail. The hangers-on soon dropped off to search out their own warthogs, but, even discounting the loss of part of a tail on the smaller piranha, I had scored doubles on my first cast with a fly! It was a moment to be savored.

With the innocence and creativity of youth, I had re-created that moment in history when the lone Macedonian angler dipped the first imitation fly into the River Astraeus. I was at once a transplanted Halford experimenting along the banks of the Itchen and a young Theodore Gordon of the tropical rain forests, independently discovering a new tactic to meet the angling needs of a new world.

While I had not expected anything more than a small brass plaque, I was disturbed to read, years later, that the name of the Commewijne River had been changed, and not to mine. Revisionists had taken over the seat of government in Paramaribo, changed the country's name to Suriname, and had proceeded to rewrite both geography and history.

Since then, fate and three decades have brought me, by ambience if not merit, to the Olympian preserves of fly fishing. I have sat at the side of Arnold Gingrich, Esquire, at the tables of the Gordon Flyfishers in Manhattan as he recounted tales of pursuing the elusive grayling of the Upper Traun in Austria.

I have walked along the banks of a Colorado stream with Ernie Schwiebert as he discoursed on the master Atlantic salmon of the fierce Laerdal that he had brought to heel under the pressures of his relentless rod, and I have rested on the banks of the storied Letort with master-angler Charley Fox as he recalled high moments spent with Hewitt and LaBranche.

Angling Olympus is currently headquartered, I suppose, in a hotel suite on the Place Vendome in Paris, and presided over by the current Zeus of anglerdom, M. Charles Ritz. Yea verily, I have knelt at his feet while he told me of his early exploits on the Beaverkill and the chalkstreams of Normandy and Hampshire.

And through all this, knowing my place as a mere Boswellian Recorder of Deeds, I have held my tongue. But someday, the propitious moment shall present itself. And then I will move in.

It will probably be in the dimly lit bar of an exclusive angling club along the storied Upper Neverkill, to which I have been invited by a respected member who is still negotiating with me for the negatives I retained that show his leaving a Catskill fish market with a heavy creel.

Glasses will be raised in a comradely "Hear, hear!" as one of the members, a crusty old slogger who has fished everything except the River Styx and is now working on that, had just finished his eleventh recorded version of the landing of a monster brown trout in the Vale of Kashmir. All the major prophets of angling are there, and a few select disciples. In general composition, the gathering parallels Da Vinci's rendering of The Last Supper.

Then there is silence. I break the perimeter of the Inner Circle of flydom and casually push my glass across the table for a refill as I calmly allow the electricity to build.

"Rather reminds me," I will begin softly, "of the summer of '37. I was fishing the headwaters of the Commewijne—just upstream from Moengo, y'know. Piranhas rising everywhere. Worked up a quick tie streamside, dropped it on the edge of the school, picked up doubles the first cast."

A short pause for effect and a sip of scotch. "Devilish little creatures, those piranha. Really work over a hook. You must always retrieve quickly. They bit through a 9/0 hook in a matter of seconds."

It's now very quiet around me. Two prominent members of the Angler's Club of New York have already started toward the door, probably preparing to place themselves on the inactive list the next day. The Hero of the Kashmir is slumped in his chair, bleating weakly into his brandy. There is a general nervousness among the others.

"Really a rather simple tie. Been meaning to pass it on to Darbee." I will then rise, a sipping rise as I drain my glass in finality, and call it a night. But not before I add a final comment.

"Really haven't had it, you know, until you've fished the Upper Commewijne. Especially during the warthog hatch."

Before retiring to my room, I will raise my glass in final camaraderie to the Company of Anglers grouped before me.

"As we used to say on the Commewijne . . . 'Shibet slingrer voldsömt'!" And it had, very much.

In Praise of Smallmouth— and Me!

(*1974*)

As I'm writing this, the smallmouth season is about to open in our parts, but on our old home waters in the Ozarks, and specifically the beautiful Buffalo, the stripe-siders have been displaying their wares to knowledgeable anglers for two weeks. And it's the first time since I picked up my typewriter and other assorted paraphernalia and moved the magazine to New England that I've really been homesick.

Not that I don't miss many friends of many years standing—and wading—the latter category including *Fly Fisherman* magazine associate Bob Bassett who remained behind to hold down some of the pools we staked out together years ago. But come June—even the name "Bassett" conjures visions of lesser but not-to-be-ignored smallmouth, and I'm off again to float and wade the Buffalo and relive one of my major—and shockingly few—angling triumphs.

I will proceed to bore you, and please myself immensely, by recounting it. I had flown down to the Buffalo near the Missouri-Arkansas border from St. Louis with a delightful chap— on the ground—who must have been the illegitimate issue of a union between Amelia Earhart and "Wrong Way" Corrigan. He had talked as if he had been the navigator in Jimmy Doolittle's lead B-25 in the Shangri-la Tokyo raid, but after an hour or two in the air I discovered that he had just gotten his cross-country rating the week before. He didn't specify what country.

We landed at three different airports along the way by mistake, not including two airstrips obviously designed primarily for model airplane rallies and that would have been summarily rejected by any of Doolittle's crippled craft. He couldn't have made his way cross-town in Roscoe, New York, without falling into the Beaverkill.

I hadn't learned until after we finally landed that he was

also, besides being the country's worst navigator (on the return trip he couldn't find St. Louis at all and made a forced landing with one gallon of gas in the deep dusk some hundred miles south; he took us back to St. Louis by taxi and we made him feel every tick of the meter), he was also a spincaster of the most blood-thirsty variety. I suggested that his great clump of under-water hardware had thrown off his compass, and he leaped on this excuse with reckless abandon. Typical of that class, you know.

Well, so there we were, floating the rock-walled confines of the enchanted Buffalo River valley. The john-boat ahead of us held an advance party of anglers from our little safari who had beaten us by a day—but not by many fish. I took the stern posi-tion in our float boat while Prince Henry the Navigator plied his trade with little success from the bow. I always use the ex-cuse of taking photographs to glim the competition when I'm fishing with an unknown quantity of fisher-folks—and I define "competition" as any group including anyone other than me—unless it's Bassett!

But on this day, a few hours later, my only competition was myself—and I was up to the challenge. The water was cold, but low and gin-clear, laced with a little vermouth. The fellows in the boat ahead of us were both experienced—including a plug-caster who had obviously plunkered for lunker largemouth be-fore. He was dropping them in all the places I'd go if I were a bass, but with no success. And he was giving the bluegill and punkinseeds coronaries with his well-placed depth bombs.

As the afternoon wore on, the efficiency of the fly rod was paying off, and respectable one-pound-plus "brownies" (as Ozarkians call smallmouth) were falling prey to my mighty Muddler in a 3-to-1 ratio over the other three fishermen put together—and I wish they were.

And then—the feeding activity seemed to drop to nothing. An hour and one wayward stripesider and a few suicidal blue-gills. Dusk was nudging the deepness of the bluffed-in river valley of the Buffalo, and one of the slackers up forward was even suggesting putting in at the next gravel bar—and was complaining about the mosquitos! "Big ones all around the banks—they'll be on us in a minute!"

Just as he had pleaded his case—I heard a "slurp" and

then a "slop" and a dark shape rose to one of the "mosquitos."

Well, back East they call them "Hendricksons," and I just happened to have a few little lovelies left from the vise of Roscoe's Walt Dette—sweet #16's and never been kissed. Our guide grabbed an overhang and held us against the current— he had learned the peculiar needs of fly fishermen in float boats—and I dropped one into the grisly looking jet of water just ahead of a great gnarled oak that, with a many-branched willow, ruled the water for a radius of thirty feet. The Hendrickson had scarcely wet its hackle-tips before the "slop" resounded against the bank—no "slurp" this time—all "slop!"

The situation was designed for disaster. Submerged roots, dangling willow fronds, an uncertain fishing platform—for the guide, who was not a verbal person, was trying to instruct me, through noises and hand-signals, in rites for which neither of us, being mortals, were properly prepared.

I've had twenty-five-pound crick tarpon on in tight waters, I've taken several dozen torpedoing bonefish, and I've vied with sounding jack crevalle—but the current, the size of the bass, and his deep-bodied profile combined with the cunningly placed natural booby traps to make this the most memorable angling adventure of my life. Never had nature, animate and inanimate, conspired against me so.

My rod was underwater—under limbs, under roots and under the boat—more than it was above, as I remember. Thank the good patron Peter and his colleagues, I was too overwhelmed to think. I reverted to animal reflexes; I did everything right. Forced into a corner, I must admit that I don't remember what I did, of course, but the other members of the party and the guides did, and I encouraged them to reveal the details of the event that night after the manner of the Wagnerian Ring Cycle, with special emphasis—with drinks all around—when we got to the "Ride of the Valkyries." Even during the tussle, I seemed to remember hearing heavy brass choruses—with tympani.

Well, it was a 4½-pound smallmouth, deep of belly and hard of flesh—until cooked that evening. And six more in the one- to three-pound class, all on Hendricksons (plus one Red Quill; by then it was dark and Dette had let me down), proved that it was not just the luck of the lame and the halt. A year later, on Wisconsin's Wolf River below Langlade, I re-proved to myself the selective nature of smallmouth when treated as first-class citizens.

Driving back—in the taxi—I found that I had made some converts among the spincasters. But the only time I saw Prince Henry the Navigator was on a TWA flight to LaGuardia—which, in spite of him, landed on the runway of the field of the same name!

Catch and Release—But
First, Catch
(1977)

As HE LINGERED OVER a last sip of claret at table in the London Flyfishers' Club, Nick Lyons' recently acquired "steely-eyed gaze"—usually guaranteed to curdle the blood of any Henrys Fork trout or send a Big Hole brownie into the final stages of the *delirium tremens*—had taken on the glazed aspect of a freshly beached carp.

And with good reason, for he had just fished the Kennet, one of England's most leveling chalkstream waters, and was still receiving consolation and partial absolution from his companion of that day astream, English angler John Goddard. Relaxed now that the Bicentennial Year had passed, Goddard smiled quietly at the plight of the cocky Colonial as Nick recounted those desperate hours. He will possibly, when all is recollected in tranquillity, discourse further on his experiences in his guise as "The Seasonable Angler."

Lyons and I were lunching with some of England's most expert and literate anglers—such hardy types as T. Donald Overfield, who writes of "Trout Flies of Yesteryear" so knowledgably in these pages each issue; Brian Clarke, an innovative disciple of the demanding stillwater discipline now being developed in Britain; Goddard, of course, also known to many of our readers as one of that country's ultimate fly fishers; Dennis Bailey, the brilliant English custom rod maker; and Timothy Benn, a major British publisher and angler of note who dissolves into a lump of Silly Putty whenever fly-fishing is on the agenda and defers wisely to this growing stable of angling writers.

Now this is a somewhat less motley crew than Lyons and I usually hang out with, but we're in a business where we have to sacrifice personal pleasures occasionally to run off to far-flung wilderness areas such as the Mayfair club-district of London and southern England's chalk waters. It's a living.

And you learn things, even lagged by jetting as both of us were. Things such as the fact that Walton's leather creel, served under glass in the Flyfishers' Club library, reveals on further inspection that it contains the shrunken remains of a human hand, not that of Walton, nor Cotton's, nor even that of a hapless poacher of the Dove, but an anonymous amputee from the Battle of Trafalgar! The British don't throw anything away.

Nick's experience on the Kennet with Goddard was an eye-opener for him, as he had just written a piece for our Late-Season Issue titled "Rights and Restrictions," which suggested that, when the sport of angling threatens its own existence, a conflict arises between these rights and restrictions. Apparently the River Kennet offered up few rights to Lyons and was fraught with restrictions, but this is healthy for a fellow who has recently taken a quantum leap from fisher of the Hudson River at 84th Street to "steely-eyed" apprentice guide on Western trout waters.

A few days later Lyons did manage some time on Dermot Wilson's Kimbridge stretch of the Test, a somewhat friendlier flow, where he apparently enjoyed unspeakable triumphs. I tried to pump him as to the measure of his success, and I distinctly heard him whisper hoarsely, in a burst of self-plagiarism: "Thirty-two!"

Actually, his article, and an accompanying editorial request for comment by readers on "catch-and-release" fishing, drew considerable mail, and these comments were duly read and included in a paper delivered for us by West Coast Field Editor Ron Cordes to a national symposium of fish-and-game officials in California in early September. All this will be reprised in an article in our January 1978 Pre-Season Issue, with appropriate comments by steely-eyed old Nick Lyons.

Casual banter about "fish-for-fun," "trophy stretches," and "catch-and-release" regulations is certainly no replacement for their use as intelligent and thoughtful fisheries management techniques. I know, because they were integral to the developmental stages of my own fly-fishing career, a pursuit I had taken up when middle age was approaching and blondes weren't. It's a sordid tale, basically, but one which perhaps will add another dimension to trout conservation.

UNLIKE MOST OTHER angling greats, I had no early mentor to guide me. I learned about fly-fishing in the gutter. I had to pick up scraps of knowledge from the streets, from rumors, folk myths and old fishwives' tales. In my early years, I had found no streamside companions, for I had not yet learned that fly fishermen could be identified by their residual odors—a delicate blend of trapped wader sweat, silicone and stale bourbon. As I gradually became able to sniff them out, I was eventually able to engage them in productive discourse—some of them even fished with me, usually just once. They taught me many things of considerable moment, but one of the most important things I learned was the uniquely lofty level of my own incompetence.

But—the other important thing that I soon learned was that *competence* wasn't really *important*. For more than two years of fly-fishing I had been catching more on my backcasts than on my forward casts. The expectantly moist grasses and ferns lining the bottom of my creel had turned to dust by the end of each fishing trip. My return home from the river to the bosom of my family was a journey into humiliation and disgrace.

But then I learned about conservation. "A trout," Lee Wulff told us, "is too valuable to be used only once." That was certainly a step in the right direction, but my limited skills had not yet forced me into such a moral confrontation—although I'm certain I would have reflexively made the right decision.

Soon I heard about the philosophy of "Limit Your Kill— Don't Kill Your Limit." At first I was indignant that someone would even *suggest* that I would do such a thing as take my limit of trout. In fact, to say that every time I waded into a trout stream I was striking a blow for ecology would be an understatement. I was the only angler on our stream who could rest a pool by fishing it. Knowledgeable fly fishermen vied to fish in my wake, knowing that they had everything to gain and nothing to fear—except, of course, my lethal backcast. But, by God, I was limiting the hell out of my kill!

But the Rosetta Stone that opened up my window on the world of fly-fishing was the philosophy of "catch and release."

By that time I was sufficiently sophisticated to realize that one need not follow the *letter* of that most holy of laws. Since no one would fish with me anyway—or if they did they wisely kept their distance—it was none of their damn business whether I "caught," "released" or quite possibly *none* of the above.

Quickly my return from the river became a moment to be savored. When the wife, family or neighbors inquired as to the extent of my catch, I would merely sigh and remind them somewhat cryptically that "a trout is too valuable to be used only once."

I found this also to be equally true of Lee Wulff's convenient quotation, until I eventually found it necessary to improvise on this theme. When comments on the emptiness of my creel became caustic I would reply by telling my family that "if they were that hungry I would take them all to McDonald's."

Even to this day, an era in which I have actually been known to catch fish, I still wear my treasured fishing vest, replete with a montage of declamatory patches and buttons displaying the sanity of my conservation policy, the purity of my soul—and frequently, the lingering emptiness of my creel.

I find "trophy trout waters" especially attractive. I fish them frequently, confident that the big ones have already been taken out early in the season by hardware merchants, poachers and Ernie Schwiebert. Besides, anything over fourteen inches would, under normal conditions, bring on immediate cardiac arrest.

No, I would rather think of fishing in terms of quality, not quantity. Through an intelligently applied program of "catch-and-release" fishing, we can keep both anglers *and* trout coming back for more. Anglers, like trout, are too valuable to be used only once.

The Joy of Tying One On
(1981)

I<small>T IS FEBRUARY THE SECOND</small>, and I was up with the groundhogs this morning to see my shadow. Actually, I did, but it came from our basement light just before the floodwater shorted it out, and my forecast is that there will be two more months of plumbing bills to come.

Our considerable inventory of Vermont snow had been washed away overnight by a heavy thaw and warm rain, a good portion of it draining into my basement. This dank cell and its contents is now tributary to the East Branch of the Battenkill, which is just a few hundred yards west of our house toward Mother Myrick's Mountain, the steep slope where this saintly old lady of yore grazed her deformed cattle.

There had been no warning groan from our vintage sump pump during the night. It has always given our house that lived-in sound, much like the first radiators of autumn and the reassuring drip-drip-drip from the upstairs bath onto the livingroom ceiling. Usually the pump sounds like an elephant dropping a calf, with a comforting thud at the final coda, but no such reassurance visited us during the Night Of The Deep Water.

The event did give me a chance to discover which pair of waders had the leak. Luck had it that I found out on the first try; nothing like it at dawn to start those old juices flowing, I say. Happily, there were just a few inches of water around the oil-burner motor, but our basement slants—*all* of Vermont slants—and there was a dark pool at the other end that could easily have harbored a hold-the-press entry in the spring *Orvis Record Catch Club News*.

There was even an uneasy moment when I detected a rise, but it was just a tributary leak from the root cellar. It was obviously the time for a high-density sinking line, but the only one available was an old floating line that happened to be floating by at the time. Also floating in the scummy surface film was an

212

old wader sock, a package of emergency flares, a dead mouse, and that lovely old blue-dun cape I had been looking for, floating high as a cotton seed.

I HAD NOT ACTUALLY anticipated the great Groundhog's Day Flood of '81 to the point of building an ark, but some primal reflex had sent me down into the dungeon a few weeks before on a mission to liberate my old accumulation of fly-tying equipment. Long before the start of *Fly Fisherman* I had fallen into fly-tying, and even though my concoctions made a bigger splash than I did, I knew I had found my calling. After a year or two of intensive practice I was at the stage in which I could knock out an acceptable Quill Gordon in less than two or three hours—faster than I was able to catch trout.

Even so, by default I had learned what a good fly should be, how a dry is tied to float high on the water, how a certain hook controls the "bite," why the relative proportions of a pattern—the tail, the hackle, the wings and the body—are so important in instilling that consummate death-wish in the myopic eyes of a lurking trout.

I would have learned even more, perhaps, if it hadn't been for my mentor. I had early learned that the fly-fishing shelf of my local library was not state-of-the-art, when a fishing companion explained to me that it was not necessary to keep a Bible under my arm when making a cast, and I soon consigned to the back shelves both the casting book and that particular Bible, the latter sweat-stained and profaned by a nervous armpit. My knowledge of gut and greenheart, although profound, was, I learned, of little use in today's angling scene.

Thus, in the first few years of my skill-honing, I threw myself on the bad offices and worse shop of a most uncivil old man I shall not name, although several occur to me. He was also unwashed, but this was no problem amidst the overriding ambience of his shop. An immersion of sheep-dip would have improved things immensely. I was later told that he had, in his youth, studied taxidermy by correspondence and had flunked out, possibly because he couldn't read very well. He had kept all of the birds and animals, however, in great jars and flagons on floor-to-ceiling shelves, picking out a quill of owl feather here and a patch of squirrel tail there. It was a never-ending supply of fly-tying materials that seemed to have a half-life of their own.

He was very attached to his stock. Every customer was suspect of breaking-and-entering, and it often took several hours to convince the Old Crud to sell you something. He marketed his own brand of thread wax, but always seemed to be out of stock; I suspected that he had merely run out of Q-Tips, because there was a mother lode of the stuff in his ears. Other vital supplies were contained in giant Mason jars on the top shelves, far beyond the timberline as defined by his double hernia. Occasionally a vitamin-deficient little neighbor boy, playing an unwilling Oliver to his Fagin, was pressed into service to ascend the heights, and the local jungle telegraph soon warned of the imminent availability of furnace hackle and jungle cock.

I eventually learned that Old Crud was not only a flunked taxidermist, but also a failed author—but not until I was well into chapter one of his own catchily titled opus, *How to Tie a Fly*.

"Hold the hackel clip in you're left hand, mean while wraping the tinsle forward around the hook shank untill you reach the bend of the hook(!)."

Then he totally lost me when he continued in his stylish prose: ". . . and then with the other hand . . ."—but by then I began to feel like a character in an Addams cartoon.

His "E-Z Step By Step How To Ills" gave one little more confidence. Gouged crudely into dried-up duplicator stencils, the "Step By Step Ills" lead one quickly into purgatory. They had the clarity of a short-wave radio schematic, with captions translated literally from the original Japanese. Wrapping-thread blended with knuckle-wrinkles on the tier's hands (one of which had only three fingers, with the thumb at the bottom), and hooks changed directions from one E-Z Step to another. "Forward" became an option, "clockwise" an elective move on the tier's part. Old Crud never honestly confronted the concept of a third dimension, so the rendering of a closing-off half-hitch became undecipherable and the knot quickly disappeared into thin air in practice.

My first—and last—E-Z fly pattern, purporting to be a March Brown, turned out to be a hyperthyroid creation resembling the anchor from a ship model tied palmer, and sporting two wings with the delicate structure of the south end of a ravaged tournament dart. The experience was the lowest ebb in my fly-tying career, but I became because of it, if not a better fly tier, a better editor.

I MUST CONFESS that this stroll down Memory Lane is triggered by a happy event. After nearly a decade of understandable disuse, I recently rescued my considerable cache of fly-tying equipment from the pre-flood cellar and brought it over to a little room next to my office, where it now enhances five shelves and a desk—an accumulation of nearly twenty years of everything a resurgent fly tier needs to get himself back into all kinds of trouble.

For ten years I have threatened to return to the bench, but only now is it possible. I am about to tie again, as soon as I straighten things out. I won't be taking out any ads in the magazine, nor will I accept any advance orders. In fact, I will give only one piece of advice to fly tiers, or to anyone thinking of beginning a magazine covering his hobby or recreation interests—and that is: Don't! I won't even give reasons, although I will pass on a bit of magazine-trade gossip—that Hugh Hefner has to eyeball five centerfolds and several years of *Playboy* calendars to work up a good leer.

But now, as I attempt to organize my little disaster area, all comes back in a flood. It's like falling from a high place.

- Here's a tin of Old Crud's ear-and-thread wax, never to dub again.
- And there's a piece of polyethylene tubing, suitable for a streamside tracheotomy but slipped to me from an envelope one evening by Charles Ritz. He had taken me aside during a cocktail party to tell me of his latest discovery, the tube-fly, which, if the netters and long-liners didn't get there first, would make a substantial dent in the world salmon population. (It's not on the condemned list of the Atlantic Salmon Association, but of course I haven't tied one yet.)
- Over here, safely tucked in a drawer, are several dozen jungle-cock eyes from the last legal shipment into the United States—and a few more dozen from the first illegal one.

- And a miniature metal crossbow, presented to me at an angling show by a friendly con-man as a prototype model of a device to finish off fly heads quickly and neatly. It turned out to be Frank Matarelli, and his whip-finisher (an appropriate name for a device used in this masochistic calling) is now a must item, in several sizes, for any but the most spartan fly tier.

- An assortment of some four-dozen vials of mixed dubbing material—"guaranteed," wrote the donor, "to get you back into fly-tying." It almost did—or at least out of the magazine business, because the "donation" was made in lieu of back ad bills amounting to many thousands of dollars.

- And down there—two copper-wound Sawyer nymphs, one tied by me, and most closely resembling the tuning coil of an old crystal radio set; the other tied by the late Frank Sawyer himself and looking exactly like a Sawyer nymph.

- Now, those wild-looking creations in the top-left drawer. They're not in their original state. I had the idea of performing autopsies on my flies instead of on my fish (the latter technique had always disappointed me; for the first few years most of the fish I took appeared to be starving to death). I took flies tied by such experts as Jorgensen, Harrop, the Dettes and the Darbees, then stripped them down, hackle by hackle, thread by thread, until I arrived at the Ultimate Truth. The Truth was that these people were better at it than I was.

- But then you ask about that looming wooden object, still damp at the base from this morning's flood, but rescued in time. That, ladies and sirs, is the world's largest pre-owned fly chest, and one appropriate to Pandora had she been a fly fisher. It was acquired on Sunday afternoon, July 20th, 1969, and this day is recorded in the *World Almanac*, and in mine, under "Memorable Dates."

IT WAS THE DAY that Harmon Henkin walked on the moon. In the *Almanac* only Neil Armstrong and Edward Aldrin are credited, but in my personal records it's Harmon Henkin who will eventually have a modest lunar crater named after him. Harmon was an angler in all aspects of the word. He was also a part-time newspaper man, fly tier, sometime fishing writer and later a book author, but I think of him most often as the first angling groupie.

He had arrived in St. Louis a few months before after having spent an enriching few weeks camped out on Ed Zern's lawn in Scarsdale. I learned about his availability for more productive work when I had a call from our neighbor, a Concerned Scientist named Barry Commoner (than which there is no one less, as people now know). It seems that Harmon had been hired by his organization to work on its magazine, *Environment,* but that the editor felt that Henkin might be more useful to our fledgling publication. We needed anyone we could get at that time, and we found him to be the most charming con-man we had ever met—handsome, boyish-looking though in his late twenties, and including in his entourage a pretty little Indian wife and tiny papoose.

We gradually learned, however, over a period of several days, that Harmon's prose style was unencumbered by those irritating little disciplines that so often bog down other writers—facts, spelling, punctuation and grammar. It was rumored that he had once worked for a national news service, but if so he was the only rewrite man with a back-up rewrite man. But he was a fund of fishing gossip for a magazine landlocked on the banks of the Mississippi, and we managed to adjust to the pressures of his strong personality until a long, hot St. Louis summer loomed ahead.

It was in the middle of the summer that I had taken a Sunday off after putting the third *Fly Fisherman* issue to bed, never certain that it would rise again. A life-long follower of things astronomical, I had spread a composite chart of the moon, measuring some ten feet square, on the living-room floor.

Astronaut Armstrong was just preparing to take his "giant step for Mankind" when Harmon Henkin burst into the house and beat Armstrong to the punchline. He traversed the Sea of Tranquillity and the great crater Copernicus in a single bound, then negotiated the lunar Appenines, doing great violence to the just-completed lunar maps prepared by the Air Force's Aeronautical Chart operation in St. Louis.

"I'm going to Montana tomorrow," he said, "and I'm going

to let you have first crack at the world's greatest fly-tying chest."

Only this announcement saved his life—at least for the moment.

It was one of the weirder moments in a life already rich with bizarre recollections. One-hundred-degree heat, man landing on the moon, Houston chatting with Apollo II, and Harmon Henkin trying to sell me a three-foot-long chest stuffed with the most unbelievable assortment of fly-tying and fishing paraphernalia known to angling man. Orvis could have opened a Midwest branch around it. Harmon told me that it was custom-made for him by a mountain craftsman, but it was more likely that he had rolled an itinerant carpenter.

But to me it was a symbol of liberation, and worth the price. I paid him what he felt he needed to get to Montana, and then purchased a stubby old cane rod "by one of Montana's greatest rod makers," whose name he couldn't remember. I wanted to make certain he got to Missoula.

But even that wasn't to be. On the way out of the house, my check in hand, he made a deal to buy our next-door neighbor's Bronco, which he picked up the next day and totaled a few days later at the Montana state line.

Harmon eventually made it to Missoula, polished his prose, attached himself to novelist Tom McGuane, and published a book on tackle in which he gave no credit to what now is sadly called "The Harmon Henkin Memorial Fly Chest." For Harmon Henkin totaled another vehicle last year in Montana, and himself along with it. Harmon was a free spirit, and the fly-fishing world needs a few people like that. It's just that I didn't at the time.

THAT EVENING I found myself staring at the fly-tying chest, wondering if I'd ever plumb its depths. Then I remembered the words of Old Crud. "Now you've compleated Chapter One. Why not tie one on yourselves?"

Only good advice we, or I, ever had from him. And we did.

Epilogue:
Fly Fisherman at Fifteen
(1983)

SOMETIMES IT FEELS LIKE FIFTY YEARS, other times like five. But, in all the truth that is in us, it was exactly fifteen years ago this April 15th that *Fly Fisherman* was unleashed on an unsuspecting world. This event, however, was crowded off the front pages of the newspapers, because on that same day a U.S. reconnaissance aircraft carrying thirty-one passengers was shot down by the North Koreans over the Sea of Japan. (It must have been a CIA charter tour!) The U.S. commitment of troops to Vietnam had peaked earlier that month at well over half a million men, even though peace talks had begun in January. On the brighter side, there was talk of an imminent recession.

The Vietnam war we outlasted and the recession we didn't even notice. We had our own built-in recession. Today, a financial analyst would describe our growth plan as "bankruptcy-at-birth." Our long-term marketing plan was to publish the next issue. To raise additional funding, we sold life subscriptions, but only for the life of the magazine; it seems we lost on that deal.

However, within this very sentence we shall suddenly switch from the editorial "we" to the first-person "I"—because I was the first person to stir up all this trouble and I don't want anyone else to take the blame. Picture if you can a 45-year-old man with a wife and four teenage children, until a few months before quite satisfied with a comfortable and stimulating job of a dozen years, a man who one day walked out of a restaurant after a few medicinal martinis and turned left in search of a mid-life crisis.

Of course, my dissolution had began many years earlier when I first accepted an invitation from friend and neighbor Bob Bassett to go fly-fishing on a small trout stream near St. Louis. I caught a fish and he didn't. Perhaps it was the wind in the trees, but I seemed to hear trumpets blare. Of course, there is no such thing as "just one trout," and I soon became addicted. "Yes, I'm a fly fisherman," I replied to my shrinking circle of non-angling friends, "and I admit this freely."

I was soon able to tie wind-knots with one hand. I was releasing most of my catch, often before they were even netted. My employers were personally moved over my increasing concern for the marketing and public relations needs of our smaller outlying soft-drink bottlers in such places as Oregon, Montana, Colorado—and Vermont. My travels also enabled me to fall in with fly-fishing's faster crowd in New York and San Francisco, even though they took a little while to sniff me out. Within a few years I had been skunked on some of the country's greatest trout streams, from the Madison and the Big Hole to Michigan's Au Sable to the revered Beaverkill. Anyone trained in deviant psychology could have predicted my eventual end.

BUT I REALIZE as I write this that there is no way I could possibly convey to you the sordid and sleazy story of *Fly Fisherman*'s early days—and if I could, there is no way you as a reader could possibly be interested.

How to explain the near-meltdown of the core of my nuclear family when I drove up one afternoon with a large rental truck? The printers had experienced a breakdown of their press—which I believe they had purchased on time from Gutenberg—and could not finish printing our newsstand copies until Saturday. I had a very important meeting in Chicago on Monday, the day 20,000 magazines had to be on the docks of our newsstand distributor on Houston Street in lower Manhattan—by noon. The plan was for my two sons, already on the most-wanted list of the local traffic officers in our St. Louis suburb, to drive the truck and magazines to Manhattan. I left for Chicago the next morning, and heard no more until early Sunday evening when I had a call from somewhere in New Jersey.

"Dad," shrilled the voice of my 10-year-old daughter, "we're in a motel here and Mom has already had two big martinis and she says she's going to hurt all of us!" It turned out that old Mother Earth had decided to put the girls in the station wagon and follow the boys in the truck from St. Louis to Manhattan. Somehow they had separated during a torrential rain-storm on the Pennsylvania Turnpike after driving all night, with our younger son at the wheel and our girl riding shotgun. After several hours of throwing up roadblocks, the sterling men of the Pennsylvania State Police located the suspects and brought them back to Mother for grilling and sentencing. Sentencing was apparently having to spend a night with her in the New Jersey motel room. Beyond this, I've understandably never asked any more questions, except to learn that they also got lost in Greenwich Village on Monday morning, but did eventually find Houston Street, learned its proper pronunciation from a cabbie and delivered the 20,000 still-wet magazines just before noon.

The magazines did get out and sold very well. Our first subscription-promotion mailing, 10,000 pieces assembled on Bob Bassett's ping-pong table, returned more than 50 percent in subscriptions, with the second one of 15,000 doing almost as well. Subscriptions were $7 per year, the newsstand price 75 cents, and the first issue contained articles by such budding writers as Charlie Fox, Tom McNally, Ben Schley and Roderick Haig-Brown—plus a department called "Anglish Spoken Here." Apparently we did something right, because fly fishermen soon had a flag to rally 'round—and here we all are, talking about it a decade-and-a-half later.

BUT—I'VE TOLD YOU more than you want to know. Really more interesting, even to me, is a look at the rather significant developments in the world of fly angling over these past fifteen years . . . most of them very good, a few questionable.

The arrival of graphite on the scene. The replacement by graphite and other fibers of bamboo and fiberglass rod materials has probably been the greatest change over the past fifteen years. This development of the middle 1970s allowed rodmakers to fabricate rods with many of the qualities of bamboo, but much lighter and with slimmer butt sections than the cane rods (and dramatically so in the case of most fiberglass rods). Graphite is cheaper, is readily available, is easily worked, has a quick return after the cast, and is relatively indestructible (except for those early few which tended to self-destruct when overloaded with great leviathans).

Sinking fly lines. Although sinking fly lines have been used for a century or more, the 1970s saw the development first of fly lines that sank at various rates and then of such lines with the additional benefits of tips of various lengths and sink rates—all in designer colors! It's about as complex as buying a pack of mentholated, 100mm, extra-slim, filter-tipped cigarettes, and much better for your health. They're especially important for stillwater fishing.

Fly-tying materials. Except in a few hard-to-locate tackle shops, fly-tying materials, accessories and tools were difficult to locate fifteen years back. Buying by mail was a risky proposition, and about as dependable as those correspondence schools advertised side-by-side with them in the classified-ad sections of outdoor magazines. Today, except for a few protected exotics, you can find hundreds of good suppliers of materials from anything that crawls, creeps, crows or flies. Vises and other tying accessories are now of surgical quality. You new guys don't know what it was like back in the good old days.

Books on angling. Fly fishing has always enjoyed a high-quality and voluminous literature, but in the 1970s book publishers' presses exploded with angling tomes. Not an angle has been overlooked, not a stonefly unturned, and I'm certain that at least a thousand volumes have hit the store shelves in the past fifteen years. The only book on fly-casting I could find in 1961 demonstrated the proper arm-position with a sketch of a bearded gentleman holding a Bible under his armpit.

Changing demographics. Fly Fisherman made several in-depth surveys of readers throughout the 1970s. The average age dropped from 43 in 1970 to 34 in 1977—it would have been even more dramatic if some of our original subscribers had just acted their age and given up. Although harder to detect, the increase in women fly-fishers was obvious to anyone who hung around with that type—wives, daughters and girlfriends were soon netting their own. Now they have designer waders.

Along with the arrival of younger anglers, the piscatorial center of the United States moved steadily westward, and the Rocky Mountains and the West Coast increasingly became areas of frenzied and creative angling activity. Fly patterns, for years *adapted* to western rivers, soon became *developed* for those waters. Fly-rod artisans seemed to spring up from the earth, working in glass, cane and fiberglass, to produce some of the finest fly rods available today—and probably *more* rods than the eastern two-thirds of the country produces. And, as for the western anglers themselves, their writings on indigenous entomology, techniques for fishing the spring creeks and the serious exploration of mountain lake-fishing have given us a great store of new and original information.

Concern for the environment. In all regions of the United States, fly fishers have stopped paying lip service to environmental problems and started paying attention. In the East, a few pioneers in the late 1960s were concerned about the increasing acidity of their streams, but today, working with state and federal authorities, cooperating anglers have brought the problem of acid precipitation to a high boil. But old problems also remain—those of effluents, insecticides, and the ever-increasing nervousness of the Corps of Engineers at the sight of free-running water. Trout Unlimited and the Federation of Fly Fishers are gathering momentum each year, and regional or local groups of fly fishers, such as the Catskill waters militants, are zeroing in on such encroachments with dramatic effect. Most of us are really beginning to worry about where our next trout is coming from.

AND THERE ARE A FEW CONCERNS. I have a fear that the art of fly-fishing is becoming *over-technical*—easy entrance to the sport was from the earliest days clouded by ritual and mysticism, but now potential converts could well be frightened off even more by the high-tech aspects of today's world of the fly. Angling is still a happy fool at one end and a fly at the other.

Aren't we *over-publishing?* Many publishers, unfamiliar

with the market but eyeing the burst of books in the '70s, have leaped on any new angling manuscript, any fresh new author, and during the past several years these books aren't selling in the same numbers they were ten years ago. We must become a bit more selective in our publishing, and in our purchasing.

In fly fishing, the *competition* is with the trout, not with other anglers. I see trout derbies sprouting up about us, and wonder if commercial tournaments can be far behind. ". . . and now, ABC's 'Wide World of Sports' . . . with Howard Cosell . . ."

Is there a fear, among fly fishermen, of *bass-fishing*? Many of us have available splendid natural smallmouth and largemouth waters, possibly better than our local trout waters. Some of my most memorable moments have been spent fishing for smallmouth on those lovely Ozark mountain rivers, or bugging the shores of Florida lakes for largemouth. Share them with me.

And finally, do we *wade with blinders on*? Admittedly, not all good fly-angling waters are on the edge of town, and few of us are free from worldly chores—our stream-time ticks away and we do our best to amortize the investment. But fly-rod gamefish live in wondrous places and the fly-fisher's world doesn't end at the riverbank. Let's pause a bit more frequently to catch that first burst of wildflowers, record the upstream flight of mallards, supervise the work of that beaver or kingfisher, or savour the sweet smell of a spring pasture. (But watch out where you're stepping; that ain't second base.)

FLY FISHERMAN MAGAZINE is in good hands. Over the years, a good magazine changes character and new voices are to be heard. My voice changed at fifteen, too, offering exciting new challenges. So, this character has stepped down, and other characters, led by long-time FFM-er John Randolph, are in charge. May St. Peter have mercy on their tortured souls.

After fifteen years as a piscatorial "recorder of deeds," in which capacity I made a serious effort to observe the angling scene and its hazards—some 100-plus columns of which many readers apparently took to be humorous—"Anglish" will no longer be "Spoken Here." This department has become a bit confining in its discipline, and I think it is time to wander about a bit more aimlessly, tripping and stumbling into more varied forms of trouble than "Anglish" allows. If I continue, I'm afraid the column would have to be changed to "Anguish Spoken Here!"

For a year the editors continued to recognize my association with *Fly Fisherman* with a rather austere "Founding Editor & Publisher" on the masthead, but this made me a bit nervous— as if they were just sitting around waiting to fill in the dates on the tombstone. D.D.Z.